THE CASE OF THE MISSING MADONNA

THE CASE OF THE MISSING MADONNA

A Patrick de Courvoisier Mystery

Lin Anderson

Severn House Large Print
London & New York

This first large print edition published 2016
in Great Britain and the USA by
SEVERN HOUSE PUBLISHERS LTD of
19 Cedar Road, Sutton, Surrey, England, SM2 5DA.
First world regular print edition published 2015 by
Severn House Publishers Ltd.

British Library Cataloguing in Publication Data
A CIP catalogue record for this title is available from the British Library.

ISBN-13: 9780727894861

Severn House Publishers support the Forest Stewardship Council™
[FSC™], the leading international forest certification organisation. All
our titles that are printed on FSC certified paper carry the FSC logo.

MIX
Paper from
responsible sources
FSC
www.fsc.org   FSC® C013056

Typeset by Palimpsest Book Production Ltd.,
Falkirk, Stirlingshire, Scotland.
Printed and bound in Great Britain by
T J International, Padstow, Cornwall.

For Sharon and Christine who love Cannes and for my friends in Le Suquet who inspired this series, in particular Christine Blanc and the real Pascal, not forgetting Oscar.

One

On their approach to Heathrow the captain had informed his passengers that the weather in London was cloudy, with a temperature ten degrees cooler than Patrick de Courvoisier had left behind in Nice. Adding for good measure that there was a strong possibility of rain. The resulting groan from his fellow passengers had mirrored Patrick's own thoughts exactly.

Now, emerging from Victoria underground station, he was met by a chilly wind and a few drops of the forecasted rain. Not quite the right weather for a Buckingham Palace garden party. The Queen of England could invite her subjects to attend, what she couldn't do was guarantee them good weather, even in June.

Patrick exited the shelter of the underground station and headed for Grosvenor Gardens, intending to deposit his overnight bag at the hotel. After which, he would have a stiff drink and make his final decision. He was still being tempted by the idea of not turning up as requested (ordered), although he suspected the Foreign Office already knew he'd booked an airline ticket from Nice and a hotel room near the palace for tonight.

His former bosses, despite recent cuts to their budget, could still do what they deemed was in their best interests. They also disliked rogue

1

employees, as much as they disliked rogue states. So although he could tell himself he no longer worked for Her Majesty's government, his position was rather like becoming a lord. Once you were in, only death could put you out.

Having left his bag at the hotel reception, Patrick declined the opportunity to view his room and headed back out, intent on having his drink a little closer to his destination.

The bar he finally selected was peopled by a number of couples who Patrick suspected were headed in the same direction as himself, mainly because of their mode of dress. Not many men wear a top hat and tails to work on a Thursday afternoon. Nor do women wear tiny net hats and impossibly high heels unless going to a wedding.

Patrick ordered an Islay malt at the bar, added a little water, then carried it and a bowl of savoury nibbles downstairs. From his memory there was rather poor fare on the food front at a royal garden party, particularly for commoners, and definitely no alcohol, hence the gathering of attendees in the bar prior to their royal engagement.

The diplomatic tent would no doubt produce better offerings. As for what was served in the royal tent, Patrick had no idea, although he was amused at the idea of Her Majesty eating little square chocolate cakes with her initials stamped on them.

Apart from a similarly dressed couple at the foot of the stairs, the lower area was empty. Patrick located the most secluded alcove and bagged himself a table. It was difficult to believe that a little more than four hours ago he'd been breakfasting on board *Les Trois Soeurs* in the old harbour at Cannes, with Oscar, his French bulldog, spread out frog-like at his feet. It already seemed a world and a lifetime away. Or had his eighteen-month sojourn in Cannes on board his beloved gunboat been merely a break in his career? That's what London chose to think, and by coming back to order he would appear to be endorsing such an idea.

Patrick let his anger settle a little before sampling the whisky, then sat back in the chair to contemplate his plan. The royal invitation had arrived in the midst of a rather delicate and complex job, which had involved finding a missing starlet and a black pearl during the Cannes film festival. Angered at the none too subtle order to return to the London fold, Patrick had torn the gold-rimmed card in two and thrown it in the bin. He'd hoped ignoring the summons might be the end of the matter, but unfortunately he'd been proved wrong.

It was partly his own fault it had come to this. Had he kept his head down more, he might have escaped notice a while longer. However, his actions during the case of the black pearl had served to expose him to his former bosses and thus put his 'retirement' in jeopardy.

Although he wasn't entirely the one at fault.

Lieutenant Martin Moreaux of the French Police Nationale had played a part in his summons to London. Patrick was certain of that. Thinking of the detective now brought a clear picture of him to mind: short and lean, with iron-grey hair. Patrick could almost smell the cheroots Moreaux favoured. Moreaux, he was sure, would have welcomed the possibility of his departure from Cannes, and had therefore disclosed rather more about Le Limier's activities to his former employers than Patrick would have liked.

His French nickname, which translated as 'the Fixer', had been bestowed on Patrick by the residents of Le Suquet, the medieval district of Cannes in which he now lived. Born and bred in Le Suquet, Lieutenant Moreaux considered Patrick an irritating incomer who interfered in business best left to himself. The two men had worked together in the past, particularly during the case of the black pearl, but the arrangement was definitely not a marriage made in heaven. And given an opportunity of divorce, it seemed Moreaux had jumped at the chance.

Patrick drank down the malt as a waiter approached, and ordered another one, then set about consuming the nibbles. He would make his visit to the diplomatic tent as short as possible. He would listen to whatever they had in mind for him, then politely decline. They could pressure him to work for them, but they couldn't make him. They knew things about him they could make public, but then again he knew things about them, too. And in this new internet age it had become easier to expose those in power, for the manner in which they handled that power.

Patrick didn't fancy a fight. He just wanted to live the life he'd chosen in Cannes. One that suited him very well. There, he was his own boss. He decided when he would use his skills, how much he would charge, and best of all exactly who he would work for. In his previous employment there had been no choice, and duty had been cited as the only explanation for doing it. Patrick had seen how empty such a term was, especially when it played havoc with ordinary people's lives. So he'd switched his allegiance to ordinary people, and was glad that he had.

The second malt arrived with a small jug of water, just as two hatted women clattered down the stairs, heading for the Ladies. They reminded Patrick of exotic butterflies, their head attire like colourful wings. Patrick didn't envy their chances in a windswept garden with little cover apart from the tea tent, in which there would be no room to sit.

Queuing in the rain for a cup of tea, a cucumber-and-mint sandwich and a tiny chocolate square, with EIIR on it, didn't seem worth the effort. Still, the garden parties did wonders for dress and hat sales in the more exclusive London shops, and suggested to those who attended that they had at least reached the bottom rung of the ladder that led to the royals.

It was also good PR for the House of Windsor and gave a semblance that we were 'all in it together'. When the Romans had worried about the allegiance of those they'd conquered, they'd simply made them Roman citizens. Better to keep your enemy in the tent pissing out, than outside pissing in.

Which was no doubt exactly what his former employers were thinking about him.

Cynicism gave the next mouthful of whisky a

bitter taste. Patrick resolved not to think in a scathing manner any more, but to enjoy the remainder of his drink then head for the gate and get things over with.

The nibbles had done little to assuage his hunger, but he had no desire to eat a proper meal between the flight from Nice and the garden party, knowing that he wouldn't enjoy the food, however good it might be.

So he had thus made up his mind to wait until after the proceedings then head for a little French restaurant he knew close to his hotel, where he could pretend he was already back in Cannes. Between then and now he would just have to fill the gap with miniature sandwiches, cakes and a pot of Earl Grey.

As he walked briskly towards the garden entrance, Patrick considered who would be there to greet him. Forsyth was the obvious choice, but unlikely to get the result they wanted. If intelligence prevailed, they would send a more diplomatic diplomat. An image of one came to mind, causing him a little dismay. Should it be Charles Carruthers, that might prove a problem. Patrick had a great deal of respect and time for Charles.

They would know that, of course, so the odds were on Carruthers, but only if he agreed. Patrick recalled their last meeting at Carruthers' club, when over drinks Patrick had informed him he was resigning. There had been a short silence while Carruthers considered this. No bluster or arrogant dismissal of Patrick's supposed stupidity, as would have occurred with Forsyth. Charles had eventually given a wry smile and said 'What about your pension?'

'I don't care about it,' Patrick had answered.

Charles had nodded, accepting that. 'It's not usual, you know, to leave us,' he'd said, thoughtfully.

Patrick had shrugged, past caring about what was usual or acceptable. 'Will they try to stop me?' he'd asked.

Charles had savoured his brandy before answering. 'I think they'll watch you go and await your return' had been his reply.

'I won't come back.' Patrick had been adamant.

And yet, here he was.

A queue had formed at the garden entrance. Patrick went directly to the front, where two smartly dressed gentlemen were examining invitations similar to the one he'd torn up. As he approached, one of the men appeared to be listening to a voice in his earplug. He looked up at Patrick.

'You're to go straight through, Mr Courvoisier. They're waiting for you in the diplomatic tent.'

Patrick nodded, unsurprised. No doubt every entrance had been watched for his arrival. Either that or he'd been tailed on his way here – something he hadn't noticed, which suggested he was out of practice.

Stepping through the gate in the tall wall that encircled the palace and its grounds was a bit like falling down the rabbit hole. The reaction of those who'd entered in front of him convinced Patrick of that view. Outside was a busy London. In here was an entirely different and extremely

7

privileged world, which a few hundred people would catch a glimpse of today. The sight of a group of four marching yeomen, the Queen's bodyguard, with their spears and red-tapestry tabards, further enforced the image. The only things missing, were Alice, a knave painting the roses, and the Queen herself.

Patrick glanced at his watch. By his reckoning, the royal party would be arriving shortly. They would appear at the rear entrance of Buckingham Palace, then make their way fairly swiftly on a predestined route through the crowds to the royal tent for tea. Whichever family members had been chosen to speak to a few selected dignitaries would pose for photos, then head for the tent, too.

The weather had brightened a bit, the rain had held off, although there was still a stiff breeze to ruffle the waters of the lake. The queues at the tea tent were long and there were a few pinched faces. The low temperature was proving too much for the flimsy female outfits. The suited men, on the other hand, were faring better.

Patrick had chosen to be as casual as was permitted and since national dress was allowed – witnessed by colourful saris and Nigerian robes – had decided to don a kilt and a smart jacket, plus a shirt and tie. The outfit had seen him greeted by smiles, from Cannes, through Nice airport, to Heathrow, particularly when he'd produced his passport from his sporran.

The tartan, a McInnes, came from his mother's side of the family, who'd hailed from Speyside, in the Highlands. Her childhood home had been in the village of Carrbridge, a McInnes stronghold.

He spotted two more kilts on his walk across the grass, but their wearers had gone for more military jackets and one of them was sporting an impressive row of medals, suggesting he'd been at war most of his life.

Having reached the diplomatic tent, Patrick paused at the red-carpeted entrance and listened to the low buzz of voices from the interior. Whoever was waiting for him would be aware he'd be arriving shortly. Patrick had always made a point of being first at similar meetings. He preferred to be the one watching the other participant arriving. In this case, that wasn't possible. Unless?

Patrick skirted the tent, which was set close to the lake, and made his way to the back, where from memory there would be a discreetly placed set of upmarket toilets. There would also be an exit point from the tent, for those who wished to use them.

Patrick approached the toilets and went inside.

A brigadier whom he didn't recognize emerged from a cubicle as Patrick rinsed his hands. Patrick let him leave, then followed, entering the back door of the tent close on his heels. The tent was busy. The waft of expensive male cologne mingled with equally costly female perfume. There were no queues in here for the food, the expanse of which definitely exceeded the number of guests who would sample it. However, as in the commoners' tent, only tea or a cold non-alcoholic drink was being served.

For a moment Patrick stood surveying the room, looking for a familiar face and seeing none. He did, however, observe a tall, striking woman with long dark hair who was studying him. She was wearing a beautifully cut green dress, with a silk scarf draped round her neck. The eyes that surveyed him with candour were also undoubtedly green. Having studied the details of his face, her eyes now descended to his kilt, and Patrick saw a small smile play on her lips. Yet another positive aspect of wearing a kilt was the way in which it encouraged strangers to ask about it or make some wry remark.

From this intriguing woman, Patrick decided, either would be welcome.

However, having satisfied herself as to his face and attire, she turned away and headed for the food table. Patrick contemplated following her, but thought he might save that until after his meeting. Just as he made that decision, a hand touched his arm. He turned to find the man he was hoping they wouldn't send.

'Courvoisier,' Charles Carruthers said, 'it really is good to see you again.' His broad face broke into a grin as his large hand encased Patrick's.

Patrick saw a smile in his friend's eyes and knew that he meant those words.

'It's good to see you too, Charles.'

'You look well.' Charles glanced at the kilt. 'I see you came dressed for battle.'

'As did you.' Patrick indicated Charles's tails and top hat.

'The auld enemy?'

Patrick laughed. 'Not you and I.'

'Are you ready for some Earl Grey?' There was a twinkle in Carruthers' eye.

'Only if it's very strong,' Patrick said.

'I'll have a pot sent outside. There's a table awaiting us under a particularly beautiful weeping willow.'

They exited the way Patrick had entered and, as Carruthers described, found a willow and under it a table enclosed by an awning.

Charles looked up at the threatening sky. 'We don't want to be rained on.'

'Heaven forbid,' Patrick said.

Carruthers indicated he should take a seat. There was a few moments' silence as a silver tray arrived complete with a selection of tiny square-cut sandwiches and equally small cakes. At the sight of them, Patrick experienced a sudden desire for a large Bridie or a Scots pie.

Carruthers waited while the waiter poured tea into the delicate china cups, then declared that was all they needed and let him depart. Before Patrick spoke, Carruthers pulled out a silver hip flask from a trouser pocket, poured the Earl Grey on the grass, and filled the cups with a pale-brown liquid.

'They serve the beer in a teapot in Kano now. Sharia law,' he added by way of explanation. 'This, of course, is a fine Speyside malt.'

Patrick tasted it. Speyside malts were essentially 'sweet' with little peatiness, though a little 'smoke'. He recognized this one right away.

'Macallan?' he said.

Carruthers nodded. 'I was up there recently. Did the tour.'

'Not all forty-six distilleries?'

Carruthers gave a big belly laugh that seemed strange coming from someone wearing a top hat. 'No, just half a dozen. But I made a point of sampling them all.'

His friend was intent on breaking any ice that might have formed between them. He was also alluding to Patrick's roots and his love of whisky. It was classic stuff, intended to put him at ease. He would have used the same tactics had he been in Carruthers' shoes. Patrick finished what was in the cup and set it down on the saucer. Promptly, Carruthers refilled it.

There was a moment's silence, which suggested they were about to get to the main point of the proceedings. Patrick waited.

Eventually Carruthers asked, 'How well do you know the Esterel mountains?'

Patrick was surprised by the sudden mention of the Esterel Massif, the red volcanic coastal mountain range that touched the sea just west of Cannes. Its rugged terrain, oak forests and deep gorges provided an ideal location for climbers and walkers such as himself. He shot Carruthers a glance. Was he still making small talk? By the look on his friend's face, he wasn't.

'Pretty well,' Patrick said guardedly.

'We have word of some treasure hidden there, which we're interested in finding.'

'Treasure?' Patrick laughed. 'Is this the pitch for a new James Bond movie?'

Carruthers didn't smile. 'No. It most definitely is not.'

Patrick considered this, his mind going into overdrive. The Esterel mountains were peppered with caves, many of them undiscovered. They were known to be dry, with an even temperature, and much used during the Second World War to house resistance fighters and, in some instances, Nazi treasure stolen from the rich of conquered Europe. Was that what Carruthers was referring to?

'Nazi gold? I thought that had all been located.'

'Not gold. Paintings.' Carruthers took a swig of whisky. 'We are interested in one painting in particular.'

'Is that the royal "we"?'

To Patrick's surprise, Carruthers nodded. 'I shouldn't be saying this, of course. Forsyth wouldn't have,' he added with a smile.

'You think telling me that will influence my decision?'

Carruthers shook his head. 'No. I just believe in being straight with you.'

'How did a Windsor painting get among a Nazi hoard?' Patrick asked drily.

'That you don't need to know.'

'They don't have provenance?'

'Let's say it's a family heirloom that went walkabout during the German occupation of France.'

Patrick swallowed the remainder of his whisky. Neither its flavour nor the aftershock removed the bad taste from his mouth. This was an offer of redemption. The proposal, not uttered in so many words, was that he take on this special task and remove the blot from his copy book by doing the Windsors a favour. It was a decent proposal, which he had no intention of accepting. Before he could say so, Carruthers spoke again.

'Before you give me your decision, there's someone I would like you to meet.'

Seamlessly, Carruthers produced his *pièce de résistance*.

How she was aware they were at this point in the proceedings Patrick had no idea, but right on cue the woman in the green dress presented herself in front of them. Both men rose in unison, Carruthers going forward to greet her. A third chair appeared and was placed next to the table.

'Grazia Lucca, meet Patrick de Courvoisier.'

They eyed one another again.

Patrick held out his hand. 'I had a feeling we were destined to meet.'

'After I studied your kilt?' she said in perfect English.

They each settled in their chairs and a short silence followed. Eventually Carruthers spoke.

'Grazia is an art historian,' he informed Patrick, with a twinkle in his eye.

'Really?' Patrick said. 'How interesting.'

'She is helping us with a little research.'

'Into missing paintings, I expect.'

The irony of the two men's interchange wasn't lost on Grazia. She raised a delicate eyebrow and awaited further developments.

'Patrick and I were just enjoying a secret dram together,' Carruthers said.

Grazia smiled. 'I hope there's some left?'

14

'You like whisky?' Patrick said.

'I come from Barga,' she laughed, 'the most Scottish town in Italy.'

Carruthers was doing well with his bombardment, just as Patrick knew he would. A pardon subtly offered, a whisky with which to perhaps celebrate. And now a beautiful woman had been added to Carruthers' enticements. It would be difficult to refuse such an offer. But refuse he would, nonetheless.

Patrick rose and glanced at his watch, as Carruthers retrieved the hip flask once more.

'I'm afraid I have to depart, so I won't be able to share the rest of the contents of Charles's hip flask with you, despite the fact it's a Macallan. I wish you both well in your search for lost works of art.' He turned specifically to Grazia. 'It's been a pleasure meeting you, Miss Lucca.'

With that, Patrick departed. What he really wanted to do was sprint round the lake and vault the wall. However, that wasn't possible, so instead he headed for the main exit, which involved walking through the rather threadbare public rooms that formed the tourist entrance to the palace. No one prevented his departure, although a couple of guards looked askance at his leaving just as the Queen was making her way to the royal tent.

Patrick emerged from the building to find a small crowd of sightseers busily taking photographs of the front of the building. The appearance of a man in a kilt caused some further photographic interest. Maybe they thought it was Prince Charles in his Highland garb. If they did, they were disappointed, as Patrick was soon recognized as being neither a royal nor a celebrity, minor or otherwise, and the cameras and mobiles stopped clicking.

He was aware that his abrupt departure had been rude, but Carruthers' introduction of Grazia Lucca into the proceedings had been one step too far. Turning down the job and giving his reasons why, which would have involved raking up the past, had been rendered impossible by her arrival. Which was, of course, why Carruthers had arranged for her to appear just at that moment.

Charles Carruthers was excellent at his job, but in this instance diplomacy had not been the main reason for the meeting, thus stronger measures had been deemed necessary, even emotional blackmail. Patrick didn't hold this against his friend and former colleague. As far as he was concerned, he'd come as ordered and had given his answer.

Checking his watch, Patrick realized he was a little ahead of his table reservation, so, having made a visit to his hotel room, where his brown-leather overnight bag had already been deposited, he decided to have a drink in the bar. This time he opted for a vodka martini, the memory of Scotch and diplomacy being too vivid in his mind.

He watched while the martini was expertly mixed, indicated his approval, and took it, along with a small bowl of olives, to a corner table. The hotel bar held a sprinkling of other customers, some of whom he suspected had been at the garden party and were now making up for the absence of alcohol.

Having sampled the martini and staved off his hunger with some olives, Patrick made a phone call. There was a pause before connection, then he heard the distinctive sound of a French phone ringing. Pascal took a few moments to answer.

'Pascal, it's Patrick.'

'Oscar's fine,' Pascal said, before Patrick could ask. 'Very well, in fact. He's been fed and is lying in the sunshine in the courtyard.' A pause. 'How was the Queen?'

'Very well, I think, although I saw her only briefly. She's very sprightly for her age, especially when heading for the tea tent.'

Pascal made a sound that could have been approving or disapproving, it was hard to tell.

'I'll be back on the morning flight tomorrow, so I should see you around noon.'

'Have some lunch first,' Pascal suggested. 'Come for Oscar around four. We'll be back from our walk by then.'

Patrick might think the French bulldog belonged to him, but since Pascal had been called upon to look after Oscar, injured in the line of duty, he rather thought of him as his own.

'OK,' Patrick conceded.

'Oh, I forgot to say. Someone phoned the hotel looking for you.'

It was common knowledge that Patrick kept a room in Pascal's small establishment, Hôtel Chanteclair, which he made use of when the winter set in and the boat proved too cold. But it was unusual for someone to try to contact him there.

'Who was it?'

'Brother Robert from the abbey on St Honorat. He would like Le Limier to visit the abbey as soon as he returns to Cannes.' Pascal sounded intrigued, as was Patrick.

'Did he give any indication what it was about?' Patrick said.

There was the sound of the door buzzer in the background.

'I have to go,' Pascal said. 'Guests have arrived.'

Before Patrick could respond, Pascal hung up.

Patrick slipped the mobile into his sporran and considered this new and welcome development. Things had been quiet since the black-pearl case had reached a conclusion. The crowds that frequented Cannes during the biggest film festival in the world had departed. Le Vieux Port, where the gunboat was tied up, had relaxed into early summer and no one from Le Suquet or elsewhere had sought out Le Limier with a job. Patrick wasn't short of cash, the previous job having paid very well, but he preferred being busy. Also, the fact that he'd been contacted by a Cistercian monk intrigued him, almost enough to take his mind off London-centric matters.

The Île de Saint-Honorat was one of the two Lérins islands, which lay off the coast of Cannes, the other being the Île Sainte-Marguerite. Ste Marguerite was the bigger of the two, nearer to Cannes and more popular with visitors, especially the French, who liked to picnic there. The island was a nature reserve, covered with fragrant pines that bordered numerous small rocky bays, offering excellent snorkelling and fishing, with stone tables on which to eat your picnic. Fort Royal, an ancient fortress facing Cannes, provided a historic monument to visit, alongside a row of restaurants ranging from simple fare to gastronomy.

Honorat, on the other hand, was home to a working abbey, where the resident monks tended nearly eight hectares of red and white grapes from which they made world-renowned wines, in demand internationally and available in the monastery's shop. There was also a very fine restaurant that served delicious local produce accompanied by St Honorat wines.

A visit there in June would be a definite improvement on a royal garden party. Patrick's spirits lifted. He finished his martini and headed for the French restaurant near the hotel.

Two

Settled at his table, the wine chosen, Patrick awaited the arrival of the first course. He'd chosen the set menu, similar to that of his favourite Cannes establishment, Le Pistou, which was frequented predominantly by connoisseurs of French food.

There had been three choices for each course, all of them good. He settled for a *soupe de poisson*, followed by a lamb-and-artichoke stew. While waiting for the food to arrive, he found a missed call on his mobile from an unknown number. This puzzled him for a number of reasons. He kept a selection of mobiles and this one he only used while in London. He didn't give out this number readily, and those he'd given it to were listed on his phone.

There was no message left with the missed call, so Patrick decided to ignore it and concentrate on the soup, which had arrived. Traditionally, *soupe de poisson* was served with croutons, *rouille* and grated Parmesan. The idea was to smear a little *rouille* on the croutons, float them in the soup as a garnish, and sprinkle cheese at will.

As he set about doing this, he took time to check out his fellow diners. The restaurant was small, hidden up a side street, and definitely not pretentious. In fact, it had more of the air of a French café. The voices he could make out were a mixture of French and English. There was a large contingent of French people living in London now, somewhere between 300,000 and 400,000. As a result, London had been dubbed 'France's sixth biggest city'.

Patrick had just finished the main course when she arrived.

Grazia Lucca had changed her outfit, from green to chocolate. The effect was equally stunning. She spoke to the *maître d'*, who indicated Patrick's table and seemed quite relaxed about sending her over – which made sense, it wasn't

20

the first time Patrick had had an assignation in this establishment.

'May I join you?'

She sounded a little nervous, as though she thought he might refuse.

'Of course,' Patrick said with a smile. It wasn't her fault that Charles had sent her in search of him.

He waited until she'd settled herself opposite, before saying, 'I was just about to order dessert. In fact I was considering the chocolate delight . . . and here you are.'

She looked a little nonplussed by the remark. 'Charles told me where I might find you.'

'Charles had me followed?' Patrick said in disbelief.

She looked taken aback by his reaction. 'He said you often eat here when in town.'

Patrick had been unaware that that was common knowledge, although he shouldn't really have been surprised.

'I take it he also gave you my mobile number?' he said drily.

Grazia flushed a little, which confirmed Patrick's suspicion that she'd been the missed call.

Just then, the waiter arrived to take the dessert order.

'Would you like something?' Patrick said.

'Just coffee.'

Patrick ordered two espressos and skipped the chocolate torte.

'I think you've had a wasted journey. If you remember, I turned down the job.'

'I know,' she hesitated.

Patrick waited. If that was true, why was she here?

In answer to his unasked question, she said, 'Charles wanted you to know who I will be working with in your place.'

Patrick sat back in the chair and contemplated her. His intense gaze didn't appear to intimidate Grazia Lucca.

'It won't make me change my mind,' Patrick said, knowing he sounded like a stubborn schoolboy.

'No, but Charles still thought you should be forewarned, as our paths may cross in Cannes.'

The term 'forewarned' said it all. Patrick waited, hoping he would be wrong about the name, but fairly certain he wouldn't be.

'Giles—' she began.

'Huntington,' Patrick finished for her.

She nodded, watching him closely for his reaction.

Patrick strove to display none, although he was aware his voice had been icily cold when he uttered the name.

'Then I wish you luck,' Patrick said, and swallowed his espresso in one mouthful. He waved at the waiter and asked for the bill, which was swiftly delivered.

Patrick glanced at it, then laid down enough cash to incorporate a sizeable tip, before standing up.

'I'm sorry, I have a very early flight tomorrow morning and I need some sleep,' he said to soften the blow.

'Can I walk you anywhere?' he offered as they

exited, making an effort to be pleasant despite his underlying thoughts. He suspected Grazia had been warned about his possible reaction to the news of his substitute. He also believed Charles had hoped the revelation might soften Patrick into acceptance, if only to protect Grazia from his sworn enemy.

'Thank you, no,' she said, quietly.

Patrick held out his hand, which Grazia took. There was steel in the green eyes, as there was in the handshake. Grazia Lucca, he decided, was formidable, although he doubted whether she was just an art historian.

'Perhaps we'll meet in Cannes,' she said.

Patrick gave a slight nod, while hoping that wouldn't be the case, particularly if Giles Huntington was with her.

He waited until she'd flagged down a cab and climbed inside. He would have liked to hear the address she gave the driver, but wasn't able to. He wondered if she was heading for Charles's club to discuss the outcome of the meeting.

Wherever she was going was no concern of his, Patrick reminded himself.

He watched the cab disappear into the night, hoping that was the end of the matter, but sensing it wouldn't be. His former employers were nothing if not tenacious.

As he walked back to his hotel, it began to rain. Lightly at first, then more persistently. The delight of the meal had dissipated. Now Patrick's thoughts were as dark and dismal as the night.

Three

The early flight landed in Nice at 10.00 a.m.
Patrick caught the 10.30 a.m. express bus to
Cannes and was deposited outside the Hôtel de
Ville forty minutes later. He had decided en route
to try for the midday crossing to St Honorat,
which was a possibility. He just needed to go to
Les Trois Soeurs to change out of his kilt, then
head along Quai Labeuf and join the tourists that
were gathering at the jetty to visit the Lérins
islands.

Cannes was bathed in sunlight, the entrance to
Le Suquet via Rue St Antoine arched with
flowers. He suddenly remembered it was the
weekend when the medieval town celebrated the
coming summer by decorating its narrow cobbled
streets with an astonishing variety of flower
arrangements. By midday on Sunday the event
would be over and the locals would remove whatever flowers took their fancy. He'd often decorated the boat with his own pickings, enjoying the
scent for as long as the display lasted, revelling
in the ability of Les Suquetans to relish summer
and artistic ability, while declaring the flowers
their own.

Walking along the *quai* towards the gunboat,
he was relieved to be back. With London (the
centre of the universe, as Forsyth had once
declared it to be) now a distant memory.

24

The dive boat owned and operated by his Irish friend Stephen Connarty wasn't at its moorings, suggesting Stephen had taken a party of divers out. Patrick checked the sea to the west of Ste Marguerite, where Stephen often took beginners. There was no sign of the boat there, so he assumed it had gone further afield, maybe round the Esterel headland to the Île d'Or. There was a miniature sunken underwater village near there, popular with more experienced divers.

Patrick made his way to *Les Trois Soeurs*. The gunboat was unmarked by his absence, although he missed the scrabbling sound of the small French bulldog, desperate to see him. Patrick stripped off in the cabin, then went through the old engine room to the bathroom, in the stern.

The mahogany sunken bath in the stern, for which his gunboat was famous among Les Suquetans, was infinitely preferable to any hotel bathroom. Patrick stood under the power shower long enough to revive, then dried himself and dressed. He would have loved to have breakfasted on the upper deck, on fresh coffee and a croissant from the nearby bakery, but knew he didn't have the time. He would have to look forward to lunch on St Honorat instead.

Ignoring his hunger, he shut up the boat and made his way along the *quai*.

The ferry for the larger island was in the process of boarding. Patrick bought his ticket for St Honorat and headed down the steps to berth six, where a much shorter queue had formed for the crossing to the smaller of the islands.

Patrick boarded and took a seat inside, leaving

the small number of external bow and stern seats for those keen to take photographs of a retreating Cannes and the approaching islands. He hadn't been to either island for a while. When he'd first moved to Cannes, he'd spent some months getting to know the area, as much a tourist as those that surrounded him now. He'd also taken part in the annual charity swim from Cannes to Ste Marguerite. A strong swimmer, he often swam miles along the coast west of the old port, following the line of rafts anchored off each of the public beaches.

Initially those swims had been taken as much out of necessity as pleasure. Memories of the reason for his 'retirement' had haunted him during those months, only physical exertion such as swimming and climbing in the nearby Esterel mountains had saved his sanity.

Allowing himself to recall, even briefly, what had made him leave the service immediately brought back the visions he'd fought so hard to subdue. Despite the warmth and bright sunshine, Patrick felt again the blast of a snow-laden wind and viewed again the icy look of death on the face that stared up at him from the snow.

A small girl ran past, and as the ferry hit a swell and rose she stumbled, falling on to Patrick in the process, bringing him back to reality. Helping her regain her balance, Patrick murmured a few words of encouragement in French, which made her smile. Having seen her safely off towards the bow, Patrick concentrated on the view of the approaching islands, his resolve not to get involved with London strengthened again.

The crossing was swift, only twenty minutes to curve round the western tip of Ste Marguerite, traverse the busy strip of intervening water between the two islands, and tie up at the tiny jetty that served St Honorat.

Patrick waited while the rest of the passengers disembarked, among them two women with small suitcases, no doubt heading for a few days at the abbey. Le Chanteclair was the hotel recommended by the Abbot for those en route to the abbey for a retreat. Pascal was rather proud of the recommendation. Patrick mused whether his own association with Pascal and Le Chanteclair had resulted in the summons, although why a monk from the abbey required the services of Le Limier, Patrick couldn't imagine.

The monks of St Honorat, he knew, belonged to the Cistercian order, founded at the end of the eleventh century in an attempt to ensure a stricter obedience to the Benedictine rule. The brothers lived simply, following the rule 'Ora et labora', pray and work. However, they did run the island as a successful business and had recently purchased the island ferry for €1.6 million and were running head to head with other ferry operators, offering trips to the Corniche d'Or and Cap d'Antibes. Making money didn't seem to cause them any crisis of conscience.

Climbing the stone steps from the jetty, Patrick stood for a moment to get his bearings. To his right lay the only restaurant, La Tonnelle. Had he been here for pleasure, he would have chosen to eat lunch first, then take a walk round the island. A few of the other passengers were already heading that way, having no doubt booked online to take advantage of the special price offered for a meal and ferry ticket combined.

Patrick decided he would go for lunch after the meeting, his 'breakfast' on board the flight to Nice from London now a distant memory. As he watched, a small tractor arrived and, loading the women and their suitcases aboard, turned and set off towards the living quarters.

Patrick headed inland, choosing to approach the abbey by way of the famous vineyards, which produced some of France's finest wines. On either side of the dirt track, plane trees showed off their fresh-green leaves. Here they were permitted to grow tall, whereas in Cannes they were trimmed and shaped. Among them stood olive trees and an occasional eucalyptus, lime tree or palm.

The island hummed in the midday heat. Passing the rows of vines, he saw brothers, dressed in their cream-and-black robes and leather sandals, working there. The gates to the fields stood open. Fastened to the metal was the sign of a hooded monk and the instruction that only brothers could enter.

As he approached the first building, which contained the monastery's shop, he was met by the throaty hum of bees and the scent of rosemary. Long serried ranks of the purple-flowered herb flourished in front of the shop, where groups of tourists trooped in and out of the doorway.

Unsure where he should report, Patrick bypassed the shop and made for the church. The door was closed and when he eased it open he realized a service was in progress, so he slipped into the back pew to watch. A dozen brothers, robed in white, six on either side of the simple altar, chanted and sang in low voices, standing, bowing and sitting, almost in perpetual motion. The congregation followed their lead, but the monks seemed oblivious to their presence. It wasn't a mass, Patrick realized, but one of the many services of celebration and prayer offered throughout the day on the holy isle.

The brothers filed out and the church fell silent. Patrick waited while the congregation exited, then made his way along the cloisters to a small office at the entrance, where he made his presence known and asked to see Brother Robert.

He was small and slightly built, yet had a substantial presence. Patrick decided it was all in the eyes, which were a startling blue. His head was shaved close, although it was obvious he was grey, and his face and hands were burnt dark brown by the sun.

Patrick immediately liked him.

They were seated in a shadowy room that overlooked a central square surrounded by a cloister. Through the open shutters came the quiet sounds of the abbey at work. A butterfly fluttered in at the window, bringing a delicate beauty to the scene. It settled briefly on a simple wooden crucifix hung above an equally simple desk, then exited once again into the midday sunshine.

Patrick waited for Brother Robert to continue.

They had gone through the usual pleasantries,

about the June weather, Cannes in general, his crossing to the island.

'What did you think of our new ferry?'

'Very efficient.'

'And Benedict, our captain?' Brother Robert said with a smile.

'I only remember the very large gold crucifix round his neck,' Patrick admitted.

'Yes, it's difficult to miss. A little ostentatious for a Benedictine,' he added with a smile.

Brother Robert walked to the window and surveyed the courtyard. Patrick suspected that the reason for bringing him here was difficult to discuss.

'I wonder what you know of the history of the monastery, Monsieur de Courvoisier?'

'Only a little,' Patrick said honestly.

'Have you heard the name Mademoiselle de Sainval mentioned?'

Patrick thought for a moment. 'Wasn't she an actress?'

The brother nodded. 'A wealthy and successful Parisian actress whose father, one Jean-Honoré Alziary, purchased this island after the Revolution, when it had been disestablished from the Church. Mademoiselle de Sainval lived here for twenty years.'

Patrick waited, sensing that even more intriguing information was about to be revealed.

'As well as being an actress, she was also the mistress of a famous painter born not far from here, in Grasse.'

Patrick knew immediately who the brother was referring to.

'Fragonard?'

Brother Robert nodded. 'Fragonard returned to Grasse to be near her.' He paused. 'Are you familiar with the artist's work?'

Patrick wasn't sure what to say. Fragonard, he remembered, had forsaken religious painting for erotic themes, which were more popular, similar to his master Boucher's work. In fact the two men's erotic masterpieces had been reproduced as a frieze on the stairs that led to Cannes' premier escort agency, Hibiscus, ruled over by the formidable Madame Lacroix.

'I remember *The Bathers* and *The Bolt*.' He mentioned two of Fragonard's pictures that he had viewed. Both rather good. The first comprised a group of naked, buxom women. The second a bedroom tryst between two lovers, with the image of the man bolting the door before they got down to business.

'Ah, yes,' Brother Robert nodded. 'He painted a series of works on the theme of love.' He paused again, making Patrick suspect they were nearing the reason for his visit.

'We have a Fragonard here in the monastery. A painting of the Madonna.'

This was news indeed.

'I didn't know Fragonard painted the Madonna.'

'We believe the painting was gifted to Mademoiselle de Sainval, and there is a certain likeness of her in the depiction.'

The small smile that fleetingly touched Brother Robert's lips suggested the likeness was more than superficial. Patrick found himself imagining an erotic representation of Fragonard's mistress

31

as the Virgin Mary, much like the paintings that decorated Madame Lacroix's apartment on the Rue Antibes.

'I'd love to see it,' Patrick said.

'I'm afraid that's not possible.' The wry smile was replaced by a cloud. 'In fact that is why I asked you here.'

Patrick examined the monk's worried expression. 'The painting is missing?' he said.

'Yes.'

'And you think it's been stolen?'

The monk looked distressed at Patrick's question. 'We are a small community on St Honorat, and very few people were aware of the painting's existence.'

'May I ask who knew?'

'Myself, as keeper of the artefacts. The Abbot. That's all, officially.'

'A theft of such an important and no doubt valuable work should be reported to the Police Nationale,' Patrick said.

Brother Robert looked decidedly uncomfortable at such a suggestion.

'I am afraid we are unable to do that.'

'May I ask why?'

'Monsieur de Courvoisier, this is an internal matter for our order. We trust you to keep it so.' The blue eyes were turned upon him. 'The police will not become involved, whatever the outcome.'

'You're worried it might have been a brother who took it?'

The monk nodded. 'Yes, but that's not all.'

Patrick waited.

Brother Robert went back to the open window,

where he appeared to find solace in the view of the cloisters below. Eventually he braced his shoulders and turned to face Patrick.

'No one outside the monastery must know the painting was, or is, here.'

'I don't understand,' Patrick said.

'We wish that to remain the case,' Brother Robert said.

'If you won't admit to its existence, how can I investigate its disappearance?' Patrick said, puzzled.

'I was led to believe Le Limier was skilled in such matters,' Brother Robert replied, with a smile.

Patrick acknowledged he was adept at keeping secrets, and it was perfectly possible to extract information from people without revealing why questions were being asked.

'What do you propose?' he said, aware that Brother Robert had already formulated a plan.

'Should you decide to investigate, we suggest you stay with us for a few days as if on a retreat.'

An image of hourly prayers, ridiculously early rising, and life without good food and wine didn't appeal, which must have been obvious from Patrick's expression.

'Some visitors come for the relaxation and quiet,' Brother Robert explained quickly. 'Some to do research on the monastery. Either reason would seem applicable in these circumstances.'

Patrick realized the monk was perfectly serious about this.

'Would I be permitted to question the brothers?'

'We would ask you to be discreet, but yes,'

Brother Robert said. 'We will, of course, recompense you for your work,' he added, perhaps sensing Patrick's capitulation.

A thought crossed Patrick's mind. If he was here on St Honorat, he would be less likely to meet Grazia Lucca and her associate, which was a definite positive. But there was also Oscar to think of.

'I have a dog,' he said.

Brother Robert's face broke into a wide smile. 'We know all about Oscar. In fact I've met him at Le Chanteclair. He is most welcome to join you here.'

It seemed the monk had thought of everything.

'May I have an hour to consider?' Patrick said.

'Of course. I suggest you have lunch at La Tonnelle. I will call and tell them you're on your way.'

That was one proposal Patrick had no wish to refuse.

Four

Patrick had already decided to accept Brother Robert's offer of work before he sat down to lunch. However, having sampled the menu at La Tonnelle, he warmed even further to the prospects of a few days' stay on the island.

He'd been warmly welcomed by the head waiter on arrival and a table had been ready for him.

34

'Brother Robert suggested you might like a bottle of our own rosé.' The waiter indicated the wine already chilling in an ice bucket.

Patrick wondered whether he could eat here every day, or would it have to be the refectory and much more simple fare? He decided to make the most of it and chose the asparagus soup followed by the sea bream, which was served with flowering baby courgettes in a light batter.

Around him the other tables buzzed with conversation and the healthy sounds of good food being enjoyed. At the neighbouring table there was a family of five adults. Below sat a small white terrier, who occasionally reminded his owner of his presence in the hope of a titbit, which was obligingly given. Patrick couldn't imagine such a scenario in London.

Allowing dogs in shops and restaurants was another indication that the French made their own rules – along with speeding, and parking wherever they pleased. That thought led Patrick to remember his own car, languishing in the garage, bullet-ridden and possibly beyond repair.

His much loved Ferrari 330 GTS had probably saved his life and in the process lost its own, but he hadn't given up hope on it yet. It would take time and money but it could be restored, or so Daniel at the repair shop on Rue Hibert had told him as he hovered round the car like a mother fretting over a sick child. It was Daniel who'd rescued the sports car from the mountain gorge and brought it back to Cannes. If he could accomplish that, then Patrick was more than happy to let him loose on what was left of it.

After lunch, for which payment was waived, Patrick asked the head waiter to inform Brother Robert that he would be back tomorrow, then headed for the ferry.

The return journey, it being early afternoon, was much quieter. Most visitors travelled to St Honorat to spend the day there, and would return by a later boat.

Patrick decided this might be a good time to make himself known to the captain. Approaching the cabin, he called in, giving his name and suggesting Brother Robert wanted them to meet.

Benedict indicated Patrick should negotiate the metal chain that barred his entrance and join him. Swarthy, his skin burnt dark by salt and sun, at close quarters Benedict was an imposing figure. Patrick had already come to the conclusion that, like many Cannes inhabitants, he had North African ancestry. Although in Benedict's case, the rather large ornate crucifix round his neck indicated he wasn't Muslim.

When he spoke, the voice was guttural, the language well sprinkled with local dialect. Patrick suspected his own ability with the local language was being tested, so answered appropriately, adding a sprinkling of swear words. At this, Benedict emitted a hearty laugh and nodded.

'Brother Robert is right. Le Limier is one of us.'

Patrick found himself rather pleased by the comment, even if it had been said to flatter him

36

and probably to encourage him to take up the job on offer.

'Brother Robert says you're to stay with us for a few days.'

Benedict sounded so certain that Patrick wondered if word had come down from on high while he was eating lunch and supposedly making up his mind. Either that, or divine intervention had assured he would say yes.

Patrick had his cover story ready.

'The island has a fascinating history. I'd like to study it at closer quarters.'

'A worthy project,' Benedict suppressed a smile. 'But plenty of time too, I hope, to take an interest in the present-day activities of its inhabitants?'

'Of course.'

'On your return, Monsieur, I suggest we share a glass of wine.'

An offer Patrick was pleased to accept.

Deposited back on the *quai*, he headed for the Irish bar. Stephen's boat was back in its mooring, the wetsuits hung out to dry. So the most likely place to find him would be inside, having a pint of Guinness.

Stephen was indeed sitting in his usual corner in the dark shadows of the interior, whereas the barrel-style tables, with high chairs, outside were occupied by smokers and by visitors who didn't come to Cannes to desert the sun.

'Welcome back. How was the Queen?'

It seemed telling Pascal where he was going had meant telling the world, or at least the world of Le Suquet.

'I didn't really see her.'

'It's a poor party where you don't get to meet your host.'

'I agree. Fancy another pint?' Patrick diverted the conversation.

'Sure thing.'

Minutes later, settled at the table with a half-pint of Guinness for himself, Patrick queried Stephen as to what had happened in his absence.

'Daniel wants to speak to you about your car.' Stephen paused. 'So why were you on Honorat?' When Patrick raised an eyebrow, Stephen said, 'Benedict is a distant cousin of François, who supplies fish for the monastery.'

François Girard, a local fisherman known as Posidonie, had been of help to Patrick in his last case, secretly transporting him to a Russian yacht anchored in the bay. Posidonie had also performed another vital job during that investigation which would forever remain a secret between them.

'Word gets round fast,' Patrick said.

'This is Cannes,' Stephen reminded him. 'So, anything I can do to help?'

Patrick considered the offer. 'Report back any gossip about what goes on on St Honorat.'

Stephen's eyes lit up. 'With pleasure. I have an acquaintance working there.'

'May I ask who?'

'Monique Girard is now second chef at La Tonnelle,' Stephen said with a broad smile.

Monique was François' daughter. Patrick had first met her on the Russian yacht when she'd been called in to replace an absent chef for a big dinner party. Now this was good news. Patrick regarded Stephen's smug look.

'You two are an item?'

'We are.'

'Since when?'

'Since after the black pearl.'

So the outcome of that job had proved satisfactory to more people than just Patrick.

'Good luck with that.' Patrick refrained from adding 'You might need it!', although that was true. François was a man of few words, but his daughter was the opposite. Small, dark-haired and very attractive, she was every inch a Suquetan. Had she been alive during the war, Patrick imagined she would have been heading a resistance cell and blowing up railway lines.

Having given Stephen a job, Patrick took leave of him. It was nearing four o'clock and he was keen to see Oscar again. He entered Le Suquet via the archway of flowers, the scent of lavender as strong here as it had been in the buzzing midday heat on St Honorat. All around him were sounds of chatter and clinking glasses. Lunchtime over, late afternoon presented residents and visitors with an opportunity to sit and watch the world go by while enjoying a glass of wine or a coffee.

As Patrick passed Le P'tit Zinc, Veronique, its proprietress, deigned to give him a nod – although not a smile, as smiles were not in her nature. It was too early to find his friend Chevalier at his usual table, but he noted that Veronique had placed a reserved sign there in anticipation of Chevalier's arrival.

He turned into the narrow Rue de la Miséricorde and within minutes was at the door on Rue Forville that gave entry to a set of flats and the courtyard of Le Chanteclair. Being a part-time resident of the hotel, Patrick had his own key and duly used it. He was barely through the intervening short passage before he heard a joyful grunt, which served Oscar as a bark, and skittering paws quickly deposited Oscar's sturdy muscular body at his feet.

Patrick greeted the little dog with pleasure. In response, the snuffling noise Oscar emitted through his flat nose became even louder. Having welcomed him in style, the dog led him like royalty into the courtyard.

Pale-pink roses in full bloom climbed the right-hand side of the handsome frontage of the old building, their fragrance captured and held within the walls of the courtyard. To either side of the entrance stood Pascal's prize lemon trees, on which a few lemons still hung, ready to be plucked and sliced to add to a gin and tonic if required.

Patrick stood for a moment, drinking in the scene. Cannes might be noisy and busy outside these walls, but here in the courtyard all was calm. Just like the cloisters of the abbey on St Honorat.

Pascal, having heard his arrival, appeared from reception. He gave Patrick the once over, as if meeting the Queen of England might have changed his appearance in some way, then seemed satisfied that it had not.

'I've just brewed some coffee. Would you like a cup?'

'I would.'

Pascal waved him to a seat at one of the four tables where he served breakfast, and guests might eat their evening meal. Patrick settled himself below the shuttered window of his room, which was on the second floor.

The cafetière arrived, emitting the strong, aromatic scent of fresh coffee. Pascal poured them each a cup and sat down.

'I'm waiting on two more guests then we're full,' he said.

'You know you can use my room if you need it,' Patrick told him.

'I prefer to keep it empty in case you turn up unexpectedly,' Pascal said, his look reminding Patrick that such a thing had happened before now, and recently. 'So how did it go with Brother Robert?'

'Fine,' Patrick replied, without being more explicit.

Pascal wasn't going to be put off that easily. 'And what is the job he has lined up for Le Limier?'

Patrick decided the best thing to do was to give enough information to keep Pascal happy.

'There's been a theft. He wants me to find what's missing, but not involve the police.'

'Mmm.' Pascal considered this. 'He thinks it was one of the brothers?'

'He doesn't know.'

'And how do you aim to find this missing item?'

'He's asked me to stay at the monastery for a few days and see what I can discover.'

'And Oscar?'

'He's also invited.'

'Is that wise?' Pascal said. 'You can hardly creep about the island listening in to monks' conversations with Oscar in tow.'

It was a valid point, yet the dog's presence might also allay suspicion about his reason for being there.

'I think Oscar might be an asset,' Patrick said. 'And Brother Robert made a point of inviting him.'

Pascal looked a little crestfallen.

'Thank you for looking after him,' Patrick said to ease the pain. 'I appreciate it.'

Pascal nodded, apparently resigned to the loss of 'his' dog again. 'And what is to be your cover story for the visit?'

'I'm researching the history of the monastery.'

Pascal rose. 'I can help you with that. I read a great deal about Cannes and the Lérins islands when I came here from Nice.'

He disappeared into the hotel to emerge minutes later with a couple of books.

'You may borrow these if you wish. They'll provide you with enough to sound knowledgeable.'

Patrick thanked him again, finished his coffee, and made to go. Oscar, sensing their departure, hastened towards the exit without a backward glance at his foster parent. Patrick made a swift farewell, hoping Pascal wasn't too hurt by such a quick transfer of affections.

He wandered back towards the harbour and was pleased to note that Chevalier was now settled at his favourite table outside Le P'tit

Zinc. Chevalier – or Le Chevalier as he was affectionately known in Le Suquet – was smartly dressed as always, in a lightweight jacket, brightly coloured shirt, cravat and matching top-pocket handkerchief. Owner of the premier estate agents nearby and the magnificent glossy black Yamaha TMAX parked in Rue de la Miséricorde, Chevalier provided more than just local colour.

'Ah, de Courvoisier, you're back from your royal appointment, I see. How was Her Majesty?'

Patrick wondered how many more times he would be asked this question and wished he hadn't been honest when asked why he was visiting London.

'She sends her regards to the King of Le Suquet,' he replied, which brought a wide smile to the lips below the sleek black moustache. Then Chevalier dropped his voice to a more serious tone.

'And the real reason you were there . . . I trust that matter has been dealt with satisfactorily?'

Chevalier knew enough about him to guess that Patrick's summons to London had been more than just an invitation to a garden party, however important the host might be. Chevalier had played a prominent role during the case of the black pearl and would guard his back whenever necessary.

Patrick hadn't wanted the job London had tried to foist on him, but he couldn't prevent Huntington from turning up in Cannes asking questions. And the less time Huntington spent doing that, the quicker he could return.

43

'What do you know of the Windsors' connection with Cannes?' Patrick said.

'I know that the Duke of Windsor once sat here eating sea urchins in aioli while his security people scoured the hotels on La Croisette looking for him. According to local legend, when discovered he informed them that Cannes was like a beautiful woman – charming but full of secrets.'

Veronique's appearance prevented Patrick from responding to this tale. Without enquiring what he would like to order, she delivered a half-carafe of red, a glass and a bowl of crisps. Unruffled by this, Chevalier thanked her, poured a glass for Patrick and topped up his own, and then dropped a few crisps to a waiting and eager Oscar.

'I take it you're expecting visitors,' Chevalier said, after sampling his wine and dabbing his moustache dry with his handkerchief.

'I plan to be on St Honorat when they arrive.'

'And what do they seek in Cannes?'

'There's likely to be a woman and a man. The woman is an Italian art expert, Grazia Lucca by name. The man is known as Giles Huntington.' Patrick heard his tone change on the second name and couldn't prevent it.

'And they're interested in art?'

'Stolen art.'

'The Nazi collection?'

Patrick nodded.

'Then they're on a fool's errand.'

'I think so.'

'So you want them to leave swiftly?'

'That would be good.'

44

Chevalier's piercing black eyes stared into his. 'And you will be permitted to remain here?'

Patrick couldn't answer that question, but there was one thing he was certain of. Had he taken the job, he wouldn't have been permitted to resume his life here afterwards, despite what Charles had said. His only hope of staying was to appear useless in their eyes. An operative who could no longer operate.

Then they might leave him alone.

The alternative was to give up his home and life in Cannes and go to ground. It was an option he'd considered before coming here. Then he'd seen the gunboat, and realized he might settle here and live on her.

And so he'd stayed, promising himself to keep his head down. Provide a service for the locals. Hence he'd become Le Limier, the fixer, until the case of the black pearl had brought him back into the limelight, both with the Police Nationale and his previous masters.

'If I'd stayed off the radar, this wouldn't have happened,' Patrick said bitterly.

'You had no choice.' Chevalier's voice brought Patrick back from his dark thoughts. 'Because of Marie Élise.'

As Chevalier said her name, Marie's image presented itself to Patrick. At first alive, her bright laughing eyes fastened on him across the table as they ate together on *Les Trois Soeurs*, then naked and dead in his bath.

'Her death wasn't your fault,' Chevalier said.

'No. But perhaps I could have prevented it.'

'As could I.'

They acknowledged their shared guilt for a moment.

Chevalier changed the subject. 'When do you go to St Honorat?'

'Tomorrow.'

'We'll keep in touch. Now I have to leave. I have a dinner date.' Chevalier rose, placed some money on the tray, and rewarded a patiently waiting Oscar with the remainder of the crisps.

Patrick watched as Chevalier deftly mounted his motorbike, roared off down the cobbled street, and took a swift left, heading for the Voie Rapide.

Five

On his way back to the gunboat, Patrick picked up a *fruits de mer* platter and a chilled bottle of dry white wine. He had no wish to eat out tonight, but wanted to sit on the upper deck under the awning, with Oscar at his feet. To relish his return, until he had to leave again.

The platter too was symbolic, it was in memory of Marie Élise. They'd shared one below deck the night she'd answered his call for help in finding a missing starlet. He had known that, as one of Madame Lacroix's girls, Marie Élise would be both intelligent and beautiful. What Patrick hadn't expected was to fall in love with her a little. Nor to lose her so soon.

Patrick lowered the gangplank and Oscar ran on board, sniffing and snuffling as he re-established his presence. Patrick climbed to the upper deck and laid his platter on the table, then fetched a glass and a bottle opener from the cabin.

Once he was seated, Oscar sprawled across his feet as if to prevent his escape, Patrick opened the wine, tasted it, then set about the langoustines. Evening had settled on the *quai*, the glare and heat of the sun dissipated, a breeze lightly shaking the palm fronds. Groups of people walked past in their evening finery seeking the perfect place to dine.

For Patrick, this was perfect enough.

By the time he'd finished his meal, it was dark enough to require a light if he was to peruse the books Pascal had given him in preparation for tomorrow. He lit a small lamp and, having refilled his glass, settled down to read.

St Honorat, like St Columba, had been of noble birth and each founded a centre of Christianity, the one in the far south and the other in the far north of Europe. Whereas Columba had chosen the cooler northern isle of Iona, off the west coast of Scotland, Honorat had chosen a warmer clime, although it seemed his selected spot had been swarming with serpents, which crawled through the Roman ruins littering the island.

St Honorat had disposed of the snakes, just as St Patrick had done in Ireland. Since St Patrick had, apparently, been educated at the monastery on Honorat, perhaps he'd learned his 'banishing' skills there.

The monastery had grown rich and very powerful, at one time owning most of the coastal land between Grasse and Barcelona and becoming home to 4,000 monks, which seemed surprising considering its land mass. Patrick imagined it as an island city back then, rather than the tranquil and verdant place it was now.

Such riches had been a great temptation and resulted in attacks by pirates and incessant arguments with the Pope. By the end of the seventeenth century, the monastery had fallen into decline. Disestablished in 1787, during the French Revolution it had become the property of the state and had been sold to Mademoiselle de Sainval, the wealthy actress who Brother Robert had told him was the mistress of Fragonard. She'd lived there for twenty years. Certainly long enough to have her portrait painted. Eventually, the Cistercians bought the island in 1959 and rejuvenated it through hard work and prayer, perhaps bringing it back to what Honorat had envisaged in the first place.

As Patrick laid down the book, Oscar stirred at his feet, anticipating their late-night stroll prior to bed. The *quai* had quietened now to the steady hum of conversation from the diners at the outdoor tables. All had now been fed, but a few still lingered enjoying the night air.

Patrick indicated with a low whistle that Oscar was to get his wish. The little dog sped down the gangplank, and once on the *quai* turned towards the beach with Patrick following. Of the line of yachts moored beyond *Les Trois Soeurs*, some were familiar and some new. Patrick registered each of them, always keen to know who his current neighbours were. By the time he

48

reached the avenue of palm trees that skirted the shore, the steady beat of the sea had taken over from the quayside chatter. Patrick stood for a moment at the slipway leading to the beach and listened to the sea's comforting rhythm. Tonight there were no energetic waves pounding the pale sand, but merely a steady lapping, almost a caress.

Eastwards, the dark landmass jutting out into a silky grey sea was like an outstretched arm. Lights twinkled along its shore, but in the high reaches of the Esterel mountains the only light came from the stars and the half-moon that hung above.

Oscar had already visited the beach and now came running back to encourage Patrick to follow. And follow he did, having decided that a night swim might be in order. He stripped to his boxer shorts, told Oscar to wait, and waded into the water. When the water lapped at his thighs, he dived under, registering the 'not yet summer' temperature.

He struck straight out until he passed the curve of rocks that sheltered the beach and kept the sand from departing, then turned to the right, intent on a steady crawl along the neighbouring beaches of the eastern seaboard for maybe fifteen minutes before turning back. Oscar would patiently wait there for him, but Patrick didn't want the little dog to think he'd been deserted yet again.

No yachts were anchored here, their owners preferring the shelter of Cannes harbour, or in the bay just outside for those craft too large to

49

enter. Towards the end of June diving rafts would be towed out and secured at regular intervals opposite each popular beach, but for now the stretch of water before him was invitingly empty. Patrick could make out nothing below the dark water, but was pleased to note shoals of small sardines jumping and diving nearby on the moonlit surface of the sea.

Ahead, further out, Patrick spotted a local fishing boat already at work. Cannes' small fleet of fishermen had their berths just beyond the gunboat. Small in size and number, they seemed at times to be a throwback to the past, when Cannes had consisted only of Le Suquet with its cluster of houses on the steep hill that led to the castle, and the surrounding land on which the famous La Croisette stood had been a reed-studded marsh.

Yet a continual supply of fresh fish was required to grace the tables of the rich and not so rich of Cannes, although the fishermen themselves rarely became wealthy by catching them.

The water in June was still chilly, especially when the sun went down. Patrick turned and headed back the way he'd come. As he drew near the shore, a plane flew overhead, its landing lights flashing as it approached Nice airport, reminding Patrick that the London visitors might soon be arriving, if they hadn't already. That thought made him decide to catch the early ferry to St Honorat.

Oscar came bounding towards Patrick as he emerged from the water, the dog's grunts indicating his pleasure that his master had returned.

There had been times during the last job when that hadn't happened, and Oscar had a long memory.

Patrick praised the little dog for obeying his command, picked up his clothes, and began the walk back along the *quai*, looking forward to a hot shower and bed. What little he required for his time on Honorat he could pack in the morning.

After midnight now, only the Irish bar still had customers. As Patrick approached *Les Trois Soeurs*, a figure detached itself from the group outside and crossed the road towards him. Patrick didn't have to see the man's face to know who it was. The short neat figure was instantly recognizable, as was the scent of the burning cheroot in his right hand.

Rather than greet Patrick, Lieutenant Martin Moreaux ground out his cheroot then bent to ruffle Oscar's ears. The bulldog was the only positive link between the detective and Patrick, having been bred by Moreaux's wife, Michelle. Patrick believed that should he appear not to be taking good care of Oscar, his own life would be on the line.

Having satisfied himself that Oscar was in tiptop condition, Moreaux viewed Patrick, still dripping from his swim.

'The last time you swam at this late hour something bad happened as I recall,' he said drily.

'You came to arrest me for murder. I hope that's not the reason for your visit tonight?'

'You look cold. Shall we go on board?'

Patrick contemplated telling Moreaux to get

51

lost, but curiosity got the better of him. He lowered the gangplank and, with Oscar leading, they all trooped aboard and down into the cabin.

'Help yourself to a drink,' Patrick said, 'while I take a quick shower.'

Moreaux nodded and immediately headed for the wide selection of bottles on the bar next to the cooking area. Patrick left Oscar with him and went through to the bathroom, his mind already trying to work out why Moreaux should turn up here, and now.

Under the brief but very hot shower he came up with three possible scenarios, the first being that Moreaux had learned of Patrick's London trip, perhaps even its outcome. The second was that the detective's network in Le Suquet had got wind of his summons by Brother Robert. The third possibility was that the London team had already touched down in Cannes and asked some pertinent questions.

All three scenarios were possible. But whether Moreaux chose to tell him the real reason for his visit was another matter. The Lieutenant was a good detective because he rarely gave anything away yet managed to acquire the information he desired.

A trait I can match, thought Patrick.

Drying and dressing swiftly, he re-entered the cabin to find Oscar sitting at Moreaux's feet, much as he liked to sit with Patrick. Judging by the bottle on the counter, Moreaux had chosen to drink whisky. Patrick decided to do the same. He poured a large measure, added a little water, swirled it round the glass, then savoured it. Now warmed inside as well as out, Patrick waited for Moreaux to tell him why he was here.

Eventually the policeman spoke.

'How was your London trip?'

'Brief and uneventful,' Patrick said evenly, while wondering exactly how much Moreaux might be aware of concerning his summons to the garden party.

'I thought you might be preparing to return home,' Moreaux sounded almost wistful.

'I am home,' Patrick said, indicating the interior of the gunboat with a wave of his hand.

Moreaux gave a low grunt that resembled the sound Oscar emitted when he found Patrick irritating.

'The business with the black pearl—' Moreaux began.

'Is over,' Patrick finished for him.

Moreaux shrugged an acceptance. 'And your current plans?'

'To swim, visit the casino, and drive when I can resurrect my car.'

'Ah, the car. It is repairable?'

'Daniel believes so.'

'And what of your desire to climb in the Esterel mountains?' Moreaux said, catching Patrick's eye.

'That too, once I can access them again,' Patrick said carefully. 'Why do you ask?'

'If I recall, that particular location proved dangerous for you,' Moreaux said grimly.

'Fortunately you were watching my back on that one.' Patrick gave him a grateful smile.

'We cannot always be watching your back, Monsieur.' Moreaux's voice had an edge to it.

'I wouldn't expect you to.' Patrick finished his drink, hoping to bring an end to the matter.

But it seemed Moreaux wasn't yet ready to leave. He swirled the remaining whisky round in the glass, watching it rise and fall like a small wave. Eventually he appeared to come to a decision and, giving a typical Gallic shrug, downed the remainder of his drink and stood up.

'Then I'll bid you goodnight.'

Patrick stood back to let him exit. Following Moreaux on to the deck, he watched as the iron-grey head went ashore. Moreaux stopped for a moment to light another cheroot before turning to Patrick.

'Please give Brother Robert my regards when you see him tomorrow. I hope Oscar enjoys his sojourn among the vines.' And with that he departed on foot along the *quai* in a fragrant cloud of smoke.

Patrick stood for a moment assimilating what had just happened. It appeared from Moreaux's oblique references that two of the scenarios he had considered while under the shower were correct.

The detective was aware that Patrick and Oscar were headed for St Honorat tomorrow and had also mentioned Brother Robert, but that didn't mean he knew why Patrick was going there. As for the Esterel connection, that had been more tenuous. Patrick had nearly lost his life in the mountains and had Moreaux to thank for saving it. And the lack of a car? That had been a slight impediment to his movements in Moreaux's territory recently – something he suspected the detective might have liked. It was easier to keep an eye on Patrick when he remained in Le Suquet. Maybe that was the only reason for the subject being raised.

Oscar had already taken up residence in the corner of the bedroom and was snoring softly. Opening the porthole a little, Patrick stripped off and climbed into bed, allowing the gentle sound of water lapping at the hull to lull him to sleep.

Six

He was awakened by the throb of engines as the fishing boats passed by on their way out to sea. The rosy light of dawn spilled through the porthole, reddening the room and Oscar's sleeping body. Patrick rose, went through to the cabin, and put the coffee pot on before getting dressed. The first ferry to Honorat left at eight o'clock and he had a visit to make before then.

Before taking his coffee up on to the deck, he went across the road for a couple of fresh croissants to go with it. By the time he returned, Oscar had stirred and was taking advantage of the food laid out for him. Twenty minutes later they were heading up the hill to the Place du Suquet in response to Daniel's summons about the car.

On Rue Hibert, the garage door had already been raised and there was the sound of men at work inside. When Patrick entered, he made straight for where he'd last seen the remains of his car. What stood there now was almost unrecognizable.

'What do you think?' Daniel asked, having noticed Patrick's arrival.

'It's magnificent!' Patrick said and meant it. 'How did you—'

'I have a friend in Paris who shipped me some second-hand replacement panels. He's a collector of old cars. I haven't managed to remove all the bullet holes, but they are scars to be worn with pride. Not many men survive what you did.'

'And the chassis and undercarriage?'

'Sturdy as ever. It's a solid car, even if it has had a rough time.'

'I can't thank you enough,' Patrick said feelingly. 'You must give me the bill.'

'We'll discuss the bill another time,' Daniel replied. 'I have a little job I need you to do for me.'

They adjourned to the tiny office at the rear. Once inside, Daniel shut and locked the door, then explained why he required the assistance of Le Limier.

Patrick and Oscar made the eight o'clock ferry with only seconds to spare. Had Benedict not seen their mad dash down the steps to the jetty, they would have had to watch it depart and wait an hour for the next one.

Once they were aboard and Benedict had

56

steered the ferry free of the harbour, Patrick made his way forward to say thank you. There were few passengers, most of them, Patrick suspected, workers from the restaurant and the monastery shop.

He did spot one person he was acquainted with. Monique Girard was exactly as he remembered her from the night they'd met aboard the Russian-owned yacht named *Heavenly Princess*. Petite and curvaceous, on this occasion she wasn't encased in a fitted white chef's jacket but wore a lightweight top and jeans. Her jet-black hair lay loose on her shoulders rather than rolled into a tight knot, but the full lips were painted a rich red as before.

Those lips broke into a smile when she spotted Patrick.

She rose from the seat to greet him and Patrick bent down to receive her kisses.

'I hear you're on a job,' she whispered as he did so.

Patrick viewed her animated expression.

'You've been talking to Stephen.'

Monique shrugged. 'That and other things,' she said coyly.

'He's a lucky man.'

Monique's expression suggested she agreed with him.

'So how can I help Le Limier?'

Monique was in a good position to offer aid, but Patrick had given his word that he wouldn't reveal the real reason why he was on the island and he had every intention of keeping it.

'Just let me know the gossip.'

'Everything?'

'Everything,' Patrick assured her.

'Do you want to start now?'

Patrick abandoned his decision to talk to Benedict and took a seat beside Monique instead. By the time the ferry approached St Honorat, Patrick had been brought up to date on the sexual liaisons of the entire staff of La Tonnelle, as well as the abbey's ground staff and those who manned the monastery shop. Monique kept the monks until last.

'Including the Abbot and Brother Robert, there are twenty-five brothers on the island,' she informed him. 'Of all ages. Some I like, others not so much.' She pulled a face. 'A few of the more reclusive ones I haven't yet met, so must go with the general opinion. As Cistercians, they've all sworn to remain celibate.' Monique's face wore a bemused expression as she said this. 'It seems they're adhering to their vow.'

'So no gossip about the brothers?'

'I didn't say that exactly.'

They were drawing alongside the jetty now.

'It'll have to keep until later,' Monique said with a conspiratorial smile.

'When?' Patrick said.

'I have a break after lunch, for an hour, around three. A water taxi takes me back to Cannes at ten.'

Patrick had no idea how his own day would pan out and told her so.

'I'm working the next three days in a row,' Monique said with a shrug. 'I'll see you when I see you.' She bid a fond farewell to Oscar and gave Patrick a parting wave as she disembarked, then set off along the path to the shoreside restaurant.

Patrick sought out Benedict. 'Thanks for waiting for me,' he said.

'Brother Robert thought you would be keen to get started.'

'Can we have that glass of wine together later?'

'Come to the jetty at nine,' Benedict told him.

Patrick clipped Oscar's leash on, as demanded by the local regulations. Oscar seemed a little surprised by this but didn't complain vocally. Patrick suspected that once inside the grounds of the monastery the dog might be given more leeway, but he didn't want to arrive in a manner that suggested he was already breaking the island's rules.

The small tractor that had transported the two women the day before now arrived for his luggage. Since he was carrying nothing but a small backpack Patrick waved it away, indicating he would walk to the monastery.

The morning was fine with a clear blue sky. He took the same route as before through the fields of vines. His study of the island had armed him with plenty of information as to the layout and he now knew which vines were grown and where.

On his immediate right there was Chardonney Clairette, for white wine. Beyond them Syrah, for the red wine. A mix of Syrah, Mourvèdre, Clairette and Chardonnay was grown to the east of the monastery grounds. All in all there were eight hectares under cultivation, half for red and

59

half for white. The brothers also made a range of flower and fruit liqueurs, one of which, Lérincello, was a favourite of Patrick's.

Having extended the dog's lead to its full length, a snuffling Oscar was free to examine every olive, lemon and lime tree that lined the path. A mix of scents enveloped Patrick. With the only sounds birdsong, the rustling of fragrant leaves and the steady, distant beat of the sea on the shore, the island was living up to what it claimed to be – a calm and verdant oasis, minutes away from the bustle of Cannes.

Patrick stopped for a moment to allow Oscar to investigate a particularly interesting scent, and used the time to briefly contemplate his earlier meeting with Daniel. He'd never imagined that his car could rise from the dead like Lazarus. It had, and with it an intriguing proposition.

It seemed Daniel, a confirmed bachelor, had finally found the woman of his dreams. He'd shown Patrick a photograph of her. She was indeed beautiful, as Daniel had declared. She was also living in France illegally. Daniel was concerned about her status, but that wasn't the main reason he'd spoken to Patrick.

The Riviera was rife with immigrants from North Africa, legal or otherwise. They worked in people's homes and restaurant and café kitchens the length of the Côte d'Azur. This particular young woman had apparently been in Cannes for three years and had worked in a number of establishments, some quite prestigious.

The danger to Fidella wasn't the fact that she was illegal, but that she was being pursued by the men who'd brought her to Europe then forced her into prostitution, instead of offering her the work they'd promised. Her escape from their clutches had been difficult and daring, but she'd managed to stay free of them until now. Having discovered Fidella's whereabouts, they wanted their original investment back, plus the money she would have earned for them in the interim, with considerable interest.

If not, they'd threatened revenge on both Daniel and his new-found love.

Patrick didn't doubt their threats. Neither did he question that he would help Daniel. Exactly how he wasn't yet sure, although he had the beginnings of a plan.

Reporting at the small office in the outer cloister, Patrick was greeted with an interested look by the young monk on duty, who had apparently been told to expect him.

'Monsieur de Courvoisier, welcome to St Honorat and in particular to the monastery. I understand you're staying with us for a couple of days?' He suddenly noticed the dog and came round the desk to greet him. 'And you must be Oscar.' He bent to pat Oscar, who accepted the approbation with aplomb, suggesting Patrick may have been right in bringing the dog along with him. His presence certainly seemed to disarm.

'Your room is ready. If you'd like to follow me.'

Patrick followed Brother Thomas, as he'd introduced himself, through the main cloister, emerging into the inner gardens and sanctum of the

61

monastery. The scent of lavender and a multitude of other herbs, the busy hum of bees, and the warm sun reflected back from ancient stone walls would, he felt, be enough to lull anyone into a sense of tranquillity.

Walking through the gardens, he could hear the sound of chants from the church as yet another short service of prayer began. Patrick understood perfectly at that moment why a retreat from the real world could be desirable. After all, he'd sought something similar when he'd deserted London for a gunboat in Cannes.

Brother Thomas approached a low stone building with three doors leading on to a cloister that encircled the inner garden.

'This will be your place of peace,' he said, opening the door. 'Brother Robert will see you when you've settled in.'

Patrick thanked him and entered his designated abode.

The room was small and square with a single narrow window. Above the wooden bed hung a simple crucifix. A door to the right gave on to a small toilet and shower room. Shadowy, with the scent of warm stone mixed with that of lemon, the room would do very well, he decided.

He set his backpack by the bed, washed his hands with the soap that bore the stamp of St Honorat, and headed back to the main cloister. This time there was no Brother Thomas on duty in the office, so Patrick made his own way up the stairs.

Pausing outside Brother Robert's room, he heard the low murmur of male voices. It seemed

Brother Robert already had a visitor. Unsure now whether he should knock or wait downstairs for the visitor's departure, Patrick hesitated.

As one of the voices rose a little, he realized the conversation was being conducted in English. The distinctive tone was one he'd hoped never to hear again.

Patrick knocked and immediately entered.

Brother Robert stood by the window. The figure addressing him had his back to Patrick. It didn't matter that Patrick couldn't see his face, because he knew exactly who the tall slim figure in the light-grey suit was.

The figure turned, and it was clear from his expression that Patrick was the last person he'd expected to find at the abbey. There was a moment's stunned silence as Giles Huntington assessed the situation. Then Brother Robert smiled in a welcoming fashion, suggesting he was unperturbed at the meeting of the two men.

'Monsieur de Courvoisier, I see you've arrived safely. I take it Brother Thomas has shown you where you'll be staying?'

'Yes, thank you.'

'Let me introduce you both. Mr Coburn, this is Patrick de Courvoisier, who's staying with us for a few days' retreat. Mr Coburn is a buyer of our wines. An important buyer, in fact he supplies your royal household.' Brother Robert beamed at this. 'Apparently our 1979 Syrah is a firm favourite.'

The two men eyed one another as if strangers and shook hands. Huntington, alias Coburn, having masked his initial surprise, now made a quip suggesting he had intimate knowledge of each of the Windsors' taste in wine.

'And you're here on St Honorat to buy more of that vintage?' Patrick asked.

'And to taste some of the newer ones,' Huntington answered smoothly.

'Mr Coburn is also contemplating a trip to Cap d'Antibes on our new ferry,' Brother Robert said.

'No vineyards there,' Patrick said, as if confused.

'He's interested in the current refurbishment of Château de la Croë,' Brother Robert explained.

Now that was interesting, and something Patrick could tell by Huntington's expression that he hadn't wished Patrick to know.

'Château de la Croë and the Windsors . . .' Patrick smiled. 'Now there's a story to be savoured, rather like a good wine,' he said mischievously.

At his words, Patrick caught a flash of hatred in those pale-blue eyes, before the smooth diplomacy returned.

'It's a long time since a Windsor lived in the château,' Huntington said.

'And he wasn't exactly in favour at the time, having just abdicated and married an American divorcee,' Patrick added for good measure.

'A scandal of the past,' Brother Robert intervened as the door opened and the young monk appeared. 'Now, Mr Coburn, if you'd like to go with Brother Thomas, he will take you to the cellar.'

Huntington wasn't keen to leave, not until he knew why Patrick was resident on St Honorat, but he had little choice. However, he had one last try.

'I'll be having lunch at La Tonnelle, Monsieur de Courvoisier. Might I see you there?'

Patrick gave a non-committal smile.

Once the door closed, Patrick asked, 'Has Mr Coburn visited the island before?'

'No, although we've spoken on the phone. And of course we're delighted about the Windsor connection, although we French are Republicans at heart,' Brother Robert said. 'Would you like to take a look at where the Madonna was being stored?'

Patrick indicated that he would.

The air in the vault was as dry as in a cave in the Esterel mountains. In fact ideal for storing paintings. There were a number of them there. Mostly overwrought images of tortured saints, ancient French nobility, long deceased, and of course Christ on the Cross. No images of a kindly Jesus with children featured among them.

Brother Robert observed the array of canvases with a bemused eye. 'The Cistercian approach to Christianity is somewhat different, as you know. Which is why none of these are on display.'

'Was the image of the Madonna painted in a similar fashion?' Patrick said.

'Not exactly. There is a small photograph of the painting, rather the worse for wear but . . .'

He produced the snapshot from the folds of his gown and handed it to Patrick.

The colours were faded but the image was clear enough. As Brother Robert had suggested, it wasn't a standard depiction of the Madonna. No lowered glance. No expression of love, servitude or suffering. This Madonna looked you in the eye, challenging your way of viewing her. The face was beautiful and distinctive and, Patrick assumed, resembled Fragonard's mistress. No enveloping robes disguised the fact that she was a woman. The breasts were exposed, reminding Patrick of Edvard Munch's half-length nude often called *Madonna*. Munch had reworked the painting of his mistress, Dagny Juel, a number of times, and a hand-coloured print of one version had been sold in 2010 for £1,250,000. Fragonard's depiction of his mistress would no doubt fetch a handsome price, too, on the open market – and possibly even more among those buyers who preferred to bid in private and had no wish for an official stamp on their purchase.

'May I keep this until we find her?' Patrick said.

'Of course.'

Brother Robert indicated a register giving details of who had access to the vault and when. There were four names on the list besides his own.

'All four have agreed to speak to you,' he said.

'They are aware the Madonna is missing?'

'As I said, the existence of the Madonna is not common knowledge. However, a rumour of a painting having been misplaced is circulating, although it hasn't been confirmed by myself or the Abbot. The brothers have simply been told you're researching a history of the monastery.'

It was clear from Brother Robert's discomfort

that he wasn't happy about the lack of honesty surrounding the disappearance of the Madonna. Patrick wondered how much the Abbot had had to do with the enforced secrecy.

'Will I be speaking to the Abbot?' he said.

Brother Robert looked even more uncomfortable. 'He doesn't normally meet with those on retreat,' he said obliquely.

Patrick chose not to argue the point, suspecting he would learn little from such a meeting. Ownership of the Madonna seemed to be something unwished for, and its disappearance had forced them to acknowledge the painting's existence.

Or maybe their ownership had been illegal in the first place?

Oscar had accompanied him into the vault and had taken advantage of the coolness of the stone floor. Perhaps realizing patience was required while the two men talked, he'd spread himself out, just as he often did in the shade of the court-yard of Le Chanteclair.

As the two men made for the exit, Oscar jumped up.

'You may leave Oscar in the garden while you talk with the brothers. He'll be well looked after.'

'I prefer to have him with me. He seems to put people at ease,' Patrick said.

Brother Robert smiled. 'He has that particular gift.'

Patrick had chosen to speak to the brothers in the garden, rather than in his room or in Brother Robert's office. It had been a good decision. In full view of those who traversed the gardens en route to their daily duties, it looked informal and not in the least intimidating, particularly with a small dog snoring in the shade next to their bench. The glances that came their way suggested others wouldn't mind being asked to sit and chat in a similar fashion, which was of course what Patrick intended.

Brother Thomas had been the first to answer the summons. Having already made Patrick's acquaintance, the conversation was entered into easily. It seemed Thomas had joined the Order only four years ago, prior to which he'd been a music teacher and hence now led the abbey choir. It was at this point Patrick realized he'd seen Thomas in the church yesterday.

The monk also declared an interest in French history and, in particular, the story of the island he'd come to live on. He spoke enthusiastically about this until Patrick guided their conversation round to the subject of the works of art in the vault.

'I believe you help look after them?' Patrick asked, encouragingly.

Thomas nodded.

'And your favourite piece is?'

Thomas looked Patrick in the eye and said. 'The naked Madonna. It is magnificent and was, I believe, painted by Fragonard.'

Having skirted round the subject for some time, Patrick was nonplussed by this blunt admission.

The monk's face assumed a look of distress. 'That's why you are here, is it not, Monsieur?'

'I confess I would like to know more about the painting,' Patrick replied, cautiously.

'And you cannot, because it's missing,' the monk said quietly.

'You are aware of that?'

'Everyone is, Monsieur.'

'Brother Robert wished the enquiry concerning the painting to be discreet.'

Thomas gave a wry smile. 'This is a small, close-knit community, Monsieur. Our secrets are our own, and it is true that we do not care to share them with those outside. In this case, that may be necessary, if we are to restore the Madonna to her rightful place. With us,' he added firmly.

In the aftermath of his chat with Thomas, Patrick wondered how realistic Brother Robert's directions as to how to conduct the enquiry had been. He couldn't believe that Brother Robert wasn't aware that the secret was truly out, but perhaps it had been the Abbot who had laid down the ground rules.

The other three brothers whose names appeared on the register in the vault all began their conversation with Patrick as if they already knew what had occurred with Thomas. Each told him exactly when they had last seen the Madonna. It seemed that, rather than being a hidden piece of art, she was an object of pilgrimage, among the younger brothers at least.

It was even possible that for that reason she had to go.

With this thought, Patrick woke Oscar from his slumbers and left the garden, his intention being to have lunch then do a reconnaissance of the shore. The only way for the painting to leave the island was by boat. Patrick wanted to be sure he knew all the locations it could have left from. The island had a rocky shore and there were not many places a boat, however small, might approach and pick up such a precious cargo. Once away it could have met up with one of the hundreds of yachts that plied these waters for pleasure, and the painting might be anywhere by now.

Assuming, of course, it *had* left the island.

His discussions with both Brother Robert and the four young monks had cast doubt on this. From Patrick's experience, circumstances were rarely what they appeared to be. And with that in mind he allowed himself to recall the incident in Brother Robert's office.

The irony of his accepting this job to avoid Huntington and then meeting him on the island wasn't lost on Patrick. One thing he did know. Huntington wasn't here to buy wine – or at least not just to buy wine, however good the vintage and however important the client. According to Charles Carruthers, Huntington was in the area to search for a painting for the Windsors.

A job I was offered and turned down.

And with that thought, Patrick entered La Tonnelle.

Obviously told to expect him, a waiter led him to a reserved table overlooking the water. Oscar, scenting the delicious smell of food, positively swaggered in, taking up his place below the table in anticipation of what might be forthcoming.

Patrick made a point of not scanning the room to see if Huntington was there. If he was, he would no doubt seek Patrick out. He doubted his former colleague would have bought the story of a retreat as the reason for Patrick's presence, so would be keen to know the real reason he was here.

Patrick ordered the meat dish of the day and a half-bottle of the red wine that had so delighted the Windsors and ostensibly brought his old enemy to these shores. When the waiter arrived, he brought two plates, one of which was swiftly placed below the table. It seemed instructions had come from the abbey that Oscar should also partake of today's special. Either that or Monique had spied them from the kitchen. As Patrick savoured the wine, he thanked whatever deity was present that at least he didn't have to share that with Oscar.

Huntington appeared as Patrick was beginning his dessert, which was a pity because his arrival spoiled Patrick's appetite.

'May I join you for coffee?'

Patrick pushed the dessert plate away. From beneath the table came a low growl, as Huntington took the seat opposite and Oscar picked up the negative vibes radiating from his master.

'I didn't mark you down as a dog lover.'

Not deigning to answer the sarcastic remark, Patrick waved the waiter over and asked for an espresso. Huntington immediately added an Americano to the order, which suggested that he was planning to hang around.

When the waiter had gone, he said, 'I am

71

aware you failed to cooperate with London. Therefore I would ask you not to interfere with the job.'

Patrick took his time answering, studying instead the spray on the rocks a few yards from where they sat while imagining holding the smug face below the water until the pale-blue eyes popped.

'You were a fool to turn this down, Courvoisier. You could have wiped the slate clean . . .' Huntington's expression turned into a leer. 'And also had the pleasure of Miss Lucca's company.'

Patrick saw again Grazia's face across the table from him in the restaurant in London and the chocolate dress he'd used to poke fun at her, as he abandoned her to this excuse for a man who sat opposite.

'Well done, Charles,' Patrick muttered, under his breath.

'What did you say?'

'I said, fuck off. And as soon as possible.' Patrick gave a smile that his mother would have described as liable to curdle milk.

'You always were coarse, despite the fancy name,' Huntington offered.

At this point in the proceedings, Oscar threatened to show his displeasure at their unwelcome guest by cocking his leg.

Much as Patrick would have been delighted by this, he gave a sharp command that put an end to the possibility. He didn't give a damn about Oscar wetting Huntington's trouser leg, he just didn't want the dog banned from the restaurant for the remainder of their stay.

Huntington, unaware of his close call, carried on regardless.

'Why are you here, anyway?'

'I'm considering joining the order,' Patrick said to annoy him. 'Why are you visiting Château de la Croë?'

'An invitation to view its refurbishment.'

Patrick wasn't sure who the current owner of the château was, but he'd heard it had cost the Russian billionaire and Chelsea football club owner Roman Abramovich £30,000,000 to refurbish what had been until recently a burnt-out shell occupied by squatters. He didn't doubt London was on friendly terms with Abramovich, but Patrick refused to let the name-dropping rile him.

'It's rather far from the Esterel mountains,' he said.

'But much more comfortable than a monk's cell.'

They were going round in circles, scoring points. Patrick decided he'd had enough. With a short whistle he extracted Oscar from below the table and, indicating to the waiter he was finished, walked out without a backward glance.

I am here to do a job, Patrick reminded himself. I have another job to do back in Le Suquet. Both are more important than duelling with Huntington. Let him find his artwork, and I'll concentrate on mine.

With that, Patrick set off on a westward path around the island with Oscar at his heels.

Seven

St Honorat was 1.5 kilometres in length and only 400 metres wide. As well as the abbey and vineyards, there were a number of locations that drew tourists, such as a sprinkling of seven small chapels, most of them in ruins but at least one, the Chapel of the Trinity, still celebrating mass. The *fours à boulets,* at the east and west extremities, provided evidence of the defence of the island. Built by Bonaparte, they were furnaces designed to heat cannonballs until they were red-hot, in order to set enemy warships on fire.

To the south of the modern monastery was its eleventh-century fortified predecessor, which was free to explore. Perched on an outcrop of jagged rock, with exposed rock in the sea around it, the four-storey tower with chapel and cloisters had protected the monks from the constant stream of invaders that the island had attracted in its rich past.

Patrick's circumnavigation of the south side of the island with its dangerous shoreline had reinforced his belief that the Madonna had to have left from the northern side, either on the ferry or via a small craft from the nearby harbour.

If she had left at all.

The long walk – long for Oscar, at least – was taking a toll on the dog's short legs, which had a great deal of weight to carry about. Patrick took pity on a panting Oscar and headed back to the cloisters, where he handed the dog over to Brother Thomas, before heading to La Tonnelle in the hope of catching Monique during her afternoon break.

Patrick found her seated at one of the garden tables with a cup of coffee.

Monique's opening remark made him laugh, sprinkled as it was with French curses, as she demanded to know who the fool was who'd had coffee with Patrick earlier.

'A former colleague of mine,' he told her honestly.

'He asked a lot of questions about you.'

'Such as?'

'Why you are here.'

'And what did you tell him?'

'That I was your lover and you couldn't stay away from me.' Monique gave a throaty laugh.

'Well done,' Patrick said with a smile. 'Is he still around?'

She shook her head. 'I saw him get on the ferry for Cap d'Antibes.'

'Good.'

'So,' Monique said, 'you're here about the missing painting?'

'I thought it was supposed to be a secret,' Patrick said, feigning surprise at Monique's direct question.

'Brother Thomas and I are friends. Platonic, of course,' she added firmly. 'He's very distressed that the Madonna is missing.'

'She seems to have quite a fan club.'

Monique gave one of her signature shrugs.

'There's little opportunity here to view a beautiful naked woman.'

'Any idea what happened to her?'

'My father thinks she's been taken off the island.'

When Patrick asked how François knew this, Monique explained, 'There was a large yacht anchored in the bay last night. He saw it send a dinghy ashore.'

'Maybe they were just visiting the island.'

'At three o'clock in the morning?' Monique said dismissively.

Which chimed with Patrick's thoughts exactly.

'Did your father catch the name of the yacht?'

'*Hirondelle*. He says it's now in Cannes harbour.'

Patrick thought highly of François Girard. If the fisherman believed the *Hirondelle* was worth checking out, then he would do so.

'Thanks, Monique.'

'You're welcome. What are you planning to do?'

Patrick asked Monique to call the monastery and let them know he was headed for Cannes. 'I left Oscar with Brother Thomas. Will you tell him I'll return later?'

'The last boat back's at five thirty,' she warned him.

Patrick joined the queue of visitors waiting by the steps as the ferry approached. This time Benedict wasn't at the helm, replaced by a younger man, so there was no chance to find out whether Benedict knew anything about the

Hirondelle or to warn him that he might not make their glass of wine together.

Patrick decided on the return journey that staying on St Honorat might hamper the investigation unless he had quick and easy access to the mainland. His best bet would be to ask to borrow Stephen's motorboat, which was small enough to tie up in Honorat's tiny harbour. Pleasure craft weren't generally permitted to use the harbour, but under the circumstances Patrick thought Brother Robert would agree.

An impatient twenty minutes followed as he watched while the ferry slowly approached Cannes. There was no sign of the *Hirondelle* at the western end of the harbour, but most of the larger yachts tied up in the eastern area.

Patrick disembarked and swiftly made his way round the bay. Entering it next to the casino, he walked the length of the L-shaped quay. There were a dozen yachts tied up on this stretch. All large, all luxurious, but none of them were named *Hirondelle*. The outer wall had only one yacht, which he recognized as *Le Ciel Bleu*, its current caretaker being Hercule Allard, a man Patrick knew well.

Disappointed, Patrick considered his next move. The yacht in question might be anywhere by now, but there was a way to find out when it had departed and maybe even its destination. Patrick made for the harbour office, hoping that Jacques Dupont was on duty.

'*Mon ami*, I heard you'd gone to London,' the big burly figure gave him the statutory two kisses.

77

Patrick prayed he wouldn't be asked about the Queen yet again. Thankfully he wasn't.

'What can I do for you?'

Patrick had helped Jacques out a few months back, when he'd got into debt at the casino. The money involved wasn't a large sum, and at the time Patrick saw it as a goodwill investment. He also knew he could win it back, being a better poker player than Jacques, who wore his thoughts on his face. A bad feature for a gambler to have.

'There was a yacht anchored here last night, name of *Hirondelle*. Has she gone?'

'Let me take a look for you.' Jacques punched the name into the computer log. 'Here she is. *Hirondelle*, one night only. Took on fuel and water. Left this morning.'

'Any idea where she was heading?'

'Cap d'Antibes.' Jacques smiled, knowingly. 'You on a job?'

'You could say that,' Patrick said. 'Can you tell me the owner's name?'

Jacques glanced at the screen again. 'It's registered to a company called Blue Water Holdings.'

'Did the captain say anything about his passengers?'

'No. Very discreet.' Jacques paused. 'I could check with my friend at Port Vauban. See if they're berthed there.'

'That would be very helpful.'

Patrick thanked Jacques, although he'd already decided that since his car was back on the road he might as well take it for a spin and check the yacht's whereabouts on Cap d'Antibes for himself.

78

He called Daniel in advance and asked if the car was ready to go.

'Sure thing. When are you coming for her?'

'I'll be with you in ten minutes.' Patrick's heart lifted at the thought of driving his beloved Ferrari again. Bullet-torn and pushed off the road as she was, Patrick had kissed her goodbye that day in the mountains as he'd tried to save his own life.

Yet here was the Ferrari, almost good as new. Lovingly polished, she gleamed in the sunlight. Daniel had done a fine job on her. One that Patrick would repay in kind.

'I've been considering your problem and think I may have a solution,' he told Daniel. 'When are you expecting them back?'

'They gave me thirty-six hours to come up with the money . . .' Daniel wasn't easily frightened, so if he was showing fear, there was a good reason.

'That place we discussed?' Patrick said. 'I want you and Fidella to go there tonight. I've told Jean-Paul to expect you. Stay until I contact you.'

'What about the garage?'

'Put up a closed sign.' Patrick told him. 'I'll call you when it's OK to return.'

Daniel looked as though he might ask for more details.

'It's better you don't know,' Patrick said firmly.

Daniel nodded. 'Thank you.'

'You've thanked me enough already.' Patrick indicated the gleaming car.

Settling himself inside, he took a few moments

to savour the pleasure, then made a phone call. Jean-Paul answered immediately.

'They're heading your way tonight,' Patrick told him.

'When do you need me?' Jean-Paul asked, sounding excited by the call to arms.

'I'll be in touch,' Patrick promised.

There was a grunt of agreement and Jean-Paul rang off. A man of few words, but when he gave his word he kept it. He and his English wife, Joanne, had a small beach restaurant with cabins in the hamlet of Le Dramont, a short drive west along the coast road. Jean-Paul's grandfather, a resistance fighter during the Second World War, was a son of Le Suquet and had a cobbled alley leading to the castle named after him, because of his heroic exploits during that war. His father had served in the Foreign Legion, and Jean-Paul, following in his father's footsteps, had served in France's special forces. Now he did what he loved most, preparing and serving the dishes of Provence in his small restaurant on the beach where the American forces had landed.

Jean-Paul was, like his father and grandfather, not a man to get into a fight with, unless he was on your side.

Patrick sounded the horn as he drew out into Rue Hibert and gave Daniel a farewell wave. Within minutes he had wound his way through Le Suquet and on to the Voie Rapide, en route to Antibes. Joining the coast road once outside the town, he made his way past the luxury villas that dotted the hillsides of La Californie and Super Cannes, with their views of the passing superyachts that ploughed the Côte d'Azur.

Luxury yachting had always been a part of the Riviera legend and its harbours were open to anyone wishing to take a closer look at the lifestyles of the rich and famous, unlike on land where their villas and châteaux were hidden behind security gates and high walls.

Although Cannes and Monaco had a reputation for berthing luxury yachts, Port Vauban in Antibes was the true centre of Mediterranean yachting. Patrick's intention was to check Port Vauban first. If the *Hirondelle* wasn't there, then she might have chosen to moor either side of Cap d'Antibes.

As he approached Juan-les-Pins, his mobile buzzed an incoming text from Jacques. Glancing at the screen, Patrick noted that word had come back from Jacques' friend at Port Vauban that the *Hirondelle* wasn't berthed there, but had anchored off Hôtel du Cap-Eden Roc on the western side of the peninsula. Patrick silently thanked Jacques for sparing him an unnecessary journey, and at the junction near the casino headed south on to the peninsular.

Eden Roc was one of the most famous hotels in the world, especially popular with Hollywood stars, particularly during the Cannes film festival. It had been the setting for Scott Fitzgerald's *Tender is the Night*. You didn't anchor off such a hotel, Patrick reasoned, without intending to visit it.

The original hotel, a stately white Napoleon III building, was reached by a wide avenue through the extensive gardens. Beyond this, a further avenue led you to the newer buildings, which clustered above the rocks and around an organic-shaped pool that overflowed into the sea. These were the rocks that Scott Fitzgerald's 'mad' wife Zelda had dived from. Patrick had done so himself, and thus admired her fearlessness.

He handed the car over to a parking attendant and walked through the gardens towards the glistening sea and the sight of a large white yacht, which with the aid of his binoculars proved to be the *Hirondelle*. It stood three storeys high and had its own helipad.

Pleased to have located the mystery yacht, Patrick made his way up to the Champagne Lounge. Perched above the pool, with a clear view to the jetty below, it would provide a vantage point from which he could watch any comings and goings involving the *Hirondelle*.

It was at this point Patrick noticed a woman standing at the far corner of the terrace, gazing out to sea or, perhaps like him, towards the yacht. This time Grazia Lucca was dressed in glorious red. Despite the fact that her back was towards him, Patrick recognized her immediately, by her height, the way she held herself, and her luxurious long dark hair. His surprise at discovering Grazia here immediately gave way to caution. Where Grazia was, Huntington might also be.

Patrick sat down at the bar, keeping his face averted. When asked what he would like to drink, Patrick requested the champagne menu, to give himself time to decide his next move. He had no wish to meet Grazia again, at least not in such circumstances, and was even less enamoured at the prospect of encountering Huntington. But he was here for a purpose and didn't want to leave yet.

As it was, Patrick didn't get to decide how to play this, because Grazia suddenly appeared beside him.

'Grazia! Where did you spring from?' Patrick said, feigning surprise.

As those green eyes surveyed him, Patrick imagined what she might be thinking. That de Courvoisier had finally been brought on side and was now here to offer his help in searching for the House of Windsor's stolen painting.

'Why are you here?' Grazia asked sharply.

'I live near here, remember? And this is one of my favourite places to drink champagne.'

Hearing this, the barman approached, anticipating that Patrick was ready to place his order. Patrick did so.

'A bottle of the Cuvée Paradis, *s'il vous plaît.*'

'Two glasses, Monsieur?' the barman said with an enquiring glance.

Patrick turned to Grazia. 'Would you care to join me? It's a nice champagne.'

Grazia indicated her acceptance, although she seemed ill at ease at the turn of events.

'Is Huntington with you?' Patrick said, when the barman went to fetch the champagne.

'No.'

'May I ask when you expect him?'

Grazia hesitated, before finally meeting Patrick's eye. 'He was supposed to meet me here at lunchtime but didn't arrive, and now he doesn't answer his phone.' A flicker of concern crossed her face.

'Giles isn't known for working well with others,' Patrick said. 'But I assume Charles warned you of that?'

At this moment, the chilled champagne arrived, preventing Grazia's response.

Patrick sampled it, pronounced it satisfactory, and asked that it be brought to a table at the seaward side of the terrace. Once they were settled there, Patrick took stock. He'd told no one he was coming to the Eden Roc, although Huntington had made a point of his own intended afternoon visit to the nearby Château de la Croë. Patrick assumed that was where he was now, but why then arrange to meet Grazia here at lunchtime, when he was in fact visiting the monastery on St Honorat?

Patrick toyed with the idea of revealing what he knew of Huntington's movements, but decided not to for the moment.

'If you're concerned about Giles, you could always check with London,' he suggested.

'I don't think that's necessary,' Grazia said firmly.

Patrick recalled his first impressions of this woman and the term formidable sprang to mind again. Perhaps Huntington had met his match in Grazia Lucca. Patrick hoped so.

Patrick refilled their glasses. As he did so, he noticed a motor launch swiftly approaching from the *Hirondelle*. Using his binoculars, he scanned for passengers. There was only one figure on board apart from the pilot. A man, whom he didn't recognize.

84

He looked round to discover Grazia was watching his actions intently.

'You're on a job?' she said.

'Yes, but my paymaster isn't London,' Patrick assured her.

'So it has nothing to do with what you discussed with Charles?'

'Nothing at all,' Patrick said honestly.

The launch had docked and its sole occupant was disembarking. Patrick watched the tall figure climb towards the promontory.

'I need to check out this man,' Patrick told her.

Before Grazia could respond, the man appeared at their level. Tall, darkly tanned, wearing a smart cream suit. His eyes swept the room, and settled immediately on Grazia.

He walked swiftly towards her.

'Grazia!' he said, his face beaming with pleasure.

From Grazia's expression, Patrick was certain she did know the man but had not anticipated this meeting. Either that or she was a very good actress.

She finally rallied. 'Marco, how good to see you again.'

They embraced, then Marco turned to Patrick and held out his hand.

'Marco Fratelli. Mr Coburn, I presume?'

Patrick registered the Coburn name and immediately accepted the firm handshake. 'Delighted to meet you.'

It appeared from Grazia's reaction that she had no knowledge of the *nom de plume* Huntington had bandied about on St Honorat and so assumed Patrick was posing as Coburn.

Patrick gave her a conspiratorial smile, hoping she would play along with him.

Grazia might be puzzled, but she was no fool. 'You two haven't met before?' she said.

'No,' Marco said. 'But I'm delighted to be working with you.'

His eyes lingered on Grazia.

He's been her lover, Patrick decided. And would like to be again.

'I see you've already ordered,' Marco said, noting the open bottle of champagne. 'May I ask what you chose?'

'The Cuvée Paradis,' Patrick told him.

He nodded. 'A serviceable wine, but perhaps we might try something a little more exciting.'

'What do you recommend?' Patrick asked.

'The 2003 Dom Pérignon Rosé?'

'Sounds good,' Patrick said, aware that Marco's choice of champagne cost four times as much as his own. It seemed he was keen to impress. Whether he was trying to impress Mr Coburn, that connoisseur of wines and supplier to the House of Windsor, or Grazia Lucca was still to be established.

When Fratelli went to the bar, Grazia turned on Patrick.

'He thinks you're Giles,' she said.

Patrick opted to stay as close to the truth as possible. 'Maybe,' he admitted. 'But I need to speak to the owner of that yacht, and this provides an opportunity to do so.'

'How has Marco got anything to do with the

job you're on?' When Patrick hesitated, Grazia added, 'If you don't tell me, then I'll tell him who you really are.'

Patrick glanced at the bar where Marco was deep in conversation with the barman. He decided to come clean.

'A valuable painting has gone missing from the monastery on St Honorat. I think the *Hirondelle* may have been used to take it from the island.'

Grazia looked shocked by this. 'You must be mistaken,' she said.

'Who exactly is Marco Fratelli?' Patrick said.

'He's an eminent Italian art dealer.'

'Well, I have it on good authority that a boat went from his yacht to the harbour on St Honorat at three o'clock yesterday morning,' Patrick explained. When Grazia didn't look convinced, Patrick added, 'And Giles was also on St Honorat this morning, masquerading as a Mr Coburn, purveyor of fine wines to the Windsors.'

'What?'

'He was having lunch there, when he should have been meeting you.'

Patrick felt suddenly sorry for Grazia. If she was indeed an art historian and that was the only part she'd been given to play in this project, then discovering her colleagues were being anything but honest with her must be unsettling.

'I don't understand . . .' she began.

'Neither do I,' Patrick admitted. 'Perhaps Marco can explain.'

Marco was now on his way back, accompanied by a waiter bearing the bottle of choice. As the waiter prepared to pour the champagne, Patrick decided to open the proceedings.

'So, do we get to visit the *Hirondelle*?'

'Of course,' Marco said. 'I was going to suggest we eat on board. The restaurant here is excellent, but the yacht is more conducive to private conversation.' Marco directed his smile at Grazia.

Now was the moment Grazia might tell him the truth. Patrick prepared himself for that to happen, and was relieved when it didn't. Whatever Grazia had decided, it wasn't to out Patrick at this moment in time. That didn't mean she didn't plan to do so once they were aboard the *Hirondelle*.

As they drank the champagne, they talked a little about the hotel, its history and its art collection. Marco, Patrick decided, was extremely knowledgable and might be a useful ally in their search for lost works of art. He also seemed to have accepted Patrick at face value. Either that or he was fully aware Patrick was a fraud.

If so, then Giles was almost certainly aboard the *Hirondelle*.

Patrick decided it was time he found out. Draining his glass, he said, 'That was delicious. Shall we head for the yacht now?'

Eight

His mobile rang as they made their way to the jetty. When Patrick checked the screen and saw Jean-Paul's name, he answered.

The stream of rapid Cannois caught him unawares, tuned in as he had been to the English conversation in the Champagne Lounge.

'Slow down, Jean-Paul. What's wrong?'

'Where are you?' Jean-Paul demanded.

'On Cap d'Antibes.'

'Then look across at Cannes.'

Patrick did as requested. Even without the binoculars he could see the billowing cloud of smoke rising from the top of Le Suquet. With the binoculars, even the sparks that rose from the leaping flames were visible.

Patrick's cursing outstripped even Jean-Paul's.

'Daniel's place?'

'The bastards set the garage ablaze. It's spread now to the flats above and alongside.'

'Where are you?' Patrick demanded.

'Place Suquet.'

'And Daniel?'

'With Fidella at Le Dramont.'

'Stay there. I'm on my way.'

Grazia and Marco had reached the jetty and were waiting for him. Patrick beckoned Grazia over and speaking in low tones, explained he had to go back to Cannes immediately. Her face clouded over and he caught a flicker of fear in her eyes.

'What will I tell Marco?'

'The truth. That London wanted me on the job, but I wasn't keen and they shipped in Giles. Then you can lie and say I'm considering taking on the job after all.'

She didn't agree, but also didn't disagree. Instead she said, 'Can I ask what's wrong?'

'A friend's in trouble,' Patrick told her.

'Not too serious I hope?'

'More serious than a missing painting by Fragonard.'

Grazia started at his words. 'The painting from the monastery is a Fragonard?'

'It is.' Patrick caught her eye. 'If you can find out why the *Hirondelle* sent someone ashore in the middle of the night I'd appreciate it.'

'How can I contact you?' Grazia said swiftly.

'Use the number Charles gave you.'

At this, Patrick turned on his heel and headed up the steps without looking back to view Marco's reaction at his sudden departure. Frankly he didn't care what Giles was up to with Marco Fratelli. Even the missing Madonna would have to take second place. A stolen painting was unfortunate, an attack on a friend went way beyond that.

Anger and adrenalin resulted in his return journey taking half the time of the outward one. Approaching Cannes by the coast road, he was struck by the amount of smoke now visible. The street that housed Daniel's garage was a tightly packed narrow thoroughfare, like the majority of streets of the medieval Le Suquet. Directly above the garage were three floors of small flats, including Daniel's own home. On either side of the garage was the same. Access for large fire-fighting vehicles would be difficult.

Patrick cursed himself for his delay in dealing with Daniel's tormentors. Had he enacted his plan immediately and confronted the enemy, it would never have come to this.

Screeching to a halt next to the gunboat, he jumped aboard for what was required. The old engine room that sat midships was exactly how it had been when the gunboat was in operation, although no longer used for its primary purpose. Secreted within it was Patrick's stash of various currencies and a variety of passports and mobile phones, including the one Grazia might contact him on.

He retrieved the bag of money he'd prepared earlier, the mobile and a handgun. Normally Patrick didn't carry a weapon, but if the gang he had to deal with were willing to burn people out of their homes it didn't look as if they would be open to honest persuasion.

Using the London mobile, he sat in the cabin and made the necessary calls, noting as he did so Oscar's water and food dishes. In the circumstances it looked increasingly unlikely that he would be back on St Honorat before morning, but he trusted Oscar was in good hands.

Back on shore, he was acutely aware of the pall of smoke that smothered the harbour, bringing a bitter taste to the tongue and stinging the eyes. The quayside restaurants were still serving, although many of their clients had chosen to move inside to avoid the discomfort and the smell. Those more interested in what was happening on the hilltop were on the move, climbing the various steep inclines that led there. Patrick ignored the obvious and busy routes, choosing instead the quieter Rue Forville, reaching the Place du Suquet from the east.

Entering the square, he found Jean-Paul seated at a table outside the café-bar Los Faroles. Of average height, but with his upper body predominantly muscle and his skin burnt dark by the Mediterranean sun, Jean-Paul appeared a force to be reckoned with. Particularly now, when anger blazed in those dark eyes.

'*Mon ami,*' he said, rising on Patrick's appearance. They exchanged a Cannois greeting, then Jean-Paul indicated he would fetch a drink for Patrick and renew his own. Patrick agreed, choosing a beer, keen to replace the acrid taste of smoke with something more pleasant.

On Jean-Paul's return, Patrick took a long cold drink, while Jean-Paul muttered a number of expletives about what he planned to do to those who had set fire to the garage.

'You're sure the fire was deliberate?' Patrick said.

'Daniel had a threatening call. I persuaded him to stay with Joanne while I came back. I saw the smoke from the coast road.'

'No one knows he and Fidella are at Dramont?'

'No,' Jean-Paul said.

'Right.' Patrick drained his glass. 'Let's go.'

The two men involved Patrick knew to be North African in origin and probably in Cannes with no passports or at least false ID. The Police Nationale would be less than keen to round them up for that alone. Immigrants from all parts of Europe and further afield came and went in the busy ports of the Côte d'Azur, largely ignored until brought to the attention of the police through criminal activities. Even then they might be disregarded, if they kept their activities under the radar or paid off the right officials.

Payback for Patrick would be personal, but would perhaps require the added element of police involvement – and that would entail the assistance of Lieutenant Martin Moreaux.

As they moved through the darkness of the harbour, Jean-Paul didn't quiz Patrick, preferring it seemed to await instructions. On the outer wall, Patrick approached the yacht he'd already selected for the showdown. Smaller than the *Hirondelle*, it was nevertheless a handsome craft. Manning it was a solitary individual, placed there to maintain and guard it until its owners should find time to visit.

Hercule Allard, like Patrick, was a keen diver who liked to spend any leisure time he had out with Stephen on the *Diving Belle*. He also had a penchant for the gaming tables of the casinos both in Cannes and Monte Carlo. With his bed and board supplied by the owners of *Le Ciel Bleu*, his salary could be used in other ways. And use it he did, not unwisely. Hercule, like Patrick, was known to profit by gambling, winning more often than he lost. Sitting guard on some rich man's yacht offered little excitement, so Hercule wasn't averse to being offered an interesting pastime other than playing poker or diving beyond his depth.

For this reason Patrick had chosen Hercule and *Le Ciel Bleu* for his meeting with Daniel's tormentors.

*   *   *

Le Ciel Bleu was in darkness. When Patrick gave a low whistle, a light came on and the gangplank was lowered.

Once inside the cabin, Patrick introduced the two men. Both were immediately wary of each other, Jean-Paul probably the most. Then again his part in the proceedings probably held more danger, or so he would think. Jean-Paul was, after all, the one harbouring the fugitives.

Patrick watched as the two men evaluated one another. Hercule was at least ten years younger than Jean-Paul, but in Patrick's opinion if it ever came to a fight between the two then, despite his youth, Hercule would lose. Hercule was fit and could handle himself well but Jean-Paul, an army veteran, would be more than a match for him.

Perhaps Hercule had also come to that conclusion, for he was the one to extend a hand first. The pecking order having been established, Jean-Paul accepted the offer in good grace, supplementing it with a slap on the back and a distinctly Cannois greeting, which boded well.

'When can we expect our visitors?' Hercule asked.

Patrick checked his watch. 'They should be here shortly.'

'So, what's the plan?' Hercule enquired.

Hercule cleans up nicely, Patrick thought, as he circled the man now dressed in one of his employer's smart Italian suits.

'I've seen this one before,' Patrick said, recognizing the blue-silk sheen.

'My favourite for a trip to the casino. It always brings me luck,' Hercule told him.

'I'll try not to get blood on it then.'

A knock by Jean-Paul on the cabin door alerted them to an approach. Patrick signalled that Hercule should ready himself. He indicated again the bag that lay on the table, and Hercule nodded that he understood.

So let the game begin.

Feeling for the reassuring touch of metal at his waist, Patrick went up on deck to await his visitors. As expected, Jean-Paul was nowhere to be seen. Patrick had urged him to find his own spot, and Jean-Paul had obviously done so.

Surveying the harbour, Patrick decided he'd chosen well. Earlier that day, when looking for the *Hirondelle*, he'd noted that the outer wall was unoccupied apart from *Le Ciel Bleu*, its nearest neighbour being four berths away.

Hercule was known to hold poker nights on board when he knew the yacht's owners were sufficiently far away not to make an unexpected visit. Currently they were visiting their luxury home in Mauritius, a fact Hercule had made widely known to anyone interested. Thus a couple of men heading towards the boat wouldn't be considered suspicious.

Patrick took up his own stance as the two figures turned the corner and began the final stretch of quay leading to *Le Ciel Bleu*. Hidden from view, Patrick sized up his two adversaries.

Neither man was tall or heavy-set. Not the bodyguard type, all muscle and slow moving.

Were he to compare them to his own team, Patrick would have said they most closely matched Jean-Paul, which suggested they would be fast and well armed. At a guess, they would carry both a firearm and a knife – equally deadly in the right hands.

Having reached the gangplank, the two men stood waiting.

Right on cue, Hercule appeared.

In the quayside light, Hercule looked every inch the gentleman. Patrick was rather pleased. After all, Hercule was pretending to be him.

There were a few words spoken in French as Hercule asked them politely to come on board. He had, he assured them, what they sought waiting for them in the cabin. Hercule's demeanour appeared to be bearing fruit, or else the two men were confident they could take him down if required.

Patrick felt a shiver of anticipation for what was about to happen. As in a game of poker, holding your nerve and self-belief were not only important, they were essential.

The three men disappeared through the glass doors that led to the main cabin.

Step one having been accomplished, Patrick and Jean-Paul moved into action. The French doors to the stateroom weren't the only entrance to the yacht. Patrick knew Jean-Paul planned to re-enter below the gangplank, via the store that housed surf boards and water skis. Patrick opted for the upper level, from which he planned to descend.

* * *

From his vantage point, the meeting appeared to be going to plan. The bag of money, having been accepted, was now being upended on the table. As the bundles of euro bills tumbled out, both men took their eye off Hercule for a second, so eager were they to check their spoils.

At that moment, Patrick chose to douse the lights.

Just as planned, the result was mayhem. Patrick let Jean-Paul enter the fray first and heard the satisfying crunch as a fist met bone. As his eyes became accustomed to the filtered light from the quay, he made out one figure on the ground and the other heading for the glass doors.

Patrick intercepted the move and, grabbing him by the scruff of the neck, smashed his head against the toughened glass, only to discover his victim's skull was just as resilient. Swinging free, apparently with his head intact, he lunged at Patrick, the flash of a steel blade coming perilously close to his face.

Next instant Hercule struck, using what appeared to be a large crystal vase, causing Patrick's assailant to halt his attack in mid air, before crumpling to the floor. Jean-Paul broke the resulting silence with a celebratory profanity and flicked the lights on.

The three men looked at one another. Jean-Paul was unmarked, as was Patrick. Hercule wore a satisfied grin.

'No blood on your lucky suit?' Patrick asked him.

Hercule gave it a cursory examination. 'Spot-free.'

'Good. Let's get this place ready.'

Minutes later, they had rebagged the money and set the place to rights, or at least arranged it in a way that suited Patrick's story.

'OK. You head back,' he told Jean-Paul. 'I'll call you in the morning.'

With a satisfied nod, Jean-Paul disappeared.

'What now?' Hercule said, his eyes glistening with excitement.

'Now you get to really perform,' Patrick said.

The flashing blue lights had brought an audience of late-night strollers, held back behind a barrier at the end of the outer quay. A fire in Le Suquet and an attempted robbery on a yacht in the harbour were more than either residents or tourists in Cannes in June were used to.

Lieutenant Martin Moreaux stood on the quay smoking his cheroot. Patrick saw no need to hurry him. Moreaux had come at his call, for which he was grateful. He could wait until the lieutenant was willing to deal with him.

The two men who'd forced their way on to *Le Ciel Bleu* had already been removed to the Police Nationale headquarters. The owner of the yacht had been contacted in his villa in Mauritius by Hercule and informed of the attempted robbery, during which only a crystal vase had been broken thanks to the fact that Hercule had been entertaining a friend to a game of cards when the men boarded the yacht. Luckily his friend, known as Le Limier, was equipped to deal with the problem and the police were already on hand.

Hercule, in the borrowed blue-silk suit, had played his part perfectly.

Moreaux, when he finally boarded, had listened to the fabricated story with his usual ironic countenance. Patrick had of course remained silent until the appropriate moment, which was now.

'I believe the two men involved recently threatened Daniel Bozonnet, demanding protection money for his business in Le Suquet.'

Moreaux hadn't expected that piece of information.

'And you believe this, why?' Moreaux enquired.

Patrick produced the two mobiles he'd removed from their stunned opponents and handed them to Moreaux.

'One of these was used earlier tonight to call Daniel and threaten him. I assume that when he didn't agree to pay up they decided to persuade him.'

'By setting fire to his garage.'

'Yes.'

'After which they decided to rob this yacht?' Moreaux said dryly.

'Maybe they thought they were on a winning streak,' Patrick said.

Moreaux looked at Hercule, who tried unsuccessfully to wipe the smile from his face, before shuffling the cards laid out on the table in the semblance of a game.

'If the light was on and you were playing cards, why did they think the yacht was unoccupied?'

'They didn't,' Patrick said. 'They thought *we* were occupied and wouldn't notice their entry via the ski store.'

Patrick got the impression Moreaux had a strong inkling about what had happened here and the part he'd played in it. What he chose to do about his suspicions was what mattered.

Moreaux suddenly nodded, as though dismissing them.

'I will expect you both to make a statement tomorrow.'

'Of course.'

Patrick accompanied Moreaux on to the quay, where the policeman immediately lit another cheroot. Patrick waited as Moreaux inhaled, sensing he had something more to say.

'Bozonnet's garage was gutted. As were many of the homes that surrounded it.' Moreaux's voice was ominously quiet.

'Clearly, they rather overplayed their hand,' Patrick said.

'As do you, on occasion, Courvoisier,' Moreaux admonished him.

Patrick accepted the rebuke without argument.

'So, are you finished on St Honorat?'

'I head back there tomorrow.' Patrick saw no reason to lie. 'To collect Oscar.'

'Ah, Oscar! Had he been here with you, the break-in might never have happened,' Moreaux said.

'Or would have been dealt with even better than it was,' Patrick countered.

Moreaux seemed to think they had danced round one another long enough. He took one more deep draw at the cheroot, then dropped it on the quay and ground it out.

100

'They will have no passports, I assume?'

'I think not,' Patrick said.

'And we cannot have foreigners breaking the laws of France. Do you not agree Courvoisier?' Moreaux didn't wait to check if Patrick had got the message, but strode off towards his car. In moments, it was roaring off along the quay.

Moreaux will let this go because he wants the men who fired Daniel's garage.

An attack on Le Suquet was an attack on Moreaux himself. About that they agreed, absolutely.

Suddenly weary, Patrick longed for *Les Trois Soeurs* and his bed. He went inside, told Hercule he had done well, and gave him a portion of the money from the bag.

'Remember to wear the blue suit when you spend this at the casino.'

'And tomorrow at the police station?' Hercule said.

'Tell them exactly what you told them tonight. No changes,' Patrick warned him.

'And you, *mon ami*?'

'I will give my statement first thing, then head back to Honorat.'

They embraced.

'We did a good thing, *non*?' Hercule said

'We did a good thing,' Patrick agreed.

Quai Saint-Pierre was deserted, its line of palm trees rustling in a light wind. Patrick could make out the sound of the waves beating the Plage du Midi like a heartbeat. He contemplated walking on past the gunboat and making for the beach.

101

A steady swim would wash away tonight and ease his body, now stiffening a little from the brief fight. The draw of the sea was great, but that of a shower and bed even stronger. Patrick pulled down the gangplank and climbed aboard.

In moments he was under a hot shower, relishing the prospect of a snack and a drink before bed. Having mixed himself a whisky and water, he set about beating four eggs for an omelette. Once it was ready, he tipped it on to a plate, cut a wedge of baguette and, carrying the food and whisky, climbed to the top deck to enjoy his supper *en plein air*.

The few hours that Cannes slept was one of his favourite times to enjoy her. Soon the fishing boats would depart the Vieux Port and the small vans and trucks arrive from the hinterland with their fresh produce for the Marché Forville. Somewhere in between, the teams of street cleaners would arrive with their high-powered hoses. To those rising later, Cannes would appear freshly showered to start her day.

Glancing towards the castle, Patrick found the night sky clear, the smoke gone. He would go up there in the morning, he decided, and see the full extent of the damage. Daniel, he knew, would be devastated by the destruction of both his home and his place of work. He suddenly thought he should have taken longer with the two men responsible for Daniel's loss of livelihood before handing them over to the police. There were a number of ways he could have indicated just how angry he was at their treatment of his friend. Ways that would not have left any mark, but would have undoubtedly left a memory.

But I don't do that anymore.

Patrick toasted that thought with the remainder of his whisky, before turning his mind to Grazia and their meeting in the Champagne Lounge at Eden Roc. He recalled her cool appraisal of the situation and the fact that she'd covered for him. Grazia would have been a good ally had he taken on the job London had offered him. But, Patrick reminded himself, he was only interested in what part, if any, the *Hirondelle* might have played in the disappearance of the Madonna. He had no wish to become embroiled in anything else.

Locking up, he gave the whistle that normally brought Oscar in for the night, forgetting the dog wasn't there to trot behind him. His final task was to check the London mobile again, in case Grazia had been in touch.

It was barely half an hour since he'd last checked, but this time he found a voicemail. Cursing himself for not taking the mobile on deck with him, he listened to the message. Grazia, her voice wary, asked him to contact her as soon as possible. He duly rang back, only to be switched to her voicemail. He told her he would be in Cannes all morning, after which he was going back to St Honorat.

As he lay in the dark, sleep evading him, his thoughts were with Grazia Lucca and why she'd wanted to speak to him so urgently.

Nine

Patrick stood beside Daniel in Rue Hibert and viewed what remained of his friend's workshop. It appeared that the fire service had managed to save the flats above and alongside, although much work would be necessary before the occupants could reclaim their homes. The garage and its contents were a burnt-out shell.

'I'm sorry,' Patrick said. 'If I'd acted sooner . . .'

Daniel cut him off. 'If I had told you of the problem earlier, it wouldn't have come to this. Fidella was so afraid of them, and of the police—'

He halted. 'The police don't know about her?'

Patrick reassured him. 'As far as Moreaux is concerned, they fired your garage because you wouldn't pay them protection money. Stick to that story.'

Daniel nodded.

'Where is Fidella?' Patrick said.

'Still in Le Dramont. Joanne has offered her work in the restaurant and us a place to stay until we can come back home.'

Patrick nodded, pleased to hear that.

He left Daniel to start the clear-up and went for some breakfast, hoping to meet Chevalier doing the same.

The restaurants of Rue Antoine were shuttered, their street tables stored inside, making the steep

104

cobbled street twice the width it normally was. Veering left near the foot of the street, he found Le P'tit Zinc open and serving, with Chevalier in his usual place a stone's throw from his estate agency. He indicated that Patrick should join him.

While they ate a *petit déjeuner* of croissants, coffee and freshly squeezed orange juice, Patrick brought Chevalier up to date on the previous night's events.

'I hear the two Moroccans involved have been threatening other businesses in Le Suquet,' Chevalier said.

'Really?' Patrick said, perturbed.

Chevalier smiled. 'No, but I have a few people prepared to say they have.'

'The problem may be if they're allowed out on bail,' Patrick said.

Chevalier stroked his moustache as he pondered such a possibility. 'I will have a word with my old friend, Lieutenant Moreaux. Tell him we were being terrorized by these men.'

'Good idea.'

'Now,' Chevalier said, 'what of other matters?'

Patrick gave him a brief outline of what had happened on St Honorat.

'The man you wished to avoid was at the abbey?'

'Posing as a Mr Coburn, wine buyer to the royal household. Apparently the Queen of England is partial to their Syrah.'

Chevalier nodded his approval. 'Then she has good taste.'

'Coburn was planning a trip to Château de la

Croë.' Patrick watched Chevalier's surprise as he assimilated this piece of news.

'How intriguing!' Chevalier said.

'Why do you think London would be interested in the château?' Patrick said.

'As you know, a former member of your royal family once made a home there. I hear it is up for sale again. Perhaps a member of the younger generation would like to return to the Côte d'Azur?' Chevalier gave a wicked smile. 'Then again, perhaps something was left behind during the war and they now wish to reclaim it.' He paused and Patrick could almost hear the wheels turning in Chevalier's wily brain.

'This man who calls himself Coburn, you're sure he wasn't on St Honorat because of the missing Madonna?'

By now Patrick shouldn't have been surprised that it wasn't only the monks who knew of the painting's disappearance. Yet he was.

'Don't look at me like that, Courvoisier. I don't plan to tell anyone.' Chevalier looked affronted. 'Unless of course that person may help find it and return it to its rightful place.'

'But how—' Patrick began.

Chevalier waved his hand in a gesture of dismissal. 'Madame Lacroix, as you know by the paintings on the walls of her apartment, is a fan of Fragonard's work. She knows a great deal about what he painted and when. She is also an authority on his mistress and her time on the island.'

'Madame Lacroix knows too?' Patrick said in disbelief.

106

'Brother Thomas and she share a love of Fragonard's work.'

'They should have hired Madame Lacroix to find the missing Madonna,' Patrick joked.

Chevalier shrugged. 'No, you are the better choice.'

Patrick wasn't sure that was a compliment.

Since Chevalier was so up to date, Patrick told him about the *Hirondelle*, which then led to the story of meeting Grazia and Marco Fratelli at the Eden Roc.

'Ah,' Chevalier said, as though something had just become clear. 'Find the Madonna and I think you may find what your London friends are looking for.'

'What do you mean?'

'Talk to Madame Lacroix. Ask her the true story of the Madonna.' He used a serviette to pat the coffee from his moustache. 'I must go to work now.'

When Chevalier departed, Patrick checked the London mobile again, to find no response to his message. Numerous calls to Grazia since he'd risen at dawn had sent him to voicemail. He'd therefore called the Eden Roc and asked to be put through to Miss Grazia Lucca, only to be told that no one of that name was resident. The name Coburn also drew a blank. By the time he'd switched to Giles Huntington, the receptionist was convinced he was a newspaper reporter chasing guests who didn't wish to be found, and politely but firmly told him she couldn't help him and not to call back.

His attempts to find the whereabouts of the

Hirondelle had also been unsuccessful. The yacht was no longer anchored off Cap d'Antibes. Neither was she in the harbour at Antibes or Cannes. By now she could of course be anywhere along the coast in either direction – although if Marco Fratelli planned to check out a location in the Esterel mountains, she might have gone west to anchor, perhaps even off Le Dramont.

The next call was answered. Jean-Paul sounded upbeat, and delighted to keep a look out for the *Hirondelle* on his stretch of coast.

'What of the bastards who fired the garage?'

'I'm just off to give a statement.' Patrick told Jean-Paul of Chevalier's intention to further their cause.

'And Fidella?'

'She's serving tables as we speak.'

'Thank you for that.'

'The busy season is about to begin. We would have been looking to hire staff anyway.'

Patrick rang off. Having walked the length of the pedestrian Rue Meynadier, he turned right, climbing the short, steep incline to Place du 18 Juin. The gaunt building that housed the Police Nationale's Commisariat Central stood on the opposite side of the dual carriageway, on the corner of Boulevard Sadi Carnott.

It wasn't the first time he'd been in the police headquarters, and it was unlikely to be the last. Moreaux never forgot a foe, even if at times that foe was a friend. Patrick gave his name at the desk and explained that he was there to give a statement. The young male officer gave him a scrutinizng look and curtly asked him to take a seat.

He was then subjected to the waiting game. Twenty minutes and three more attempts to contact Grazia later, he was finally shown into an interview room. Another twenty minutes went by before the door was reopened and a policeman came in. Patrick immediately asked if Lieutenant Moreaux was in the building and was told that he was, but unavailable.

Patrick gave his statement, which he hoped would match Hercule's.

'The accused said they were attacked by three men,' the policeman said.

'Then they were mistaken,' Patrick countered. 'And we were the ones who were attacked.'

The policeman nodded as if not really interested, prompted Patrick to sign the statement, and said he would then be free to leave.

'The two men are still in custody?' Patrick asked as he rose from the table.

The policeman gave a curt nod, which Patrick hoped, when translated, meant yes. He had no real fears for Fidella's safety now she was part of Jean-Paul's household, but if her abductors were set free they would not necessarily simply leave Cannes. Patrick had striven to hide Jean-Paul's part in last night's proceedings, but the men who'd tracked Fidella to Cannes might also be able to track her to Dramont.

Exiting the police station, Patrick tried calling Grazia again, but got only her voice asking him to leave a message. Had he been on the London job, the fact that she'd been off the radar for so long would have troubled him.

But I'm not on that particular job. If Grazia

doesn't wish to answer my calls, there's nothing I can do about it.

That inner response lasted as far as the entrance to Madame Lacroix's apartment, situated between a bank and a couturier on Cannes' most exclusive shopping street, the Rue d'Antibes. At that point Patrick made a promise to himself that if he received no response from Grazia by the time he finished talking to Madame Lacroix, then he would relay a message to Charles Carruthers. He owed his old friend and colleague that at least.

Shortly after Patrick rang the bell, the manager and owner of Hibiscus, Côte d'Azur's premier escort agency, answered. Patrick introduced himself and waited while she decided whether she would deign to invite him up.

The buzzer sounded and the catch on the door sprang open, signalling that Patrick was to be allowed entry to the hallowed halls. The last time he'd climbed the wide staircase illustrated by erotic paintings in the mode of Boucher and Fragonard had been during the case of the black pearl. Marie Élise had been one of Madame Lacroix's employees. Intelligent and beautiful, she would have been expected to work with Madame for up to five years, after which she might have married a rich client or retired with enough proceeds to marry a poor lover. Neither opportunity was afforded to Marie Élise, who now lay in a grave in the Cimetière du Grand Jas, her death a source of guilt for both Patrick and Brigitte Lacroix.

The small, slim and extremely elegant

110

dark-haired woman who opened the door to him looked just as Patrick remembered her. Back then she'd been Moreaux's mistress. Patrick wondered if she still was.

'Courvoisier!' She indicated that he might enter with a sweep of her hand, which held a burning cheroot, a habit she and Moreaux shared. Once he was inside, she allowed him to greet her properly with a kiss on either cheek, then offered him a coffee or a glass of wine.

Patrick settled for wine, knowing it would be good. When she served him a Syrah from St Honorat, he suspected she'd been forewarned of his visit.

'Le Chevalier?' he said.

She nodded. 'He says you wish to talk of the Madonna.'

An hour later, Patrick had learned a great deal about Fragonard's work and about his mistress, the actress Mademoiselle de Sainval, a miniature of whom Madame Lacroix had brought from her boudoir to show him.

The image was of a woman in a tall, elaborate white wig, standing on a stage, her hand held high as though to someone watching from a box above. Her painted face bore little resemblance to the photograph given to him by Brother Robert.

'Of course, the Madonna is more likely to be a true representation of Fragonard's lover than this.' Madame Lacroix confirmed Patrick's opinion.

'And your thoughts on her disappearance?' Patrick said.

111

'For that, I need to tell you a story.' She offered to refill his glass and Patrick accepted. The wine was a dark ruby red, full of flavour and exceptionally good.

'What do you know of this area during the war?' she said.

'The usual stories . . .'

'Poof! The ones that feature in the guide books . . . Were you aware that Winston Churchill was paying the Germans a great deal of money to leave Château de la Croë and its royal inhabitants alone?'

'No, I wasn't,' Patrick admitted.

'Then you know very little.' Madame Lacroix laughed, a deep throaty sound. She stubbed out her cheroot and immediately lit another. 'The Duke and Duchess of Windsor were ordered to take a lease on the château by the British embassy, in May 1938, so they wouldn't be in Paris for the State visit of George VI and his Queen. My grandmother was employed by the Duchess at the château. Unlike myself, she was a blonde. Everyone who worked there had to be blonde.'

'Why was that?' Patrick asked, surprised.

'Grand-mère maintained it was because the Duke had a liking for dark hair and the Duchess didn't want to be upstaged by Mediterranean beauties. The more common explanation was that to be employed you had to look Aryan to please some of their more Germanic guests.'

Patrick decided he was inclined to go for the latter explanation.

'Anyway, the Duchess transformed the château.

112

Her taste in décor was exceptional and there was plenty of money for royalty to indulge their every desire, despite the war.' She paused. 'Mistresses generally have better taste than wives, and my grandmother said the American always played the mistress, even after marriage.'

She continued. 'The Duchess bought a number of paintings for the château. Grand-mère, who loved art, used to describe them to my mother.' Madame Lacroix took a sip of wine and savoured it. 'In July 1948, with the war over and France free, Mr Churchill and his wife came to the château to celebrate their fortieth wedding anniversary. It was an extravagant affair, according to Grand-mère. The Duke attended the dinner dressed as a Highland Chief, wearing a kilt and with a knife tucked into his stocking.'

'He sported a dirk?' Patrick said in amazement.

'The bagpipes were played to entertain the guests,' she laughed. 'My grandmother liked that, although she said many of the guests did not.'

The tale of the Windsors' extravagance was entertaining, but Patrick wondered when it would link with the missing Madonna.

Then it did.

'From the descriptions given by my grandmother to my mother, then to me, I believe one of the paintings in the château at that time may have been Fragonard's Madonna.'

Ten

Madame Lacroix continued as though she had said nothing surprising. 'There is also evidence to suggest that the painting was gifted to the Windsors by Hitler, when they stayed with him at the Berghof, in Berchtesgaden, in 1937.' She paused. 'If so, then there may be some who think neither the Windsors nor the Abbey of St Honorat have first claim on her.'

It was an extraordinary tale, like many of the stories that arose during and after the Second World War. Particularly in what had been Vichy France – a no man's land, neither free nor conquered.

Yet, despite Patrick's natural scepticism, it did seem there might be a connection between Madame Lacroix's story and London's interest in a missing painting. Of course, the ideal way to find out would be to make contact with London and simply ask.

While Madame Lacroix finished her wine and cheroot, in tandem, Patrick pondered what such a move might mean for his own precarious position.

'So,' she said, 'what do you plan to do?'

'I'm not sure,' Patrick said honestly.

Madame Lacroix nodded, then rose, apparently ready to dismiss him.

'I think we would both like to see the Madonna

back where she belongs. If the abbey is no longer a place of refuge, then she could find a home here.'

She smiled and her face lit up, the shrewd dark eyes glistening with glee at such a thought.

'I wish you good luck, Courvoisier.'

As she showed him to the door, the ornate telephone on her desk rang. Madame Lacroix indicated that she had to answer it and requested that Patrick pull the door closed behind him as he left.

Back on board *Les Trois Soeurs*, Patrick made the call he'd been putting off. He'd prepared himself for Carruthers, or perhaps Forsyth, to answer and was surprised to hear a woman's voice instead. Patrick gave his name and asked to be put through to Sir Charles.

'I'm sorry, that isn't possible,' the woman said in what seemed to Patrick an imperious voice.

'May I ask why?' Patrick strove to make his tone reasonable.

'Sir Charles is away on business.'

'And when will he be back?'

'I'm afraid I can't say.'

'Charles will want to hear what I have to say,' Patrick insisted.

'Then I suggest you use his personal number.'

'Which is?'

'I assume you would know that, were you really acquainted with Sir Charles.'

Patrick swore in French.

'I speak French, you know,' she interrupted him.

'Then you'll know what I said,' Patrick retorted before ending the call.

Patrick reasoned that he'd done his best to inform Carruthers what was happening, and had been denied the opportunity to do so.

If Charles had thought for a moment I might get in touch, he would have made arrangements to allow that to happen.

The fact that Charles hadn't done so meant it was no longer Patrick's problem. Despite this, Patrick rechecked his London mobile, just in case Grazia had got in touch. But there was no response to his many assorted messages. It appeared that whatever Grazia had wanted to discuss with him was no longer urgent or relevant.

Patrick decided he would ponder all that had happened since last night over some lunch, before returning to St Honorat and discussing the latest developments with Brother Robert. He was particularly looking forward to running Madame Lacroix's story regarding the missing Madonna past the monk to see what his reaction might be. He didn't think lying would come easily to the Cistercian, although prevarication might be considered acceptable if acknowledging the provenance of the missing painting was problematic.

Five minutes later Patrick was seated outside the Cave Forville, just across the road from the market, enjoying oysters and a plate of cured meats with Christophe's recommended wine of the day while he considered his next move.

By the time he'd finished his meal, drunk the small pichet of wine, and had an espresso before him, he had come to his decision.

116

Regardless of his feelings towards his former employers and his desire not to get involved, Patrick had to admit that he could go no further with his own quest unless he checked out whether the *Hirondelle* had had anything to do with the disappearance of the Madonna.

In order to do this, he would have to locate the *Hirondelle* again. To that end, he put a call through to Jacques at the harbour office.

'I thought you'd found her at Cap d'Antibes?' Jacques said puzzled.

'She moved on, before I got on board.'

'OK, I'll check and ring you back.'

Patrick paid his bill, then made one more call to the number he'd hoped never to use again, yet still retained in his memory. This time a voice he expected answered.

'Forsyth here.'

'Courvoisier here.' Patrick echoed Forsyth's response.

'Ah . . .'

There followed a small sigh, which to Patrick's ear sounded like 'I knew you would eventually accept the inevitable'.

Patrick resisted the desire to ring off. Instead he said, 'I tried Charles earlier but couldn't get through.'

'You are *persona non grata*, Courvoisier. No direct lines through anymore.'

'Yet here you are,' Patrick said.

There was a small pause.

'Why the call?' Forsyth said in a clipped voice.

'I can't reach Grazia Lucca.'

'And why should you want to?' Forsyth said, sounding guarded.

'I have information for her.'

'Really?'

Patrick tried to ignore the sanctimonious tone. 'I believe she's aboard the *Hirondelle* with Marco Fratelli.'

'What?'

Forsyth's shocked reaction caught Patrick off guard.

'That's not where she should be?' Patrick said cautiously.

He could almost hear the wheels turning as Forsyth tried to decide what Patrick knew and what he should be told.

'I take it Huntington is with her?'

'Not to my knowledge.'

An answer Forsyth obviously didn't want to hear, judging by the resulting silence.

'Grazia couldn't reach Huntington the last time I spoke to her,' Patrick continued.

'Which was?' Forsyth demanded.

'Yesterday evening, at the Eden Roc hotel.'

Forsyth didn't respond.

Something wasn't right here.

'Who is Marco Fratelli?' Patrick asked.

Again no response.

'Grazia seemed surprised to see him. She knew him from the past, that was obvious, but she didn't expect him to be meeting her there.' Patrick waited, knowing his growing suspicion was right. Finally he said, 'Fratelli isn't one of ours?' Anger surged in Patrick as he realized he'd said 'ours', instead of 'yours'.

118

'No,' Forsyth admitted.

'He's the opposition?' Patrick said angrily.

'Maybe,' Forsyth admitted.

Christ! He hated the innuendo, the prevarication, and most of all he hated the game.

'Is Grazia in danger?' Patrick demanded.

'It's a possibility,' Forsyth conceded reluctantly.

'So where the fuck is Huntington?'

'I'll get back to you, Courvoisier,' Forsyth said and abruptly ended the call.

Bastard! Patrick uttered the word in a variety of languages, with embellishments. It didn't make him feel any better. The idea that Grazia Lucca was in danger had been planted in his mind, and the last time he'd seen her she was on her way to boarding the *Hirondelle*. He'd picked up no sense of threat from Fratelli. His reading of the man had been that he lusted after Grazia, not that he meant to harm her.

But what did I read from Grazia's demeanour?

Patrick tried to recall the scene. He remembered Grazia's surprise, and maybe concern, when she realized the man approaching them was Fratelli. When Fratelli embraced her, what had been her reaction?

Patrick suddenly remembered.

She'd recoiled, although she covered it well. And she'd definitely wanted me to go with her to the yacht.

He recalled the flicker of fear in her eyes when he'd declared his intention to return to Cannes immediately.

Patrick's anger at his misreading of the

situation was cut short by a call. But it wasn't the London mobile that was ringing. Already on the move, having settled his bill at Café Forville, he was minutes from the *quai* and the gunboat. The response to his enquiry regarding the whereabouts of the *Hirondelle* didn't come from Jacques, but from Jean-Paul.

'The yacht you seek is here, off Île d'Or.'

Patrick hadn't yet had time to garage the Ferrari in its cave on Rue Forville. The car still sat alongside *Les Trois Soeurs* on the *quai*. Patrick abandoned his plan to catch the next ferry to Honorat, but he didn't immediately jump into the car and head for Le Dramont. Instead, he took time to pack his diving gear and anything else that might prove necessary were he required to reach and board the *Hirondelle*.

Twenty minutes later he was on the coast road, heading west.

During Patrick's meeting with Moreaux after his return from London, the lieutenant had asked him if he planned a trip to the Esterel mountains. Patrick had wondered then, as he did now, exactly what the detective had meant by that. Moreaux said nothing without a reason, he wasn't known for simply passing the time of day.

Had Moreaux been aware that something was in the offing?

The answer was, of course, 'Yes'. And Patrick suddenly realized why.

London had informed Moreaux, just as Moreaux had informed them about Patrick's involvement with the black pearl. Seeing a break in the coastal traffic, Patrick accelerated, weaving in and out as he overtook.

And what of his conversation with Forsyth? Had that too been planned? Was he being set up by London, with Grazia as the decoy?

If so, she did not appear to be aware of it.

He was being drawn into something he'd sworn to avoid. But was that London's fault or the fault of the Abbey of St Honorat?

It was mid-afternoon now. The twisting coast road was busy with traffic and opportunities to overtake were rare, but Patrick took them whenever possible. The Ferrari responded immediately to his foot on the accelerator, her steering keen and true. Patrick gave silent thanks to Daniel for resurrecting her from her grave in the Esterel Massif, which rose in a precipitous jumble of red ragged rocks to his right.

As Patrick passed Moreaux's villa, which he shared with his wife Michelle, he thought of the other villa not so far away where merely a month ago he'd faced torture and death.

The physical scars of that encounter had faded, the mental ones were with him still. Patrick gripped the wheel more tightly as he recalled how the old Courvoisier had resurfaced so easily. Given the opportunity to take a life, he had done so without hesitation.

But if I hadn't, would I be here now?

Even as he thought that, Patrick knew it was an excuse. The death in the Russian's villa had been necessary for his own survival, but the underwater death earlier in the job had been premeditated and enacted for revenge.

And he didn't regret that death, not for one second.

Pulling into the car park, he found a group of tourists clustered around the Second World War landing craft, listening to the story of the Allied landings on the beach below. Passing the group, Patrick took the untarred road that wound steeply down through tall pines to Jean-Paul's place, next to where the landing craft had come ashore.

Today the beach, a mixture of shingle and patches of golden sand, held only a few sunbathers. The French weren't renowned for swimming before the Mediterranean sun warmed up the winter sea. Late July and the holiday month of August would see the beach busy, particularly with holidaymakers from the nearby campsite.

Patrick parked alongside Jean-Paul's truck and, taking his binoculars, made for the deck in front of the restaurant. There was a scattering of customers seated at the outside tables enjoying a late lunch. As Patrick approached the door, a dark-haired young woman appeared balancing two plates, the scent of which suggested a rich lamb stew. She shot him a swift glance, paused, and asked if he wished to have lunch.

'I'm here to see Jean-Paul,' he said, conscious that this must be Daniel's Fidella.

Her lovely mouth immediately broke into a smile.

'You are Patrick de Courvoisier?'

'I am.'

'I am Fidella and I want to say thank you.' She

glanced at the steaming plates. 'I'm sorry, I have to deliver these.'

'I'll be here a while,' Patrick assured her.

Jean-Paul, swathed in his apron and chef hat, turned as Patrick entered the kitchen.

'Two more to serve, then we can talk. Have you eaten?'

'Oysters at Cave Forville.'

'So you won't want the *navarin de mouton*?'

'I could manage a small helping,' Patrick conceded.

Jean-Paul immediately dished a large plateful for him and set it on the table. 'There's red wine in the pichet, but I warn you it's not from the vineyards of St Honorat.'

Patrick poured himself a glass and set about the *navarin*, as though the oysters and cured meats had been merely a starter. Jean-Paul ignored him completely until he'd prepared the meal for his final two lunch customers and delivered them into Fidella's hands. Then he helped himself to a plate of the *navarin* and sat down opposite Patrick.

'The *Hirondelle*'s anchored just west of the Île d'Or, or I would have spotted her earlier. She must have arrived there in the early hours of the morning, because I took a walk along the cliff path just before midnight and didn't see her.' Jean-Paul registered Patrick's concerned expression. 'I have good night vision, Courvoisier, as you know.'

Patrick did know that, but the cliff path that wound eastwards from here was tricky even in broad daylight. And if you slipped, there was nothing to break your fall but the sharp red rocks below.

'Has anyone come ashore?'

'They may have done during the night. As for today, no. Joanne has been on watch for you.'

'I'll go and relieve her,' Patrick offered immediately.

'Good idea. She'll be very hungry by now.'

He found Joanne seated, her back against a large pine with a view of the sea. She had a book open on her knee and a pair of binoculars in her hand.

'Patrick!' She stood up and embraced him.

'I'm sorry—' he started to apologize.

'Forget it,' she said firmly. 'I've had a lovely morning here with my book. I've avoided the kitchen at lunchtime, and washing the dishes.'

'Jean-Paul said you would be hungry.'

Joanne raised an eyebrow. 'As if.' She showed Patrick the remains of her picnic. 'Most peaceful meal I've had in quite a while,' she said with a smile.

'So, what's been happening?'

According to Joanne, nothing much. The yacht was completely enclosed and had dark windows. Even when it had drifted round so the entrance deck was in view, there had been no one visible.

'Except once,' she said. 'A man came out on the rear deck, but I think he was crew.' She apologized. 'I'm not much good on a stake-out.' She nodded at the book and the remains of a baguette and cheese. 'I get engrossed in other things, but I'm sure I wouldn't have failed to notice a trip to the shore.'

Patrick thanked her 'You go home, I'll take over here. Jean-Paul has *navarin de mouton* waiting for you.'

'As long as there isn't a pile of dishes, too.'

Patrick settled in her place and focused his high-powered binoculars on the yacht. Joanne was right. The sleek yacht was designed for privacy. Its occupants could gaze out, but sight-seers were unable to see in. The main deck at the stern, with its glazed doors, was a possibility, plus an upper deck that would normally be used for sunbathing. Neither was occupied.

However, the doors of the stern storeroom did stand open and Patrick could make out the lines of the motor launch that had brought Fratelli to the jetty at the Eden Roc.

They could, of course, have sent a party ashore during the night. But had they done so, the motor launch would most likely still be in the water.

Patrick considered his next move. In reality, there was only one option. To attempt to board the *Hirondelle*. Whether he did so in full view, or otherwise, was the question.

Eleven

Jean-Paul eased the small boat round the jagged coast of the Île d'Or and manoeuvred her into place.

'Take the wheel while I drop the anchor.'

Patrick did as requested while Jean-Paul

climbed on to the bow and, peering down into the water, chose his spot.

'Reverse slowly,' he commanded.

Moments later Patrick felt a tug as the anchor gripped, and immediately put the engine into neutral.

'Will this do?' Jean-Paul said.

They were shielded by the island from a clear view of the *Hirondelle*, but Patrick knew exactly where it was. He thanked Jean-Paul.

'This is fine.'

'How long should I wait?' Jean-Paul said.

'I'll make my own way back,' Patrick told him.

Jean-Paul looked as though he might argue, then thought the better of it.

Patrick nodded his appreciation and prepared himself for the swim. Heading to the stern, he dropped into the water and, taking care to avoid the anchor rope, struck out along the southern side of the island. The deeper water was cold, not the icy cold of a Scottish loch but cold enough for casual swimmers not to venture this far out.

Settling into a steady crawl, he made good time, leaving the shelter of the island and crossing the stretch which led to the yacht. Viewing the *Hirondelle* from the jetty at the Eden Roc, he hadn't registered just how impressive it was.

Whoever owned such a yacht had a great deal of money. But from Patrick's experience of the world, rich people could never have enough money, just as those with power always needed more.

Reaching the stern, he trod water for a moment

and established there was no one in the storeroom that housed the motor boat, then pulled himself aboard. The swim here had been the easy part, whatever happened now was likely to be less straightforward. At the rear end of the storeroom he found a couple of cubicles, some crew lockers and a supply of towels.

Drying himself, he checked the lockers for something to wear and found a set of crew's shirt and shorts that fitted well enough, along with a pair of deck shoes. The uniform might just delay his being outed as a stranger, for a short time at least. Perhaps long enough to find out who was on board.

The journey from the storeroom to the first level proved uneventful.

He noted sounds from the galley that indicated the presence of at least two catering staff. But for the size of the yacht he hadn't spotted many crew, which suggested there weren't many passengers either.

By now Patrick had reached the main staterooms. Both the dining room and the lounge were deserted. Which meant if Grazia was on board, she had to be in one of the cabins, which on most yachts of this size lay to the stern on the first level.

He made his way back down and found four cabins, numbered but with no indication who, if anyone, might be inside.

There was nothing for it but to try the doors and find out.

The first door was locked and Patrick could only hear silence within.

The second was the same, as were the third and fourth.

By now Patrick had come to the conclusion that there was no one aboard the *Hirondelle* save for a skeleton crew, which meant Fratelli and Grazia had gone ashore in the middle of the night or had left the *Hirondelle* before she anchored here.

Irritated by this turn of events, Patrick made his way swiftly down to the storeroom, stripped off, and headed for the rear platform. Just as a male voice screamed at him in French, 'Who the fuck are you?'

Patrick didn't supply an answer but instead dived straight in and, staying underwater, headed eastwards towards the island, where he could hide among the rocks until he was sure they weren't on the tail of the intruder, via a jet ski or even the motor boat.

Reaching the jagged shoreline, he sought a suitable spot, aware that a swell had built up while he was aboard the *Hirondelle* and he would be lucky not to find himself colliding with some of the sharper rocks.

Surfacing, he took a look back and, although he spotted a couple of crew members on the lookout for him, there was no sign of any craft being launched. Continuing round to the north side of the island, where he was completely out of sight of the big yacht, he struck out for shore.

The last time he'd emerged on the beach in front of Jean-Paul's place, having escaped from the clutches of the Russian Chapayev, he'd been

128

bruised, battered and half-dead. This time Patrick rose from the breaking surf little more than annoyed. He'd wasted time seeking out the *Hirondelle* and wasted more time boarding her. Wherever Grazia had contacted him from, he suspected it had not been the yacht. In fact he was now questioning whether she and Fratelli had ever gone to the *Hirondelle* after he'd deserted them on the jetty at the Eden Roc.

Bypassing the deck and its customers, Patrick entered the kitchen by the back door only to find Jean-Paul seated at the table with a man. If Patrick had been surprised at discovering the *Hirondelle* as deserted as the *Marie Celeste*, discovering the identity of the visitor sitting there imbibing red wine at Jean-Paul's kitchen table surprised him even more.

Giles Huntington looked much like Patrick had when he'd been washed up here during the case of the black pearl. Someone had obviously given him a beating. Patrick wasn't ashamed to admit he wished he'd been the one who'd inflicted the injuries on that particular face.

'Courvoisier.' Huntington acknowledged Patrick's arrival, while Jean-Paul brought Patrick a towel.

'Your clothes are in the back kitchen,' Jean-Paul told him.

Patrick took himself through the door indicated, glad of a moment to arrange his thoughts. He quickly dried and dressed, while wondering how Huntington fitted into the ever more complicated equation surrounding the missing Madonna.

Emerging, he found Jean-Paul had vacated the

129

kitchen, but had set out a clean glass for Patrick on the table next to the pichet of wine.

'Want some?' Huntington offered.

Patrick nodded, noting with some pleasure the pain it caused Huntington to raise his right arm high enough to pour. Patrick drank the wine down, then poured himself another and waited, having no wish to be the one to start the conversation.

'I assume you discovered that Grazia and Fratelli are not on the yacht?' When Patrick didn't respond, Huntington continued. 'They flew by private jet from Nice to Venice last night, after you saw them at Eden Roc.'

Patrick broke his silence. 'So, you're in touch with Grazia?'

'No. The news didn't come from her.' Huntington looked uneasy. 'Grazia is no longer in direct contact with us.'

Patrick didn't like the sound of that.

'And Fratelli?' he asked.

'As you suspected, he's not one of ours.'

'*Yours*,' Patrick corrected him. 'I'm only interested in the Madonna from the Abbey of St Honorat. Does Fratelli have it?'

'We believe so.'

'And where is the painting now?'

'In Venice.' Huntington drank the wine in his glass and replenished it. Patrick wondered if it was being used as a painkiller. Judging by the swelling on Huntington's face, he looked as if he needed it.

'Forsyth has given clearance for you to be told—'

Patrick interrupted him. 'I repeat, I'm only interested in the missing Madonna, nothing else.'

'We too are interested in the Madonna.' Huntington held up his hand to stop Patrick's immediate question. 'As are Fratelli's contacts.'

'Who are?' Patrick demanded.

'He is aligned with a Fascist group who believe the painting belongs to them.'

Patrick sat back in the chair. So Madame Lacroix had been right. There were three interested parties.

'The Madonna belongs to the monks of St Honorat. My job is to deliver it back to them.'

'There's something else,' Huntington said, 'if you're willing to listen.' He grimaced as he shifted in the chair. 'The reason why they are now in Venice.'

'OK,' Patrick conceded. 'Tell me.'

He heard the entire story en route to Aéroport de Cannes Mandelieu, via *Les Trois Soeurs* for him to pack a bag for their trip to Venice. It seemed Huntington's injuries had been obtained on his attempted visit to Château de la Croë. Huntington hadn't been willing to say more than that he'd been intercepted by two men he believed to be in Fratelli's pay.

'I'm not sure I was supposed to survive, but I did,' Huntington said wryly. 'A bit like yourself.'

Patrick wasn't yet willing to share anything with Huntington, even a joke.

'What about Grazia?' he said.

131

'I don't believe she's in danger. At least not until she's verified the paintings.'

'Paintings?' Patrick took his eyes off the road and swerved a little too near the edge, causing Huntington to grip his seat in expectation of imminent death on the rocks below.

Once they were reunited with their side of the road, Huntington answered.

'The Madonna, as you know, is a depiction of Fragonard's mistress, Mademoiselle de Sainval. Like Munch, Fragonard may have painted more than one likeness of his lover. A second painting has turned up in Venice.' He paused. 'Grazia's job is to verify which one is the original.'

Now Patrick understood Grazia's surprise at his revelation about the Fragonard missing from the island.

'She didn't know—' he began.

'Miss Lucca only knew what we were willing to tell her,' Huntington said.

'If you'd been straight with her, maybe she wouldn't be in danger now,' Patrick said coldly.

'She understood there were risks, and we were paying her well,' Huntington said.

At that moment Patrick felt like stopping the car and ordering Huntington out. Perhaps Huntington realized he'd crossed a line, because he said, 'Don't worry, we'll bring Miss Lucca out unharmed.'

Patrick wanted that to happen, but didn't like the man beside him using the term 'we'. Had he gleaned any idea where in Venice they were headed, Patrick would have chosen to go alone.

As it was, he had little choice but to play Huntington's game for the moment.

So Patrick gritted his teeth and contemplated how soon he could dispense with Huntington, and how quickly he might restore the Madonna to those he believed to be its rightful owners.

When he'd gone on board to pack a bag and pick up his passport, leaving Huntington waiting in the Ferrari, Patrick had taken the opportunity to make a couple of calls. There had still been no answer to his further attempts to contact Grazia. The second call had proved more fruitful, Pascal had immediately agreed to go to St Honorat and pick up Oscar.

'Of course I will bring him home,' Pascal said, sounding delighted at the prospect.

'Tell Brother Robert I'm on the trail of the Madonna and will be in touch when I have further news.'

'How long do you plan to be away?' Pascal enquired, sounding hopeful that it might be a while.

'Not sure. Can you look after Oscar for me until I get back?'

'But of course.' Pascal all too readily agreed to having the dog back, even if it was only for an extended holiday.

Huntington had informed Patrick that a private plane awaited them at the local airport. It would have taken Patrick six hours to drive the 600 kilometres between Cannes and Venice, depending on road conditions. A standard flight would have involved driving to Nice and accepting whatever

133

ticket they could get on whatever flight was available. Neither method would have got them there sooner than a private flight from the local airport.

Patrick suspected he was being taken along because Huntington wasn't in a fit condition to deal with whatever was awaiting them in Venice. But he had no proof that any of what Huntington had told him in Jean-Paul's kitchen had been the truth. He had only his gut instinct to go on, and it told him that the game involving the Madonna had moved to Venice.

Patrick fastened his seatbelt. In a couple of hours he would be in Venice. What happened after that was in the lap of the gods, or in the hands of the elusive Madonna.

Twelve

They took a water taxi from Marco Polo airport. Watching Huntington trying to board the bobbing motor boat from the jetty convinced Patrick he was suffering from more than just bruises. Huntington was loathe to use his right arm, and whereas no blood had been in evidence at Dramont it was now visible on his shirt near the right shoulder.

Patrick said nothing during the swift and bumpy crossing of the lagoon. It seemed to him that Huntington was gritting his teeth to prevent himself from crying out. He might not like the man, but he knew exactly how he felt in that moment and had sympathy for him. The water taxi was the swiftest way to get to the centre of Venice but it wasn't the smoothest, as evidenced by the spray that lashed the side windows of the cabin. Patrick had used his arm to wedge himself against the long seat. Across from him, Huntington seemed unwilling or unable to do the same.

Thirty minutes later they were motoring up the Canale di San Marco. Turning right into the narrower Rio della Pietà, their driver lowered the engine to a quiet purr as he negotiated the space between the tall buildings on either side.

Now Patrick knew where they were heading. The small hotel just east of this canal was favoured by London for the use of its agents when in Venice. He'd stayed there himself. Not obviously a hotel, looking more like a private home, La Residenza offered quiet, comfortable accommodation in a fifteenth-century Gritti-Badoer palazzo on the Campo Bandiera e Moro, to the east of the main hub of the tourist destinations round San Marco.

As they walked the short distance from the canal, Huntington stumbled and Patrick had to come to his assistance. He thought Huntington would reject his offer of help, but he didn't.

'We're expected,' Huntington told him.

Patrick was glad to hear it. From Huntington's pallor, he thought they would have been better heading for a hospital.

As they approached the square, Patrick noted that the plaster Madonna still stood snug in her niche high in the wall. Venice was full of such statues, painted and often crumbling, with their offerings of plastic flowers, though tonight the Madonna's presence seemed more pertinent. The large square, flanked by the church of San Giovanni in Bragora, was deserted apart from two local women sitting on a bench beneath the trees feeding the pigeons.

The hotel was exactly as Patrick recalled it – the handsome frontage, the double oak doors, the only suggestion that it was other than a private residence consisting of a discreet brass plaque declaring it to be La Residenza and instructing visitors to ring the bell for entry.

Still supporting Huntington, Patrick rang the bell. He gave Huntington's name and the big door buzzed open. Inside was the cool stone-floored room he remembered, with the red-carpeted staircase leading upwards.

The palatial first-floor room with its wall paintings of voluptuous Venetian beauties served as reception, sitting room, and home for the grand piano. It was also the place where you ate a simple breakfast of coffee and croissants. Nothing had changed since Patrick had last been here, except for some repairs to the plasterwork. Like Venice itself, La Residenza was a beautiful yet crumbling relic of past glories.

Huntington had mustered his reserves of strength and now stood before the ornate reception desk speaking fluent Italian. He accepted the proffered keys of their rooms, both of which were on the same level as the main area. Patrick followed him through a doorway just to the right of the grand piano, carrying both bags, impressed by Huntington's ability to remain upright.

136

The moment the door of the first room had been unlocked, Huntington made straight for the bed and sank down on to it.

Patrick followed him in and shut the door.

'You're next door, Courvoisier.'

'I want to take a look at your shoulder, first.'

'That won't be necessary.' Huntington shook his head.

'I brought some things from the gunboat. Dressings, antiseptic, pain relief and some medicinal alcohol.'

A flash of something resembling pleasure crossed Huntington's face.

'I'll make use of the alcohol.'

'You'll make use of it all,' Patrick insisted. 'But use the alcohol first.'

He opened his bag and produced the bottle of malt whisky, found two glasses and poured a shot in each. He handed one to Huntington. 'Drink that, then we'll tackle the shoulder.'

'I might need more than one.' Huntington tried a joke.

This time Patrick chose to share it.

'Sláinte!' he said.

'Sláinte!' Huntington downed the whisky and held the glass out for another. By the time he'd swallowed the second, a little colour was creeping back into his cheeks.

'The next one washes these down.' Patrick flourished the pain killers.

He thought at first that Huntington might refuse, but he gave him a refill anyway and laid two tablets on the bedspread beside him. A slight hesitation was followed by 'Fuck it!' and

Huntington swallowed them then, sitting up a little straighter, took off his jacket.

The shirt beneath was wet with blood. Patrick let him unbutton it, then set about easing the shirt off his shoulder. The attempt at a dressing had all but disintegrated, exposing the wound. The bullet had met the arm just below the shoulder. Luckily for Huntington, it appeared to have entered and exited reasonably cleanly.

Patrick set to work cleaning and sterilizing the entry and exit points. The gaping wound really needed stitches, but he didn't see Huntington turning up at *pronto soccorso* to have it seen to. Patrick apologized in advance for what was about to transpire, then pressed the front gash together and taped it. As he did so, a few choice words in Italian were muttered, but Huntington didn't cry out.

'Getting your own back?' he said through clenched teeth.

'I would have to do a lot more than this,' Patrick informed him as he applied a pad over the wound and taped it in place, then began on the second one.

'Stitches would have been better.'

'It'll do, thanks,' Huntington said when the torture was finished, and held out his glass for a refill.

Patrick topped him up.

'You should eat something. We both should. The café on the other side of the square does pizzas. Would that do?'

Huntington nodded.

'I'll dump this on the way,' Patrick said, holding

up the bloodied shirt. 'When I'm back, we'll talk.'

Huntington sank back against the pillow and closed his eyes. With his chest bare, the result of his beating was clear to see. His attackers had done a good job. Patrick suspected they'd been after more than just pleasure. Huntington hadn't elaborated on what had happened. But Patrick's guess was that they'd sought information about the Madonna, which Huntington had been unwilling to give. How he'd got away from them might never be revealed, but the bullet wound was testament to the fact that he had had to get away.

Patrick deposited his own bag in the neighbouring room and headed out.

Campo Bandiera e Moro had settled into night. The two women were no longer feeding the pigeons, but a scattering of people were seated outside the café, some eating, some drinking coffee.

Patrick dumped the rolled-up bloodied shirt in the nearest waste bin, pushing it down out of sight, then took himself across to the café, where he ordered two pizzas to take away. While awaiting their delivery, he chose a table and had an espresso. From where he sat, he could see the windows of the two rooms he and Huntington now occupied. Set on the western corner of the first floor, they overlooked not the square but the narrow passageway that housed the plaster Madonna. Patrick had stayed in both rooms at one time or another, but had planned never to visit La Residenza or this square again.

Yet here I am.

He took out his mobile and contemplated making a call. He had no wish to talk to Forsyth again, but he had no doubt that their last conversation had resulted in him being here. Either that or Huntington suspected he was unable to complete the job without help.

And he could be right.

He and Huntington went back a long, for the most part unpleasant, way. And there was one incident he could never forgive, or forget.

I can blame Huntington for her death, but he and I both know I was truly the one at fault.

Patrick allowed himself a moment to remember, but only a moment.

The past is over with. I'm a different man now. Or am I?

He looked up as the waiter, who'd been trying to get his attention, plonked the two pizza boxes on the table in front of him. Patrick thanked him and picking up the boxes, which were emitting a wonderful smell, headed back to La Residenza.

Patrick tried the bedroom door and found it locked.

'Huntington? I have food.'

He heard a groan, as Huntington swung himself from the bed and rose, then the padding of feet.

'You shouldn't have locked the door,' Patrick admonished him.

'I didn't want any unwelcome visitors.'

'You're expecting some?'

Huntington eyed him. 'Don't we always?'

Patrick didn't like his inclusion in the statement, although it was true.

He handed a box to Huntington, who took it back to the bed with him. Patrick chose a chair at the table by the window. The lingering smell of blood and disinfectant was now supplanted by the rich scent of tomato, garlic and cheese. Patrick would have preferred to eat *seppie alla veneziana* in the small restaurant in the nearby Calle del Dose, but the pizza was a decent enough substitute for his favourite Venetian squid and he attacked it with gusto.

Huntington was doing the same. Having demolished the pizza, Patrick replenished their glasses.

'OK,' he said, 'what happens now?'

Later, lying in the dark, Patrick revisited what Huntington had told him. The location of the other painting had surprised him. In a city full of religious paintings, many of them featuring various versions of the Madonna, he'd assumed the duplicate of the Fragonard would have been here.

But he'd been wrong. According to Huntington, the second location was Torcello, the small island where settlement of the lagoon had begun.

Despite much probing, Huntington had refused to divulge anything other than that. After this limited disclosure, he requested two more painkillers and told Patrick he needed to sleep. He obliged and, having filled Huntington's tumbler with whisky, he took what remained of the bottle with him.

* * *

Back in his own room, he showered, standing under the beating water, turning his face to the spray, remembering.

They'd chosen to eat at the Corte Sconta the first night she spent with him. The famous restaurant was just a few minutes' walk from La Residenza, provided you knew the way. Finding it in the dark, in the maze of narrow streets that all looked the same, had given them some trouble, which had made them laugh.

Finally there, though late for their booking, they had ordered the speciality, with a bottle of Prosecco di Valdobbiadene. The scallops were as creamy and delicious as promised, the asparagus fresh and delicate. But no food could compare to what happened afterwards. He'd fallen in love that night, although he hadn't realized it at the time, thinking himself drunk on good food and wine, a beautiful woman, and moonlit Venice.

Patrick turned the shower to cold and embraced the stinging onslaught on his skin, trying to obliterate memories of the past.

Stepping out, he walked naked to the window and sought the sky. The moon tonight was masked by dull cloud, much like his thoughts. Lying down on the bed, he stared at the ceiling, listening to the faint night sounds of the city – the purr of a water-taxi engine, an explosion of laughter from the nearby café, the toll of a church bell sounding the hour – and the words 'Nothing about this seems right' echoing in his head.

Thirteen

His mobile woke him before dawn. Grabbing it from the bedside table, he noted that the number on the screen was unidentified.

'Courvoisier?'

Patrick's sense of relief at the sound of Charles's voice disconcerted him.

'How is he?' Charles asked.

There was no need to use the name. They both knew who Carruthers was referring to.

'He took a bullet. I patched him up. He's asleep next door.'

'How bad?'

'It went straight through his upper right arm. And he took a beating.' Patrick paused. 'What did they want to know?'

There was a pregnant silence before Charles said, 'He's not answering his phone. Can you put him on yours?'

Patrick went next door and knocked.

'Huntington? Charles wants to speak to you.'

When there was no response, he knocked again, more loudly this time.

'Huntington.'

Patrick tried the door and was surprised to find it unlocked.

'Huntington,' he called as he flung it wide, only to discover the room empty of Giles and his bag.

'He's gone,' he told Charles.

Charles Carruthers wasn't one for swearing, but he did so now.

'What's going on?' Patrick demanded.

'I need you to go after him.'

'I'm here to retrieve the property of the monks of St Honorat. Nothing else,' Patrick said firmly.

'Then retrieve both paintings and bring Grazia back safely.'

'You bastard,' Patrick said, remembering how Huntington had asked him to leave so he could go to sleep. Patrick recalled going into the shower and turning it on to full power. If Huntington had left the hotel then, he wouldn't have heard. It seemed Huntington hadn't been as unwell as he'd pretended.

If so, why bring me along, if he didn't intend making use of me? Because I was backup. A backup he no longer thinks he needs.

No wonder Huntington wouldn't give him the full story last night.

Having been patched up, he'd decided my presence was no longer required. Either that or he feared I was only here to appropriate the Madonna and take her back.

Patrick was already down the stone steps and pulling at the heavy front door of La Residenza. Dawn was breaking in a fiery red over the Campo Bandiera e Moro. The resident pigeons rose in a fluttering cloud as he strode quickly through them. The one and only piece of information Huntington had been willing to divulge last night was that the island of Torcello was their destination.

144

He'd told Charles this. And after a short silence, Charles had responded, 'Take a water taxi to the basilica on Torcello. There's a private residence on the eastern tip of the island opposite. It has its own jetty, but better to arrive unnoticed. You'll have to find a discreet way to get across the intervening canal.'

Reaching the Riva degli Schiavoni, Patrick went in search of a water taxi. It took him fifteen minutes to find one that was manned at this early hour and ready to go, which made him wonder how the hell Huntington had left for Torcello even earlier. Unless, as he suspected, Huntington had left the previous evening, when transport was plentiful.

There was nothing good about any of this, Patrick decided, as the speedboat wound its way through the passageways of the lagoon. Charles had him operating as an agent, without the information and backup he would have had in normal circumstances. Something he'd vowed would never happen again.

I've been played like a chess piece. Maybe right from the beginning.

Huntington would never have willingly sought his help. Someone else must have wanted Patrick back in and under their command. But who? Forsyth hated him as much as Huntington did, but Forsyth hated even more the fact that Patrick had seemingly escaped his clutches. He would draw him back in, if only to punish him.

And what about Charles?

Patrick trusted Charles, at least as much as it was possible to trust anyone in this business. One thing had rung true during their conversation. Charles suspected Huntington had given away information that could endanger Grazia, and Patrick didn't want the death of another woman on his conscience.

The *vaporetto* wouldn't begin plying the lagoon until 8.00 a.m., so Patrick didn't expect any visitors to have reached Torcello's main jetty yet. From there, a short walk would lead him across the narrow island to the main tourist destination, the Basilica of Santa Maria Assunta and the surrounding remains of the glory that had once been the birthplace of life on the lagoon.

As the taxi navigated its way up Canale Borgognoni, Patrick asked the driver to drop him at the *vaporetto* stop and told him he would make his own way from there. Paying him handsomely, Patrick asked if he might be willing to return for him, if required.

'I may have to leave in a hurry,' Patrick said.

The driver handed him a card.

'I'll wait at my sister's, on Burano,' he said. 'Call me and I'll come back for you.'

Patrick thanked him and jumped ashore.

The path across the island was deserted, the adjacent canal as still as glass. The magnificent settlement of 20,000 which had preceded Venice had now dwindled to only twenty permanent inhabitants, none of whom Patrick met en route. The Locanda Cipriani, one of the scattering of restaurants catering for lunchtime tourists and the only place to stay on the island, was still shuttered.

Crossing the small canal that divided the main

146

island, Patrick hurried along the wider gravel walkway that led to the famous Byzantine church with its austere exterior and striking campanile. Yards further on, he reached the jetty Charles had spoken of.

Using his binoculars, Patrick checked out the island opposite. The narrow strip of land looked like a series of small holdings, except in the east where a tiny strip of water split the island in two. On the other side of this, an avenue of trees suggested a long drive heading eastwards. Beyond that, Patrick could make out a large white square, which he took to be a helicopter landing spot.

At the furthermost point, he saw the red roofs of the dwelling house Charles had spoken of. Closely packed bushes lined the entire shore, no doubt to discourage visitors, but there was a jetty close to the house for invited guests.

On his side of the canal two small boats were tethered at the jetty, one of which had an outboard engine and, more importantly, a set of oars.

Patrick chose that one and, with a quick look round, lowered himself in, hoping its owner wasn't in the vicinity. Had there not been any boats, he would have swum across, although he suspected that tackling the muddy weed-filled canal would have offered more danger than swimming through a rough sea off Cannes.

He aimed for the spot, just east of the intersecting canal, where the drive began. Early morning light was reflected off what might be the white gravel of a manufactured beach. He hoped he might drag the boat ashore there, or drop anchor close by. From there he might make

147

his way to the house via the tree-lined drive, which appeared to be the only concealment available.

Patrick stepped out of the boat and pulled it a little higher. Before abandoning it, he tucked a €50 note under one of the oars by way of a thank you, in case its owner should retrieve it while he was elsewhere.

The trees bordering the drive were uniform, trimmed into shape like the plane trees in Cannes. They shaded the white road perfectly. In minutes he was passing the helicopter pad and, ahead on the left, he spotted the glistening blue water of a swimming pool, surrounded by a selection of loungers, and what looked like a Jacuzzi. The pool was obviously open for use, but neither it nor its surroundings were occupied.

On his right lay the private jetty, currently occupied by two speedboats, both impressive. Whoever was here was used to travelling in style. Now it was plain why this spot had been chosen for the dwelling house that lay before him. Tucked at the far end of the island and surrounded by water and mudflats, it resembled a castle with a moat. The only missing item was a portcullis.

Patrick stood in the shelter of the trees, half expecting the howl of a dog to herald his approach, but it seemed the owners didn't think their castle needed guarding by such means.

Now he was within sight of the building, Patrick took stock and decided he would simply approach the house and ring the bell, if there was one. The main residence consisted of two buildings, of which the left-hand one faced a landscaped garden leading to the pool. The right-hand structure focused on the jetty and was connected to it with two walkways. There was a further building east of the jetty, which he assumed housed all the equipment required when you owned a boat or two.

As Patrick approached the main building, a woman appeared on the patio and began to walk towards the pool. She was tall with dark hair, wearing a robe over what he assumed would be a swimsuit. Patrick melted back among the trees and watched.

Reaching the pool, she took off her robe, exposing a red bikini. Dropping the robe and towel on a lounger, she made for the pool, performed a racing dive, and with swift strokes began to move through the water.

Patrick followed her and, having made sure that he would not be visible from the house, sat down on the lounger and waited.

The woman did a racing turn and began to plough her way back. Just before she reached the end of the pool, she spotted Patrick. To say that Grazia Lucca was surprised to find him there would have been an understatement.

Patrick put his finger to his lips.

'Stay in the water. I don't want to attract any attention,' he told her quietly.

'What are you doing here?' she demanded.

'Charles sent me.'

'Why? What's happened to Giles?' She sounded worried.

'He had an accident. I agreed to come in his

149

place,' Patrick replied swiftly. Grazia didn't look convinced, so he held out his mobile to her and said, 'You can check with Charles if you like.'

'It's OK, I believe you.' She paused. 'Does Marco know you're here?' She nodded in the direction of the house.

'Have you enlightened him about me?' Patrick asked.

'I told him what you suggested.'

'So I'll be accepted into the gang?' Patrick said with a smile.

'Unless Giles arrives and blows your cover.'

Grazia pulled herself out of the pool and put on the robe.

'The paintings. Are they here?' Patrick asked.

'They should arrive this morning.'

'Is one of them the one from St Honorat?'

'I don't know.' Grazia looked askance at him. 'You're not going to mess this up, are you?' she demanded.

'It isn't my intention,' Patrick said. 'Tell me who's here.'

'Both the *Hirondelle* and the villa belong to Marco. But besides Fratelli, there's a man here called Bach.'

'German?' Patrick asked.

Grazia nodded. 'As are the two bodyguard types who came with him. Boneheads if you go by the tattoos.'

'So the Fascists *are* involved?'

'I thought Charles had brought you up to date?' she countered.

'There was a lot to take in at short notice.'

They had reached the patio. Patrick would have

preferred more time alone with Grazia, but she didn't appear to want that. Beyond the glass doors, Patrick could make out the figure of Marco. He was on his mobile, talking in animated Italian.

Grazia slid open the door and stepped inside.

'Marco,' she called. 'Mr Coburn's here.'

Marco almost dropped the phone in surprise. Then, collecting himself, immediately said a hurried farewell to whoever he'd been talking to and came towards Patrick, holding out his hand.

'At last.'

'I'm sorry I'm a little late,' Patrick said.

'No worries.' Marco assumed a delighted smile. 'How did you arrive?'

'By speedboat.'

'It's at the jetty?'

'My driver has family in Burano,' Patrick replied. 'He's gone there to wait for me. I believe we're expecting the paintings?'

'They should be with us very soon.' Marco paused. 'We're about to have breakfast. Will you join us?'

Patrick estimated Herr Bach to be in his fifties. A man of middling height, he was in good shape and wouldn't be overpowered easily. The two boneheads had youth on their side, as well as the advantage of upper-body weight. Patrick thought he could manage one of them, but two at the same time might prove a problem.

Had Fratelli been on his side, that would have been different. Marco was proving a puzzle.

151

Forsyth had given the impression he wasn't to be trusted. Patrick wasn't so sure. Marco's frequent glances at her over the breakfast table confirmed Patrick's impression that he lusted after the gorgeous Grazia. Patrick couldn't envisage a scenario where Fratelli would want her harmed.

Bach and his men on the other hand would, Patrick feared, dispense with anyone who got in their way. Bach had accepted him as the elusive Mr Coburn, with only a flicker of interest and irritation in his eyes.

By his second cup of coffee, Patrick had come to the conclusion that none of the three parties round the table trusted one another. All had their own agenda and their own desired outcome, as did he. And all of them were waiting for a judgement to be made on the authenticity of the paintings they were about to view.

What happened after that would be anyone's guess.

Patrick stole a look at Grazia, wondering if it might be possible to speak to her alone before that event. Now that he'd weighed up the opposition, he wanted to warn her what to expect. Seated next to Grazia, he could sense her growing tension. Patrick wondered if having him there had made things better or worse for her.

Charles had tried to paint Grazia as having no more of a role than that of authenticating expert, but Patrick wasn't so sure. He recalled their first meeting back in the diplomatic tent. The impression he'd gained was that Grazia Lucca was a force to be reckoned with.

The silence round the table was broken by the thrashing sound of helicopter blades passing over the house.

'They're here,' Marco said, with a satisfied smile.

Fourteen

To Patrick's relief only he, Fratelli and Bach stood in the room with Grazia and the two paintings, the boneheads having been sent on some further mission, the purpose of which he hadn't been able to glean from the low, rapid German interchange they'd had with Bach.

Glancing round the display room, Patrick decided it had been aptly chosen, boasting as it did a stunning mosaic of the Madonna and child, a replica he guessed of the Byzantine work in the basilica on Torcello, which also housed a more famous Last Judgement.

However, the mosaic and the newly acquired paintings were not the only representations of the Madonna in the room. There was a myriad of other paintings and *objets d'art*, all of which featured the Madonna, sometimes alone, sometimes with the holy child, indicating Fratelli's passion as a collector.

The paintings in question had been hung on the wall opposite the mosaic.

Patrick immediately decided that the photograph given him by Brother Robert didn't do

153

either painting justice. At first glance the paintings looked identical, unlike the various unique renditions done by Munch of his own lover, Dagny Juel.

Patrick checked out the impact on the two men beside him. Fratelli's colour had heightened and his eyes glistened with what could only be described as desire. In Bach's case, his look suggested avarice.

Grazia's reaction Patrick found surprisingly moving. She gazed at the paintings as he imagined the true Madonna might have looked on her infant son. Her intense gaze was loving, personal and profound. He watched the pulse as it beat in her slender neck, heard her intake of breath as she absorbed the beauty before her.

Fratelli finally broke the awed silence. 'Well?'

Grazia nodded as though to herself. 'I will need time,' she said, 'and privacy to examine them more closely.'

Fratelli glanced at Bach, who gave him an almost imperceptible nod.

So Bach is the one in charge.

'Of course,' said Fratelli. 'We'll leave you to it.'

Fratelli motioned the two men away, as though it was he who had made the decision.

Patrick followed them back to the sitting room overlooking the patio and the distant pool, where Fratelli, who appeared nervous, offered them a drink.

'To celebrate,' he suggested.

He and Bach exchanged another furtive glance.

Now that the time drew near, Fratelli was deciding which side he would prefer to be on.

Patrick accepted a whisky and water, Bach declined, and Fratelli poured himself a brandy. The atmosphere in the room was as highly charged as a storm brewing over the lagoon.

How long would it be before Bach made his move?

If neither painting proved to be what the German sought, then there was no point in antagonizing the British contingent. If the opposite were the case, then he would have no qualms but to dispose of the opposition. Fratelli, Patrick surmised, was hoping he might at the very least be given the reject.

At that point, one of the boneheads entered the room and whispered something in Bach's ear. It wasn't so much the message that interested Patrick as the fact that the man had fresh blood on his knuckles.

Patrick rose, finished his drink, and told Fratelli he was going for a walk.

The Italian looked a little put out by this, but after a quick glance at Bach he conceded. Bach's easy acceptance of Patrick's departure did little to reassure him. Once out of sight of Fratelli, Patrick thought his chances of remaining unscathed would rapidly diminish.

He went out via the French windows. From the patio he had a clear line of sight to the private helicopter that had delivered the paintings. Patrick wondered if they had been the only items delivered that morning. The bonehead, from the evidence of his knuckles, had been punching

155

someone recently and Patrick had a suspicion who that someone was.

He took a swift turn to the back of the main house. Even if Fratelli knew what was going on, Patrick doubted whether he would want anyone beaten up inside his pristine home. Which meant they must have taken whoever it was elsewhere.

The block behind the main house was locked and shuttered. Patrick suspected it was used for overspill guests when necessary. He'd seen only one servant, the woman who'd served them breakfast, and gathered from her conversation with Fratelli that she lived on the western part of the island.

The last building stood by the private jetty. The shrubs that lined the shore of the island clustered round the red-roofed building. Approaching the open doors, Patrick noted that one of the speed-boats he'd seen earlier was missing from its mooring, so someone had left the island while he'd been in the house.

Patrick caught the scent of blood as soon as he entered. Sharp, metallic, it merged with other bodily odours – sweat and vomit. Patrick followed his nose to the back, past various items of boating equipment, and found a set of stairs leading downwards.

He stood at the top listening, the worrying scent in his nostrils. Whoever was bleeding was down there. The wooden steps wound round once then dropped into a stone cellar. Patrick halted at the bottom. It was colder here, the light dim. He strove to make sense of what lay before him.

One wall consisted of racks of wine bottles. The other was hung with herbs and onions, neither of which could erase the smell coming from the man before him, hanging there semi-naked, his head slumped on his chest.

As he registered Patrick's presence, Huntington strove to raise his head. The wound that Patrick had taken such care to bind lay open and pulpy, as though it had been hit repeatedly. The livid bruises on the chest had multiplied, their mass dotted by what looked like the prickings of a knife.

Patrick went forward and, lifting Giles' body, took the weight from his stretched arms and shoulders. He gave a grunt of relief as Patrick untied his hands and set him free.

'Have they found it?' Giles struggled to speak.

'Grazia's comparing the paintings now.'

Giles shook his head. 'They don't care about that.'

'I don't understand,' Patrick said.

'The paintings are not the prize.'

He heard the chopper blades as he helped Giles mount the stairs. Then he realized that whatever message had been brought to Bach had initiated the departure. Bach hadn't cared where Patrick went or what he found, because he already had what he was looking for.

As he helped Giles back to the house, the dark shadow of the helicopter made its way across the blue sky. Wherever it was heading, it wasn't towards Venice.

Once inside, he led Giles to the sofa, then went to check for Grazia.

The mosaic room they'd stood in earlier was empty, of both Grazia and the paintings. Patrick's relief that he hadn't discovered her body, either injured or dead, was immediately replaced by the realization that they must have taken her with them. For what purpose he had no idea.

Giles looked up at him as Patrick re-entered the sitting room.

'They took her and the paintings,' Patrick said.

'Bastards!' Giles hissed.

Patrick poured a brandy and handed it to him.

'Drink that,' he ordered. 'Then tell me what the fuck's going on.'

Giles's hand shook as he raised the glass to his lips. He gulped the brandy down in one.

'It's more important we follow them without delay.' He rose unsteadily to his feet.

'Where?' Patrick said.

'Cap d'Antibes. I think what they're looking for is there.'

Alberto, only minutes away in Burano, swiftly turned up at the private jetty as requested and accepted the loading of an injured man on to his water taxi without comment. By the time Alberto arrived, Patrick had patched Giles up for a second time, dressed both himself and Giles in fresh clothes supplied from Fratelli's extensive wardrobe, and retrieved his bag from where he'd hidden it by the beach.

Their return journey to Marco Polo airport was as rocky as their outward one. This time Giles made no effort to conceal his discomfort as the bow of the small speedboat thumped through the waves. Being beaten and tortured twice in succession had taken its toll. But it wasn't only pain that distressed him.

As he confided to Patrick, despite his best efforts he hadn't succeeded in preventing the two paintings from coming together. Also, he feared that under duress he'd revealed enough for Bach and Fratelli to guess where to look next. A call to Charles en route, overheard by Patrick, had confirmed Huntington's anger and despair at how things had played out. At that, Charles had asked to be passed to Patrick.

'It appears Bach and Fratelli have the co-ordinates they were looking for,' Charles said.

'The co-ordinates of what?' Patrick demanded.

'Something that should in the national interest remain hidden.'

Patrick listened to the story as the speedboat bumped through the wash of passing water taxis, the resulting spray hitting the windows. As he did so, the pieces of the jigsaw began to fall into place.

A plane was awaiting them at Marco Polo airport. Huntington climbed aboard wearily, sank into a seat, and accepted the offer of a drink. Patrick handed him a couple of his strong painkillers to go with it.

'You should have told me the truth,' Patrick said. 'Then we might have worked together.'

'The orders were to tell no one. Even you. Besides you were only interested in getting the Madonna back. Nothing more. You made that very plain.'

'So you went back alone for more?' Patrick said in disbelief.

'You would have done the same.'

It was the closest to a compliment Huntington had ever offered. After which he closed his eyes, ending the conversation.

Despite Giles's protestations, Patrick wondered if when Charles called him that morning he'd already known Giles had left the hotel. Maybe they'd cooked it up between them, to draw Patrick in. All the time, he'd suspected Forsyth of playing him. But it might have been Charles all along.

And now this?

His plan to extract the Madonna and take her home was bound up with the outcome London desired. And what London wanted, London usually got. But even now had he been told the whole truth?

Patrick extracted the photograph of the missing Madonna from his wallet and studied it. Previously, concentrating on her form and face, he hadn't particularly noticed the lower background of the painting. Discoloured by age, the details along the base were difficult to make out. Yet he could see now that it might well be, as Charles had indicated, a depiction of St Honorat, featuring the southern coast of the medieval monastery.

Closing his eyes, Patrick attempted to recall exactly what the two paintings looked like. The filtered light in the mosaic room had illuminated both Madonnas in all their glory. The right hand one, he believed, did have a medieval monastery at its base.

According to Charles, the duplicate painting had a minor difference. The image at the base of the picture was not an island but a peninsular. And that peninsular was Cap d'Antibes, the outline of the monastery replaced by Château de la Croë.

Patrick had listened to Charles's story about the original painting with interest, mainly because it mirrored Madame Lacroix's version so closely. How Hitler had initially acquired the Madonna was unclear. That he had gifted it to the Windsors when they visited him at his mountain retreat in 1937 was clearly established.

'Mrs Simpson took it, together with several other artefacts, to decorate Château de la Croë,' Charles had told Patrick as the speedboat bounced on the waves, bound for Marco Polo airport. 'The painting hung there during the war, until its true significance was realized.'

'The link between the Windsors and Hitler?' Patrick queried.

Charles ignored the question and simply continued. 'The painting was copied for safety's sake and the imitation hung in its place, the original being hidden on St Honorat.'

'I can't see how that story, however true, would embarrass anyone now,' Patrick said.

'It's not the painting which will do that, but what we suspect the two paintings will lead us to,' Charles explained quietly. 'It seems that the Fragonard wasn't the only gift Hitler gave to the Windsors. Apparently, during the occupation an item said to be of greater value and significance

161

was sent to the château as a personal present for Wallis Simpson.'

Patrick registered the distaste in Charles's voice. 'She would have made a great queen,' Patrick quoted.

'And had Hitler won the war, she might well have become one,' Charles said candidly.

'Did Churchill know about this greater prize?'

'I suspect not. I believe the Windsors kept quiet about it. Maybe they feared to reveal their continuing links with the Führer.'

'All in the past,' Patrick insisted.

'Would that were true,' Charles replied. 'Fascism in Europe is on the rise again. We cannot allow them to use this item to promote it.'

'And the Madonna?' Patrick asked him. 'Will the monks get her back?'

'That will have to be decided . . .' Charles paused. 'Should the Fragonard survive.'

The sun was setting as they approached Aéroport de Cannes Mandelieu, bathing the sea in pink and red. Patrick felt his heart lift at the sight of it. However beautiful the Venetian lagoon might be, it was nothing compared to the deep restless waters he was looking down on.

Huntington had slept for the duration of the flight. Either that or he'd feigned sleep to avoid meeting Patrick's eye or talking to him. Patrick suspected Huntington had dozed, although fitfully. Blood from the shoulder wound had made a dark stain on the crisp cotton of the shirt they'd acquired from Fratelli's wardrobe. Patrick suspected only stitches would improve the situation, but a doctor's visit might be out of the question for hours yet.

'We're coming into land,' Patrick said. 'I suggest you brace yourself. There's a crosswind.'

Huntington's bloodshot eyes flickered open. He pulled himself up, fastened his seatbelt, and clasped the armrests.

The small plane turned, angling itself into the wind, and began its descent.

There was a moment when they appeared to hover, wings tipping on either side, and then they were down, bumping along the tarmac. Huntington smothered a groan.

'We could do some work on your shoulder at the gunboat, before we head for Antibes. I have all that's necessary on board,' Patrick offered.

Huntington thought about it, but only for a second.

'No. We head for Cap d'Antibes in your car straightaway.'

'There may be other things we need. Backup, for example, and weapons,' Patrick said.

'I thought you'd retired?' Huntington replied, sarcastically.

'There are four of them, including the two boneheads who worked on you. Going into that unprepared is asking for defeat.'

Huntington's expression showed he felt useless and was angry about it.

Patrick didn't wait for a reply but pulled out his mobile and made a call as they taxied to a standstill.

Jean-Paul answered immediately. '*Mon ami*, we were getting worried.'

'There's a problem,' Patrick said.

'Tell me what you need.'

'Charles won't like you involving civilians,' Huntington said, when Patrick had rung off.

'I'm a civilian,' Patrick reminded him. 'And we can't do it without him.'

'Who is he?' Huntington demanded.

'Jean-Paul was in the French Special Forces. He's as well trained as you or I, and he's not injured.'

Huntington sat upright, annoyed at the reference to his weakness. 'Do you have anything stronger in your bag?' he said.

'I can give you liquid morphine,' Patrick offered.

Huntington gave a small laugh. 'You came prepared.'

'Without all necessary equipment I am of no use to myself,' Patrick quoted.

'Bastard,' Huntington said, but with a small smile.

Fifteen

Patrick glanced sideways as they weaved their way along the busy coast road. It seemed the morphine had done the trick, at least for the moment. Huntington was upright and bright-eyed. In the interim, he'd asked what weapons

Patrick had in his possession and what Jean-Paul might supply.

'We don't want to leave anything to clean up,' Patrick said. 'Lieutenant Moreaux of the Police Nationale would take umbrage at a mess.'

'So he favours Fascists?'

'He dislikes anyone who pisses on his patch, including Brits,' Patrick said.

'It was the Brits that rid them of the Nazis,' Huntington said.

'And Brits dabbling with the Nazis that caused this problem,' Patrick retorted, grabbing his phone as it rang.

'We're lying off Eden Roc,' Jean-Paul told him.

'How did you get there so fast?'

'We weren't caught up in traffic, not like there is on the route you're taking.'

'Can you pick us up from the jetty?' Patrick said. 'We'll be there in ten minutes.'

The *Diving Belle* sat in all her glory a suitable distance from the Eden Roc. Used to viewing sleek superyachts in the bay below, the clientele of the Champagne Lounge must have been puzzled by the arrival of the heavy-hulled and less than pretty diving boat.

Huntington's reaction was even more nonplussed.

'You have to be joking!' was his retort when Patrick indicated the *Belle* was their backup.

'She has what we need on board.'

'What, a canon?' Huntington said scathingly.

'Diving equipment,' Patrick told him.

When Stephen brought the dinghy alongside

165

the jetty, Patrick gave him a stern look, indicating he didn't want to hold a conversation in front of Huntington. Not to talk was a difficult request to make of the Irishman at the best of times. Now, excited by his inclusion in the adventure, Stephen was bursting with the desire to tell Patrick what he thought about it all.

'François is with us,' he finally said as they drew alongside the *Belle*.

'François?' Patrick repeated.

'He knows exactly where we're going,' Stephen informed him.

Being a Cannes fisherman, François Girard would know every bay, rock and inlet in these waters. What lay above the surface and what lay below.

Patrick nodded, accepting this addition, aware they would need all the help they could get. The firm set of Huntington's mouth suggested the opposite. He didn't voice an opinion, but Patrick knew he would as soon as he got Patrick on his own.

Once on board, Patrick did the necessary introductions. He could tell by Jean-Paul's expression that he didn't rate Huntington any more highly than when he'd met him at the restaurant. François replied in guttural Cannois, putting Huntington at an immediate disadvantage, and Stephen wore an open face as usual.

'Let's go below,' Patrick said. 'I'd rather any onlookers remain unaware who's here.'

As they took their places round the table, Stephen plonked a carafe of wine and five glasses on the table, plus a couple of baguettes and a large plate of *fruits de mer*, no doubt supplied by François.

'We've eaten already,' Stephen said.

Patrick, registering how hungry he was, immediately tore off some bread and helped himself to wine. Huntington thought about it for a moment, then did the same. His colour was better, Patrick decided, and he was definitely in less pain, but the morphine would need to be topped up before long.

Patrick ate while he talked. Huntington tried to catch his eye on occasion, indicating he had something to say, but Patrick ignored him. By the time the shellfish was finished and the wine replenished, the plan was laid out, or at least as much as Patrick was willing to divulge.

When the others had gone back on deck, Huntington got his chance, and took it.

'You can't be serious!' he said.

'Deadly serious,' Patrick told him.

There was a roar as the engine started up and the *Belle* began to wind her way to the chosen spot.

'We don't know there is an underwater entrance,' Huntington came back at him.

'François maintains there is.'

'It would be better by land,' Huntington insisted.

'Then we'd have to enter the grounds. The château has state of the art security systems. Besides, the co-ordinates suggest the hiding place is on the shoreline.'

'We always knew it was a cave. Just not where the cave was,' Huntington said.

'So you assumed that, like other Nazi stores,

it would be in the Esterel mountains.' Patrick paused. 'A cave on the Cap won't be dry, so I take it the item's not easily spoiled?'

When Huntington didn't answer, Patrick said, 'Are we looking for gold?'

Eventually, Huntington nodded.

'In what form?'

'That I don't know, but it'll be heavy and would therefore be better transported by land,' Huntington insisted.

'Just how friendly is London with the current owner of the château?' Patrick asked.

'Not enough to tell him he has treasure on his property and expect him to hand it over,' Huntington admitted.

'And what about Bach or Fratelli?'

'Fratelli has supplied some of the art in the château. It's possible he may have access when the owner isn't in residence,' Huntington conceded.

'And they would approach by helicopter?'

'I would assume the *Hirondelle* will also be lying off the coast.'

Patrick rose. 'Let's find out.'

Château de la Croë lay on the southern tip of Cap d'Antibes, facing the sea and surrounded by a high wall. There was no access from the seaward side, either by path or by boat, and its grounds were thick with Aleppo pines. A perfect hideaway for the Windsors and the various illustrious owners who'd followed them.

On deck now, Patrick watched as the scattered lights of the peninsular diminished in number the further south the boat chugged. There had been no sign of the *Hirondelle*, but chances were she

168

would be lying in what was commonly known as Billionaires' Bay, shielded by the narrow promontory at the far western corner.

Night diving was popular along the Côte d'Azur. A dive boat anchored off Château de la Croë would therefore go unremarked, even by the *Hirondelle*. As would a group of divers entering the water near the château.

Divers called a coastline like this a 'drop-off'. Plunging downwards via a cliff face, it offered a deep dive close to shore. François had indicated that the tunnel entrance lay at around thirty metres, although it wasn't easy to find, being hidden behind an outcrop. Using a standard fifteen-metre tank, they would have around twenty minutes of air at that depth. When Patrick questioned whether that would be enough for the return journey to the cave, François confirmed what he already knew. 'It all depends on the weight of your cargo.'

Huntington came to stand beside Patrick on deck. He had already decreed that François would take himself, Huntington and Jean-Paul to the dive spot. Two of them would enter the cave, leaving one diver outside.

'I'm coming in with you,' Huntington said.

'You're injured and you've had a second shot of morphine.' There was no need to spell out what they both knew that might mean – the bends or narcosis.

Huntington's expression was set. 'I'm coming,' he repeated.

Patrick didn't argue, knowing there was little point. And, he reminded himself, this was

London's game and Huntington was London's man. For his own part, he planned to participate only as long as it took to get the Madonna back.

The three men dropped, one after another, into the water. Patrick had dived with Jean-Paul before and trusted him. Huntington was an unknown quantity. François had taken them in the dinghy to what he said was the exact spot. Patrick only hoped the fisherman was right.

Stephen hadn't been happy to be left on the *Diving Belle*, but he'd been given an important task. One on which the whole plan hinged.

Patrick took the lead, his torch beam reflecting off the limestone rocks below the surface. On a night dive there was normally plenty to see – night creatures emerging to prey on those asleep in their burrows, and phosphorescent displays by the tiny creatures of the rocks as they detected movement, lighting up the sea like fireworks, only to disappear an instant later.

But this wasn't a normal night dive.

Patrick checked his watch and noted they were already at fifteen metres. At this point, the cliff face was traversed by a ledge, causing the waves to foam and break, hiding the air bubbles that identified the presence of divers below.

Patrick checked back on the others, giving them the OK signal. Jean-Paul responded immediately, Huntington a little later. The morphine, Patrick knew, would be dulling not only the pain but his reactions too.

Dropping lower, he checked for the outcrop of rock. François had described it as '*le doigt qui n'a pas d'ongle'*, the finger without a nail. And he was right, the outcrop resembled a large stone penis.

Indicating that the others should follow, Patrick moved behind the outcrop, flashing his torch at the rock, the beams from the other torches dancing alongside his own. This had to be the place indicated by François, yet Patrick could see nothing that suggested an opening in what appeared to be a solid rock wall.

Then he spotted something, above rather than on the same level as his current position. Rising a little, he felt a pull as a surge of water entered what had to be a tunnel in the rock.

Patrick had a sudden memory of the Bay of Skaill, in Orkney, and the waterspout on its southern rocky headland – how water surged through the tunnel at high tide to emerge in a spout from the grey rock, as though it were a huge whale.

He had no wish to be sucked in and spouted out of this tunnel.

Patrick let the swell carry him forward, then caught hold of the rock just left of the entrance. Turning, he indicated to the other two men his success.

Unhooking the nylon rope, he attached it to his diving belt and passed the end to Jean-Paul. Indicating Huntington should take hold of it, Patrick dipped his head and entered.

François had told them the tunnel emerged in a limestone cave, which lay below the outer grounds of Château de la Croë. Because of the danger of accidents, the interconnecting hole that

171

gave access from ground level had been overlaid by a grille which, before the current owner renovated the derelict property, had been hidden by undergrowth.

According to Huntington, the co-ordinates of the supposed treasure had been split between the two Madonnas, the original and its imitation. When the two paintings were identified and brought together, this was where it pointed.

The floor of the narrow tunnel was covered in white sand, the walls in little soft corals that beamed bright yellow at Patrick in the torchlight. Once or twice he spotted a patch of precious red coral, *Corallium rubrum*, its durable and intensely coloured red or pink skeleton much sought after for making jewellery.

Sudden windows or portals in the limestone gave him a glimpse of the open sea beyond, which looked for all the world like the night sky. His torch beam threw up other shapes, more monster-like than pretty. Especially the elongated shadow, resembling a Sherman tank, of a clawless lobster seated on a ledge.

Then the tunnel widened into what could be described as a shallow cave. Suddenly there was air above them, about a metre of it. The current lessened here too, its energy dissipated. Patrick trod water and waited for Huntington to follow.

When Huntington appeared, Patrick put his head above the surface, removed his mouthpiece, and took a breath of fresh air. 'There's another stretch of tunnel ahead, after which we should reach the main cave.' He didn't ask how

Huntington was, knowing it was pointless to do so.

Before moving towards the next entrance, he gave the rope two tugs, indicating to Jean-Paul that all was well.

'Let's go.' Patrick reinserted his mouthpiece.

This section of the tunnel was even more claustrophobic than the previous one. It was fully filled with water and he had to lie flat and work his way along the sand with his hands, which made it difficult to use his torch.

Eventually the passageway widened, although the height remained the same.

Patrick shone the beam ahead, hoping for a glimpse of the main cave, but all it met was a wall of rock. He swore into his mouthpiece. If this was a dead end, how the hell could they turn round in such a confined space and make their way back?

Having come to an abrupt halt, Huntington collided with Patrick's fins as a sudden swell threw him forwards.

Patrick turned his head enough to meet Huntington's eyes in the torch beam, then made a gesture indicating there might be a problem and to tread water and wait. It certainly looked like a dead end ahead. But if it was, the water would be coming back to greet them, and it wasn't.

Patrick kicked forward and just as he met the wall was suddenly swept ninety degrees to the left, indicating that the supposed dead end had merely been a sharp turn in the passageway. The tunnel roof began to rise, and then suddenly he was through and into a sizeable cave.

Moments later, Patrick came ashore on a pebble beach, where he removed his mouthpiece and mask and drew in a grateful breath of air. Seconds later, Huntington joined him. This time Patrick gave the rope three sharp tugs, hoping the signal would register across the distance between himself and Jean-Paul, indicating they'd reached their destination. Because they'd had to move so tentatively through the tunnel, Patrick wasn't sure how far they'd travelled. With the sharp bend, he suspected they'd doubled back and were now not far from the entry point, albeit with a wall of rock between.

'Look,' Huntington said, his voice echoing in the chamber. He pointed upwards to where the thick darkness had become something else. The part moon that had accompanied their boat trip was now sending them her rays via what looked like a metal grille in the roof of the cave, almost directly above them.

Patrick swore his appreciation softly in French. So François had been right, the cave was accessible from the land.

He swung his torch round. 'Assuming we're in the right place, where do we find the treasure?'

Sixteen

If Jean-Paul had followed orders, by now he would be back in the dinghy awaiting developments. Patrick checked the computer on his wrist.

They were no longer using the air in their tanks, but with the deep dive and their large lung capacity both he and Huntington had, he estimated, used up just short of half their supply, the rest of which they would need for the return journey.

They'd completed a search of the cave. At least, as much of a search as was possible with a shaft of moonlight and two powerful torches. Huntington looked pale when the beam caught his face, but for all Patrick knew he might look the same himself.

His biggest fear at that moment was to catch sight of someone at the grille above. But, he reasoned, were the opposition to locate the entrance, they would wait for daylight before entering. After all, who would be mad enough to come searching for buried treasure in the dark?

'You're certain there was nothing to indicate where the gold might be?' Patrick tried again.

'I told you, no,' Huntington said, his voice etched with frustration.

The beach they stood on was barely big enough to accommodate both men. Scraping the gravel away had revealed a layer of limestone beneath, so nothing could be buried there. The cave walls surrounding them had no niches in which to hide bounty. All in all, Patrick couldn't see where anything might be secreted.

'Of course, there's a chance it's already been found and removed, not necessarily recently,' Huntington admitted.

'Great!' Patrick said. If this was a wild goose

chase, then it wasn't the first one London had sent him on.

He sat down and began to study the cave, his torch beam playing above the surface of the water.

'If it's not above the water, then maybe it's below?' Patrick suggested.

Huntington looked as though he might dismiss such a possibility, but didn't.

'You check the left-hand side, I'll take the right,' Patrick ordered.

They'd already removed their tanks and stood them at the rear of the small beach. Patrick fixed his mask in place, took a deep breath, and sank into the water, torch in hand.

Assuming the gold was pure, then salt water wouldn't have affected it, no matter how long it had been submerged, although its hiding place might be another matter. The wall below the waterline was encrusted with barnacles. In the bright light of his torch, Patrick caught sight of the other living creatures who called the cave home. Had this been a recreational dive, he would have found the cave fascinating. Under these circumstances, he was merely irritated by what he saw, because none of it gave a hint to the presence of what he sought.

Then he did locate something, or rather his torch did. As he slammed it against the rock in his frustration, he broke through the covering of barnacles to reveal what looked like a flat, regular surface beneath.

Immediately, he freed his diving knife from his belt and began a full frontal attack on the barnacles, to expose what looked like a pane of reinforced glass. Moments later, as the water around him billowed with tiny pieces of broken crustaceans like an underwater sand storm, he was convinced of it. Desperate for more air, but refusing to give up and surface just yet, he angled his blade behind the final clump of barnacles and forced them free.

As they finally released their hold and fell away, he saw her through the pane of glass now exposed.

She stood in a niche in the stone, just like the Madonna in the corner wall of the Campo Bandiera e Moro. The Venetian Madonna was made of painted plaster; crumbling with age and damp, she seemed to symbolize a Venice past its former glory. The statue before him now wasn't crumbling or tarnished. This Madonna gleamed in the circle of torchlight as brightly as the day she had been fashioned – to reflect Fragonard's painting of his half-naked mistress.

The likeness was remarkable, but there was one difference. The face of this Madonna was not the beautiful face of the painting. Patrick, his need for air momentarily forgotten, now understood why the statue had been hidden and why the Madonna of St Honorat and its imitation had led them here.

Patrick surfaced, and quickly drew air into his empty lungs.

'Huntington,' he called. 'Over here.'

'You've found something?'

Patrick indicated that Huntington should follow him back down, without saying why. When he pointed to the cleared circle of glass, Huntington kicked forward. Alongside, Patrick watched his eyes widen, just as his own had done. Bubbles of air escaped from Huntington's mouth as he exclaimed his stunned delight.

He turned to Patrick and gave a thumbs up.

Patrick motioned that they should rise.

Surfacing, he realized that the light, or lack of it, in the cave had changed. Dawn was coming and with it, no doubt, their adversaries. They'd been down here for approaching an hour and they still had to make the return journey, this time with a precious cargo.

Neither men discussed the lack of time, just what needed to be done to get the Madonna out of her glass case and transport her along the tunnel to the waiting dinghy.

Breaking reinforced glass underwater was only the first problem they faced. Being able to breathe freely while down there would help, but they had to be sure they kept sufficient air for their journey back through the tunnel and enough to rise safely to the surface from a depth of thirty metres, carrying a heavy object.

Ten minutes later they had set themselves up on the sea floor and begun clearing the entire surface of the glass, before preparing to shatter it. Patrick estimated the Madonna to be about twenty centimetres tall, ten wide and five deep, so approximately 1,000 cubic centimetres. What that translated to in weight he would discover when she was free, but at a guess, if pure gold, it would be somewhere around twenty kilograms.

Patrick handed the mouthpiece to Huntington

and watched as he took in air. He seemed to be coping well, but the morphine would wear off soon and Patrick couldn't imagine that Huntington would be able to swing a heavy weight with that injured shoulder. As for carrying the Madonna to the surface, Patrick suspected that would be down to him.

Reigning blows below the water line was a whole lot harder than when above it, Patrick decided, as his second attempt at breaking the glass with a sharp lump of limestone rock failed. Already, daylight was entering the cave through the metal grille on the roof and filtering down through the water.

Patrick accepted the mouthpiece offered by Huntington and took a breath.

This time it would break, he vowed.

Taking up a different stance, Patrick concentrated his aim on what appeared to be a chink in the glass and swung, directing the sharpest corner of the rock at that spot.

This time he heard a crack. And moments later he saw a chequered disintegration in the surface of the glass. Patrick dropped the rock and attacked the shattered segments with his knife, until the hole was big enough to retrieve her.

Reaching in, Patrick caught hold of the Madonna and eased her forward, then tipped her into their waiting arms. He could tell by Huntington's expression that neither of them had been aware of the true weight of what they sought. Scrambling on to the beach, together they laid down their joint burden.

'Can we use the lift bag to get her out?'

Huntington said, his eyes rising to where daylight filtered through the iron grille above them.

Patrick wasn't sure if that was possible. A lift bag was essentially a balloon device which, when filled with air and attached to a heavy object, lifted it to the surface. They had to negotiate a narrow tunnel with a low roof. The bag would be no use to them in such a confined space. It might be useful once they were back outside, but using that method to lift the Madonna to the surface would only be advisable if they could be certain no one other than Jean-Paul would spot the orange balloon and realize its significance.

Coming to a decision, Patrick took off his BCD and began to undress. Losing his thick wetsuit meant dropping five or six kilos, which would allow him to ditch his weight belt. The buoyancy control device was military issue and could support just short of twenty-eight kilograms.

The water at the relevant depth was very cold. He would be taking a chance on hypothermia without a wetsuit, but then he was taking a chance on having enough air to get both him and the statue to the surface anyway.

Huntington, realizing what the plan was, immediately offered to trade places with him.

Patrick shook his head. 'I'm in better shape than you are, at the moment,' he added to soften the blow.

As he lifted his air tank on to his shoulders, a shadow crossed the grille above them. Patrick motioned to Huntington that he should step back out of sight, which he did, his own tank only half in place.

The words were in German, shouted rather than spoken, and Patrick recognized the guttural voice of one of the boneheads. A rapid exchange of voices followed, filled with excitement. Patrick reminded himself that, although they could see the light above, their adversaries would be looking into darkness.

Patrick motioned to Huntington to stay out of sight and wait, then got down on his knees in the water, lifted the statue, and secured it inside the fully inflated BCD, strapping it to his chest.

He then signalled to Huntington that they should prepare to enter the water as quietly as possible. Those above might not be able to see them in the darkness of the cave, but they would be able to hear them.

Huntington nodded and, lifting his gear to swing it over his shoulder, encountered the bullet wound. His face creased as the pain hit home, and he staggered a little. The next moment passed in slow motion as Patrick realized that the morphine had worn off and Huntington's tank was about to collide with the wall.

The resultant clang echoed like a gunshot in the confined space.

Moments later, indiscriminate firing came from above, ricocheting off the limestone walls and pinging into the water with the whooshing sound of a silencer. A bullet missed Patrick's face by centimetres and, deflected from the wall, headed downwards, entering the water close to Huntington.

Underwater they would be in danger of taking

a bullet. Up here, being hit was fast becoming a certainty. Huntington had read the situation the same way. He was fastening his tank in place and preparing to make for the water, even as the bullets continued to rebound round them in a shattering volley of noise.

Cradling the Madonna, Patrick submerged. Their attempted escape having been noticed, the bullets were now being directed at the water, making the surface seethe.

If we reach the tunnel, then we stand a chance.

Huntington had taken the lead, moving more swiftly than Patrick, with his burden. He turned and flashed his torch, and Patrick noted he had hold of the rope. Patrick could spare a hand for neither the rope nor his torch. The weight of the gold felt like a foot on his back, and he was using both hands to propel himself along the seabed towards the tunnel entrance, all the time kicking up a storm of sand.

He'd fastened the two straps of the BCD as tightly as he could, but they were no match for the relentless downward pull of the gold. The next time Patrick kicked, he lost her. Slipping out from the double straps of the lifejacket, the Madonna fell like a lead weight into the sand. His own weight suddenly lessened by twenty kilos, Patrick bobbed up to the surface.

That's when he heard it. A saw cutting through the metal grille above.

Once the opening is clear, they will be down here by rope in seconds.

Patrick let out air from his jacket, then kicked his way back to where he'd dropped the

182

Madonna and began to search frantically for her in the sand.

Then he heard shouts, and feet hitting the pebbles. One set, then another.

The boneheads will be the first down, with the guns.

Blinded by sand clouds, Patrick had to rely on instinct to find the statue.

Desperate to locate the place he'd dropped her, he began to dig like a dog scrabbling for a bone, all the time in disbelief at how far she might have sunk.

And then he found her, the hard block of solid gold.

Lifting the Madonna, he secured her inside the BCD again and swiftly reinflated it, just as a bullet swept by on his left, then another on his right. He kicked out for the darkness that was the tunnel entrance, and met Huntington's torch as he came back in search of him.

God knows how I'll deal with the tunnel, but at least I'll be free of the bullets.

But not yet free of his pursuers, it seemed.

Patrick felt the disturbance as someone entered the water behind him. Felt the approach as the water surged forward. It seemed the boneheads weren't about to give up on the prize just yet.

As Patrick, hugging the Madonna, gave a frantic kick forward, a hand caught hold of his fin and pulled him back. Jerking himself free, or so he thought, he felt something stab his leg, tearing into the bare flesh.

The beam from Huntington's torch met his mask and Patrick realized they were approaching the ninety-degree turn. Patrick kicked out, knowing that to round that corner was to leave his follower behind. As the darkness of the narrow tunnel closed about him, Patrick wondered what would await them at its exit.

Seventeen

Patrick indicated that he aimed to rise at least to the level of the underwater ledge they'd passed earlier on the cliff face. The plan was to swim along the coast in a westerly direction at a depth of fifteen metres. The surf breaking on the ledge would conceal their air bubbles from anyone on the shore looking for them.

Between the grounds of the château and the neighbouring Villa Eilenroc was a sea wall. Patrick hoped to stash the statue underwater there, then try and gain the surface before he ran out of air, or got the bends.

The boneheads had used silencers when firing into the cave, and the shots wouldn't have been heard from the water. So there'd been no warning for Jean-Paul or François that anything untoward had occurred. But once Bach knew they were in the cave he would have checked out the shoreline and seen both the dinghy and the *Diving Belle*, and surmised that if they had the prize they would be heading there with it.

Which meant they couldn't.

Huntington, knowing what was intended, gave

the rope three sharp tugs. At this depth they had no idea what was happening on the surface, but if it was Jean-Paul who held the other end then he would let it go and return to the *Diving Belle* as ordered.

Moments later, Huntington signalled that the rope had been freed.

Patrick, nursing the Madonna, kicked out for the ledge.

The confines of the tunnel had been problematic. Now the danger was that as the swell lifted and dropped him, he would be thrown against the cliff face. With the weight of the gold pulling him down, swimming at a depth of fifteen metres felt like swimming at thirty metres with a heavy boot pressing down on his back.

Checking his console, he saw that the needle indicating his reserves of air was already into the red.

Never stay down in the red.

Huntington, moving alongside, would have more air than him, but not much more. They were both running close to empty and Huntington's rise to the surface would be as fraught as his own.

The sea wall he sought was at least a hundred metres west of the tunnel, just about as far as he could manage. The pull from the Madonna seemed to be growing by the second. Patrick had an overwhelming desire to loosen the straps and let her go. But were he to do so, he would immediately bob to the surface like a cork, exploding his lungs in the process. Not something he wanted to happen.

Then he spotted it, just as Huntington turned and gave him the OK.

Before them loomed the place where he could lay down his burden.

Patrick checked his depth gauge. Had he had the air, he would have preferred to conceal her at the base of the wall, but he couldn't go deeper than this and hope to come back up alive.

To his right Huntington was busily checking out the wall, trying to find a suitable lodging place while Patrick concentrated on managing his buoyancy and staying horizontal. Were he to flip on to his back, or worse than that, spin upside down . . .

A signal from Huntington drew him nearer the shore.

A deep cleft lay between the limestone rock and the stone of the sea wall, with a ledge big enough to take the Madonna. Wedged inside, she would be out of sight to the casual eye.

Patrick gave Huntington the thumbs up, then checked his console.

Was that one bar left or five?

Aware that Huntington must be as low on air as he was, he indicated that he should go up. Now.

Huntington hesitated, but only briefly, knowing there was no other way, then began to deflate his jacket and gave a few kicks to gain his ascent.

If he didn't survive the transfer of the Madonna himself, at least Huntington knew her whereabouts.

The manoeuvre depended on timing and balance

186

of weight and air. What was required was delicate but possible, Patrick reminded himself. Simultaneously he had to move the Madonna to her place in the sea wall and compensate for the change in weight.

If he got it wrong, the Madonna would survive, but he would not.

Patrick took hold of the inflater valve with his left hand, then began to ease the Madonna free with his right. She came easily at first, then caught for a moment in the tighter strap. Two hands would have been better than one, but he couldn't desert the inflater valve. As she broke free of his body, his buoyancy rose and he immediately began to ascend.

Patrick eased open the valve and tried to compensate.

Steady again, he began to transfer the Madonna to the cleft in the rock, his fingers screaming out at the awkwardness of the hold and the weight of the statue. He held her in place for a moment before beginning to lessen his grip on her.

For a moment they were in perfect balance, but when the rock took her weight . . .

She was facing him as he sat her carefully down and he was struck again by the likeness and by the words inscribed in German along her base: *Die einst und zukünftige Königin.*

Ready now, he released her, simultaneously opening the valve to release the air that would save his life.

He was moving upwards. Too quickly, he knew. He would have to make a safety stop of at least two minutes at five metres or the dissolved gases coming out of solution would become bubbles inside his body, the result of which might be anything from muscle pain to paralysis.

He stopped his ascent, knowing that his air was almost out. The final breath from the mouthpiece would taste heavy, after that there would be nothing.

A shoal of tiny fish found him suspended there. Discovering their reflection in his mask, they tapped at it, believing they had found a mate. Above him the sun shining on the blue water, its rays filtering down, encased him in what appeared to be a golden glow.

Patrick took his last breath, as heavy as the Madonna had seemed in his arms, then began his final ascent.

Eighteen

The first thing he registered was how cold he was. Numb, bitingly cold. Then Patrick realized that if he could feel such cold he was still alive. It seemed the final breath he'd taken from the mouthpiece had turned out not to be his last.

As he strove to open his eyes, shivers wracked his body and he heard a voice say, 'He'll die if we don't raise his temperature.'

'Then you'd better warm him up,' someone replied.

The voices seemed to come from faraway,

although something told him he knew the owners of both. His eyelids finally responded to his command and flickered open. His last remembered image had been of a tiny bright-blue fish biting at his mask and the promised warmth of the sun should he reach the surface.

Although the image before his eyes was swimming, he knew he was no longer under or even in the sea. He lay horizontal on a cold, hard surface, in a shadow-filled room. Two, maybe three, faces moved above him, forming and re-forming.

'He won't be able to tell us anything if he dies.'

'Then save him.'

Footsteps, then a door slammed shut. Only one face above him now.

Another wave of shudders hit his body.

I thought the lack of air would kill me, but it's the cold that will do it.

Patrick hugged himself, drawing up his knees to his chest.

'Can you stand?' the remaining voice asked. 'We have to get you warm again.'

Patrick allowed himself to be helped to his feet, then his saviour half walked, half dragged him a few yards to what was, he discovered when he was lowered on to it, a bed.

The touch of soft warmth on his back sent Patrick into a jerking spasm again.

It's when I stop shivering that I have to worry.

Now someone was pulling off his wet shorts and drying his body. The roughness of their rubbing brought blood to the skin surface like small prickling bubbles. His brain registered this

189

and equated it to the bubbles of gas that might be in his system from ascending from depth too quickly.

Maybe that's why I'm confused.

A warm cover was pulled over him, yet still he shivered as though in his death throes. A hand touched his face gently. Patrick tried to focus on the face that hovered above him. For a moment he thought he was gazing at the Madonna. Not the cold hard version that had tried to drag him down to his death on the seabed, but the version he had gazed at in Fratelli's villa.

'Patrick. It's me, Grazia.'

'Grazia?' he said in amazement, trying to draw the moving parts of her face together. To anchor and match them to his memory of her.

'You have hypothermia. I have to get you warm. I'm going to get in beside you.'

Patrick registered the words, but not their meaning. Some moments later, he felt her warm arms envelop his ice-cold body and the heat of her breasts as they touched his chest.

As he had cradled the golden Madonna, so now did Grazia cradle him. The effect was extraordinary. Heat beat from her in waves, touching his body everywhere. Patrick imagined himself drawing out all her heat and leaving her cold and near to death, like he was, and instinctively tried to draw back.

But she wouldn't let him, clasping him to her. Gradually her heat flowed into him. Patrick felt it pass along his limbs and flood his chest, helping to pump his heart.

They were facing one another, her cheek

touching his, the warm mass of her hair caressing his shoulders. At last Patrick relaxed and let Grazia coax him back to life.

She insisted he be the one to sit on the bed, wrapped in the blanket. Grazia, dressed again, sat on the floor of the cellar, her back against the wall, observing him.

Once he was fully conscious, she questioned Patrick closely, trying, he knew, to establish whether he was experiencing any symptoms of decompression sickness. He answered honestly, because now he was warm again he could think more clearly.

'I'm OK,' he assured her. 'I think I was concussed, that's all. And frozen.' He fingered a bump on his head.

She appeared to be satisfied by this.

There was a short pause, before she said, 'You found what they were looking for?'

Grazia had saved his life, but he wasn't sure just how much of what had happened should be revealed to her, so he answered her question with one of his own.

'Why did Fratelli and Bach bring you here with them?'

'I'm not sure. Maybe they wanted me to authenticate whatever it was they were looking for.'

'They expected a third painting?' Patrick said.

She shook her head. 'I don't know what they expected.'

'London didn't tell you?'

She looked askance at him. 'Did they always tell *you* everything?'

191

'Strictly a need-to-know basis,' Patrick said with a wry smile. 'Which is what I am now applying to you.'

He tried to recall the conversation he'd over-heard in his confused state.

Who said 'He won't be able to tell us anything if he dies'? Had it been Grazia?

'Tell me *exactly* what you know,' he said.

Grazia was regarding him in much the same way as he was regarding her.

'That they found you at the location. That you escaped through the tunnel. That what they sought had gone.'

No mention of Huntington. Maybe they aren't aware there were two divers?

'What happened to Giles?' Grazia said, her face clouding over.

In that moment Patrick made a decision.

'I found his body in the boathouse. He'd been beaten to death.'

Patrick watched as the blood drained from her face.

'Oh, God.' She met his eye, her distress seemingly genuine. 'They'll do the same to you if you don't tell them where it is.'

'I can't tell them something I don't know.'

They sat in silence for a few moments, then Patrick threw off the blanket and stood up.

'Where are we exactly?'

'Somewhere on Cap d'Antibes, I think.'

'How were you brought here?'

'By helicopter, but it was dark.'

'Where are the paintings?'

'Probably here or on the *Hirondelle*.'

Patrick began to pace the basement room, conscious that movement would help pump blood round his body.

'What time is it?'

'They took my mobile. I have no idea.'

'How long have I been here?'

'At a guess, about three hours.'

Without a window on the outside world, there was no way to judge how long it had been since their escape from the cave. The plan might still be in motion, if both Jean-Paul and Stephen had carried out his instructions.

Patrick longed to know what had happened to the *Diving Belle*, but didn't want to mention it. Remembering the care Grazia had taken of him, he felt guilty denying her anything that might give her hope. And yet it was perfectly possible that, rather than his friend, she was in fact the enemy, placed here to extract information from him. Alternatively, if she was genuine and they suspected he'd revealed things, they would simply torture her instead of him.

She was watching him, trying to work out what he was thinking.

'How often do they come down here?'

'They'll come again soon,' she said. And a flicker of fear crossed her face.

It was Fratelli who came, and he was alone. Patrick was back in bed, the blanket in place, attempting to give the impression that he was in the next stage of hypothermia, namely asleep. His eyes closed, he listened to the conversation.

'How is he?'

'He'll die if we don't get him to a hospital.'
Her lie sounds genuine.
Patrick heard Fratelli approach the bed.
'His colour looks better,' Fratelli insisted.
'You realize what his death will mean?' Grazia was saying.
Fratelli was pacing now. 'I didn't want this to happen.'
'Then you'd better prevent it,' Grazia said. 'The British Government will hunt you down. Believe me.'
'He's not one of theirs,' Fratelli retorted. 'He betrayed them.'
'You know nothing.'
'I know they want to be rid of him.'
'That's not true,' Grazia said.
'You don't get it, do you? Courvoisier was set up to take the blame if this went wrong.'
'And Huntington?' Grazia tried.
'We left him at the villa.'
'Dead?'
'No, not dead,' Patrick heard Fratelli say. 'Who told you that?'

As Fratelli, suspicious now, approached the bed, Patrick prepared himself. Fratelli was tall and fit, but he was an art dealer not an operative in the field, nor one of Bach's boneheads. As Fratelli bent to check on him, Patrick made his move.

'Let him go, Courvoisier.'
Bach stood in the doorway, one bonehead by his side, his gun pointed at Grazia. Patrick had no doubt the bonehead would relish the

opportunity to shoot her, it was clear from the look in his eyes.

Patrick pushed Fratelli away from him.

'You've recovered, I see,' Bach said. 'So now we can retrieve the Madonna you removed from the cave.'

Patrick could feel Grazia's eyes on him as he answered.

'I wasn't the one who took it,' Patrick said. Seeing Bach's expression, Patrick hurried on. 'Huntington was with me in the cave. He carried the statue out.'

He watched as doubt crept in.

'I lost him when we exited the tunnel,' he went on. 'As you know, I ran out of air and had to surface.'

For a moment Patrick thought Bach might have bought his story.

'You're lying,' Bach said. 'It was your wetsuit in the cave. You needed to lessen your weight. You carried the gold out and hid it.' He paused. 'And now you're going to show us where.'

As Patrick stood defiantly silent, the bonehead raised his gun.

Grazia staggered as the well-aimed shot skimmed her cheek and embedded itself in the wall behind. The speed of the attack had surprised her as much as Patrick. She reached for her cheek, finding blood. Throwing a defiant look at Bach, she said, 'Don't do it for me.'

Patrick addressed Bach. 'If you threaten her again, I'll kill you.'

Bach shook his head in wonder. 'A forlorn hope, Monsieur de Courvoisier.'

Nineteen

Moreaux listened to the Irishman's rapidly told story, already aware of at least half of it from his alternative sources. Connarty spoke in French. Not very good French, but at least he tried, which was more than anyone calling from London attempted to do. Trying to interpret the garbled details of Connarty's story, the detective switched to English, since his grasp of that language far exceeded the Irishman's knowledge of his.

'Where is he now?'

'We're not sure he managed to surface.'

Perhaps I am rid of Courvoisier after all.

'Although we do know he escaped from the cave.'

'And Huntington?'

There was a short silence. 'We don't know where he is.'

So London's man is missing.

'And the female?'

'She left Torcello with Fratelli. We think she's still with them.'

Moreaux allowed himself a moment's relief at that news.

'Where are you?'

'Anchored in Billionaires' Bay, as agreed.'

Moreaux told him to stay there and rang off. He lit a cheroot, then indicated to Veronique that she should bring him another glass of red wine.

196

It seemed de Courvoisier had ventured rather too far in his search for the missing Madonna and collided with what London in fact sought. He had sympathy with Le Limier's predicament. Playing the British was neither easy nor straightforward, yet it had to be done. He had been aware that they sought more than the Madonna of St Honorat. He was also aware that the Nazis were involved, Fratelli's presence being proof of that.

What he didn't know was how much Le Limier knew about Grazia Lucca.

Moreaux took a deep draw on his cheroot.

He wanted Le Limier out of Cannes, yet he resented London's involvement in what he saw as a French matter. That which they sought belonged rightly to France.

And France will have it, and the Madonna of the island.

Quite how to achieve such an outcome, Moreaux hadn't yet decided.

He accepted a second glass of wine from Veronique, then waited for her departure before he made his call.

Bach pointed to the wetsuit they'd removed from the cave.

'You will find it a perfect fit.'

'I'll need a tank,' Patrick said.

'That will be provided, along with an escort.'

Patrick wondered how much air would be supplied and whether they expected him ever to resurface. As for the escort, he knew who that would be.

197

'We'll need a lift bag, to avoid the dangers of carrying it up.'

Bach considered this then said, 'You will attach a rope. We will pull it up with the vehicle.'

He doesn't want me to surface, with or without the Madonna.

'I want Grazia taken to Eden Roc. She's no more use to you now,' Patrick said.

Bach contemplated this. 'The helicopter can take her there.'

'Before I dive,' Patrick insisted.

Grazia looked as though she might argue this point, but a glance from Patrick silenced her. Her left cheek was still bleeding. Had the bonehead been aiming for the eye he wouldn't have missed.

Patrick went over to her. The movement caught Bach off guard, and he didn't prevent it.

Embracing her, Patrick whispered in her ear, 'I'll meet you in the Champagne Lounge.'

'Stay alive,' she said in return.

Patrick watched as the second bonehead walked her to the helicopter. The Eden Roc was minutes from here. Landing there wouldn't mean freedom, not with Nazi number two still with her, but it was closer to freedom than remaining here.

She's of no more use to them, so there's no point in killing her.

Patrick consoled himself with that thought as the black shape rose into the sky.

'I don't dive until I get her call,' he told Bach.

If he was going to his death, he wanted to be sure Grazia wasn't.

Bach shrugged. 'We head for the shore. By the time we're there, she will be at the hotel.'

Patrick had no idea where he'd been picked up, or whether it was close to the sea wall. If they had found him there, then diverting them elsewhere would only anger Bach and maybe put Grazia in danger.

Patrick made a decision.

He would take them to the Madonna.

The bonehead sat in the back of the car with him, gun at the ready. Patrick spent the journey imagining all the ways he might inflict pain on him – much worse than had been inflicted on Huntington.

They would be under the water together, alone. Much could happen there, unseen by those on the surface. He wondered how good a diver the bonehead was and whether any of his battles had been fought at fifteen metres with the weight of the sea pressing on him and no gun in his hand.

Then Patrick recalled the knife that had slashed his leg. It seemed a gun wasn't his only weapon of choice.

Bach's mobile rang as they offloaded the diving gear from the car. He answered, then immediately handed the mobile to Patrick.

Grazia's voice was just discernable above the beat of copter blades.

'We're coming in to land,' she said.

'Call Charles.'

'My minder won't allow that.'

'I'm sure you'll think of something.'

The mobile was taken from her as she tried to respond. Patrick handed the phone back to Bach.

'Miss Lucca isn't in danger provided you do

199

what is required.' Bach indicated that Patrick should get kitted up.

Patrick obliged, glad that this time he would be wearing a wetsuit. When they'd picked him up, they'd obviously taken his tank and BCD too. Patrick shuddered a little as he donned the life-jacket, remembering the last time he'd worn it.

The bonehead dressed swiftly. It was obvious that he was no stranger to diving, but that didn't mean he was an expert.

Patrick noted that once their hoods were on and the masks in place there was little to distinguish them from each other. Same build, same height, the bonehead's tattoos no longer in evidence.

The only thing that distinguished them was the diving knife the bonehead carried, Patrick's own knife having been removed.

'It's not wise to dive without one,' he told Bach.

'Heinrich will protect you from any fish that come along.'

Bach, speaking rapidly in German, told Heinrich he should tie the rope to the vehicle and pull the Madonna up that way. While this was going on, Patrick was imagining a different scenario.

They walked along the sea wall. Patrick checked his position, then indicated that he would enter here. Before Heinrich could respond, Patrick stepped forward to the edge and jumped into the water.

Moreaux walked swiftly to the Quai Labeuf, where a police launch awaited him. It was time to bring this incident to its conclusion. As he approached the *quai*, he noted that François Girard wasn't at his usual place under the awning in the fisherman's area, although his boat was there. The thought crossed his mind that Girard might be playing a part in de Courvosier's latest job, too. Although the idea irritated him, it didn't surprise him. De Courvoisier had somehow managed to assemble a team from a hotchpotch of Le Suquet residents, many of whom operated just this side of the law.

Once aboard the launch, Moreaux gave instructions to head for Cap d'Antibes.

Twenty

Patrick slowly descended, Heinrich alongside. The safest way to dive was with a buddy you knew and trusted. There was only one thing more dangerous than diving alone, and that was diving with someone who would like to see you dead.

Patrick wasn't sure if Heinrich had been ordered to dispose of him, or whether he just wanted to. Either way it would be relatively easy, seeing that Heinrich was the one with the knife.

The sea wall loomed large on Patrick's left. He had deliberately walked further out on the wall before entering the water, his plan being to take as much time as possible before having to hand over the Madonna, assuming of course she was still there.

He had no idea what had happened to Huntington

after he'd surfaced, or if he had surfaced. He could of course be dead and lying somewhere on the seabed, waiting to be discovered. Or he could have reached shore and tried to go for help.

If that were the case, where was he now?

Fifteen metres down, Patrick stopped his descent and signalled to Heinrich that he was going to get close to the wall. Heinrich followed. An incoming swell suddenly lifted them and threatened to throw them against the wall, then just as swiftly dropped them again. Patrick trod water and made a show of checking his depth gauge, as if unsure if he was in the right place. This didn't go down well with the bonehead, who flourished the knife at him.

Patrick ignored the implied threat and made his way to the place where the underwater sea wall met the rocky shoreline, taking the rope with him. He was well aware that he'd shelved the statue at around ten metres.

Pointing at the corner, Patrick indicated that what they sought was somewhere there. Heinrich responded by kicking in the direction indicated. The swell here had stirred up sand from the bottom, turning the sea opaque. It reminded Patrick of the harmattan, the wind that blew through North Africa bringing the Sahara with it, turning the air to thick soup.

The sun's rays penetrated the water and reflected off the floating particles, turning them to grains of gold. His friends, the vivid-blue damselfish, appeared to examine the two divers, pecking at Patrick's mask and their own reflection. As the small shoal departed, frightened away by

Heinrich's flailing arms, Patrick spotted the Madonna sitting snugly in her niche, just where he had left her.

Catching sight of her, Heinrich shoved Patrick out of the way, his eyes triumphant behind his mask, then motioned that Patrick should be the one to secure the rope to the Madonna.

Patrick approached, clear in his mind how he wanted this to play out. The bonehead was a diver but not a skilled one, and he was hampered by his need or desire to have his knife at the ready. Patrick suspected that, once the Madonna was attached, the knife would be used to pierce his buoyancy jacket or cut his air supply. Something he planned to avoid.

Reaching into the niche, Patrick made a show of attaching the Madonna, then indicated she was ready to be removed from her resting place. The bonehead waved Patrick aside, miming that he would be the one to do that. Had Patrick been able to laugh with joy underwater, he would have done so. He finned back and gave Heinrich a clear run at it.

The bonehead reached in and checked that the Madonna was securely tied, which she definitely was. Patrick had made certain of that, having had no wish to see her free herself and drop to the sea floor to spoil his plan. His moment came as Heinrich scooped the Madonna from her niche. Behind him now, Patrick chose that moment to knock the knife from his right hand and immediately looped the rope round the bonehead's neck.

As the weight of the Madonna tugged at it, the

rope began to plummet, the bonehead with it, trying desperately to release air into his jacket to fight the weight. Ten metres above them the car was already taking the strain, fighting to pull the bonehead up, even as the Madonna was intent on pulling him down.

Patrick finned to the descending knife, caught it, and anchored it in his belt. Without a backward glance at the drama unfolding as the Madonna and the car fought for possession of the bonehead, he curved round the sea wall and headed out to sea, staying just under the breaking foam to disguise his air bubbles.

Once free of this place, he would ditch the tank and swim on the surface. Let them drag up the Madonna and her victim. He had no more use for her now.

Patrick began the steady swim west to Billionaires' Bay, where he hoped the *Diving Belle* would be anchored. If that part of the plan had failed, then he would have to head for Eden Roc and his car, which would involve crossing the narrow isthmus at the northwest corner, rather than swim the distance round it to approach by sea.

The steady beat of the swimming calmed him. Above, the sun shone from a clear blue June sky. What he'd left behind didn't concern him. The golden Madonna, it seemed to him, was cursed and would have been better left in the cave. Let London sort it out now.

His only concern was the return of Fragonard's Madonna to the cellars of the Abbey of St Honorat, where she might rest in peace.

Turning into the bay, he spotted the *Diving Belle* at anchor, as arranged.

Tired but relieved, Patrick looked on the ugly, heavy-hulled boat with something resembling affection. The final yards to her side seemed to him like swimming through treacle, with every stroke an effort. Drawing alongside, Patrick hoisted himself on to the metal ladder and, having clambered up it, fell exhausted on to the deck.

'*Mon ami*,' came the shout as Jean-Paul appeared to find out who the interloper was.

Patrick was scooped up and led into the cabin, where he was stripped of his wetsuit and wrapped in towels, then handed something hot in a mug, which turned out to be Irish coffee, with more whiskey in it than coffee.

Having gulped down a mouthful, he asked if there had been any sign of Huntington.

Stephen shook his head. 'After you signalled with the rope, we headed here as agreed. We assumed you were together.'

'He surfaced before me,' Patrick said, believing now that Huntington must have perished. He had been near to death himself when washed ashore, and Huntington had been in worse shape than him.

'You contacted Moreaux?'

'He's on his way.'

'What of the *Hirondelle*?'

'No longer in these waters.'

After swallowing the remainder of the coffee, he went to get dressed and, more importantly, to make a call.

This time Patrick informed the receptionist at

the Eden Roc hotel that he was Lieutenant Martin Moreaux of the Police Nationale and intimated that he urgently needed to speak to a Mademoiselle Grazia Lucca, who he believed was in the Champagne Lounge.

This time he wasn't given the brush off.

'I'll put you through, lieutenant.'

There was a brief silence, then the barman answered. Patrick gave Moreaux's name once more, described Grazia, and asked to speak to her.

A few moments later, the barman came back on.

'The lady you describe isn't here, Monsieur.'

'Was she in the Champagne Lounge earlier?'

'I don't recall seeing her, and I have been on duty since we opened.'

Patrick described the bonehead and asked about him.

'No, Sir, I haven't seen the gentleman either.'

The helicopter had definitely appeared to be heading in the direction of Eden Roc, but once across the Cap it could have headed anywhere. Antibes, or more likely Monaco, or even Italy. Patrick tried to recall Grazia's voice. It had sounded strained, but with the beat of the blades and the bonehead beside her that was understandable.

Then another thought occurred to him. A much more troubling one.

How easy it would be for the bonehead to rid himself of his cargo above the waters east of Cap d'Antibes.

Twenty-One

The high-powered police launch was fast, yet not fast enough. During the journey Moreaux had smoked three cheroots and contemplated how he planned to deal with the situation awaiting him on the Cap.

Courvoisier's call had particularly disturbed him. If Le Limier was right and they now had the golden Madonna, then their prime aim would be to get out of French waters with the spoils.

Monaco would provide the swiftest refuge, but Moreaux suspected Italy to be their goal and had therefore sent another police launch in search of the *Hirondelle*.

Now that Le Limier had made him aware of the exact nature of the statue, Moreaux understood why the British were so keen that her existence be kept secret. Personally, he didn't care about the embarrassment her exposure would cause to the British Crown and the British Government. His only concern was that France was not dragged into it.

To that end, he was beginning to think they should let the British have the statue, provided France retained the two paintings of the Madonna, as Le Limier had suggested.

On the other hand, should he play the British game even further, he might also rid himself of

Courvoisier on a more permanent basis, which was something to consider.

As the launch entered the bay in front of the château, he saw the *Diving Belle* coming round the sea wall to join them.

On shore, Patrick watched as Moreaux surveyed the area south of the sea wall.

'And you're certain they retrieved the statue?'

'Look,' Patrick indicated the deep marks on the dirt road surface where the car had sought traction.

'It must have been heavy?' Moreaux said, surprised.

'Around twenty kilos.' Patrick didn't mention the body that he hoped had been dragged up with it.

'And how far away is the place you were held?'

There were few roads on the southern tip of the Cap. One main road and a few secondary ones used to approach the few expensive concealed villas. Patrick had memorized his route and reran it now for Moreaux's benefit.

'You won't find anything there,' he added. 'Except evidence in the basement that what I told you is true.'

'And where do you think they're headed?'

'The yacht will make for Monaco, but it won't be carrying anything. I don't think they'll use the airport at Nice to fly out. They'll expect you to have alerted security there. The helicopter's a possibility, but not for a long flight and it's easily spotted, especially if you've got a call out on it.

If it were me, I'd go by road into Italy and head north.'

He watched as Moreaux considered this.

'Once they're in Italy you have little chance of picking them up, certainly not quickly enough to retrieve the goods before they dispose of them,' Patrick went on. 'But I'm more concerned about Grazia Lucca's safety than retrieving a gold statue and two paintings,' he added.

'As am I, Courvoisier.'

Moreaux had set his men to work, sending two of them to search the villa and two divers down to check on the wall and the seabed. After which, he motioned to Patrick to board the police launch, where he gave the order to head for Monaco.

Patrick had called Jean-Paul from the fast-moving launch and told him about the police divers.

'I want you to take a look further east. If Huntington didn't reach the surface, the swell may have taken him back in the direction we came from the cave. The ledge at fifteen metres could trap a body.

'And what about you?'

'I'm heading for Monaco with Moreaux,' Patrick told him. 'Is François still with you? I need to ask him a favour.'

Moreaux was in the forward cabin setting his various plans in motion by radio. Trying to catch the lieutenant's rapidly fired French above the noise of the engine and the flying spray hitting the windows, Patrick managed to pick up the various alerts being put out. Also, the possibility that the *Hirondelle* had been located by the other police launch just off Monte Carlo and was about to be boarded. Then he caught Grazia's name.

The hope that Grazia had been deposited on the *Hirondelle* by helicopter was a forlorn one, but Patrick held on to it anyway. When Moreaux reappeared, Patrick immediately asked if there was any word about her. Moreaux didn't answer, but instead brought out a photograph from his inside pocket and handed it to Patrick.

Whatever Patrick had expected or even dreaded as a response to his enquiry, it hadn't been this. For a moment he didn't recognize her, or maybe he just didn't want to. But he did know the man beside her. Marco Fratelli had his arm around Grazia's shoulders and she was looking up at him in an adoring fashion. That was difficult enough to stomach, but what surrounded them was even worse.

Marco and Grazia stood on a platform, behind them posters proclaiming this as a rally organized by an Italian Neo-Nazi group. The crowd Marco had apparently been addressing consisted mainly of young men who looked a lot like Bach's bone-heads, their hands raised in the infamous Nazi salute.

Moreaux lit a cheroot and inhaled deeply as he waited for Patrick's reaction to the revelation. Patrick wanted to say he didn't believe Grazia was working for the other side, but found he couldn't.

So many things would fall into place if it were true. One in particular. The voice that had said the words 'He won't be able to tell us anything

210

if he dies' had been Grazia's. It seemed that Bach had given her the job of saving him, for the sole purpose of extracting the whereabouts of the statue.

And I obliged.

'That's why they took her with them?' Patrick said, dreading the answer.

Moreaux nodded. 'Yes.'

'So we don't need to rescue her?'

'No,' Moreaux said. 'Not yet, anyway.'

'What do you mean, not yet?' Patrick demanded.

Moreaux savoured a deep draw on his cheroot, before answering.

'You're not the only one, Courvoisier, capable of working for two masters.'

Patrick tried to absorb what Moreaux's words meant. True, playing two sides had sometimes been necessary in his past life. Arguably, as Moreaux inferred, he was doing it now. The question was, who exactly were Grazia's two masters?

Then a thought struck him.

Patrick flourished the photograph at Moreaux. 'London knew about this?'

'Mademoiselle Lucca isn't London's to command. Unlike you,' Moreaux said, testily.

Patrick ignored the jibe, as he tried to work out what Moreaux might mean. Finally it dawned on him. 'Grazia's working for you?'

Moreaux didn't answer the question, because he didn't have to.

My God, she's working for the French!

'In what capacity?' Patrick said.

'As an art expert. Mademoiselle Lucca has been infiltrating groups trading in stolen art from the

Second World War. The Neo-Nazis have been very busy in that sphere recently.'

Patrick glanced at the photograph again. 'That's why she's seen here with Marco?' It seemed important to Patrick to establish exactly what the relationship between Grazia and Marco was.

Moreaux gave him a shrewd look. 'If you're asking me if they are lovers, I suspect that may have been necessary to gain Fratelli's trust.'

'And her connection with London?' Patrick said.

'Her services were offered. They accepted.' Moreaux gave a thin-lipped smile. 'I did not, however, suggest you be involved. That was their idea. It seems, Courvoisier, they're quite keen to have you back in the fold.'

'Or they want someone to put the blame on when it all goes wrong,' Patrick said, sharply.

'You're sure Bach still believes Grazia can be trusted?'

'Perhaps you are in a better position to answer that than I,' Moreaux said.

Patrick replayed the scenes at the Eden Roc, then on Torcello and finally on Cap d'Antibes, and realized he couldn't be sure of anything.

'She played her part well,' he conceded.

Moreaux nodded. 'Good. The question is, can she lead us to them now?'

Grazia touched Marco's arm and he turned to give her a dazzling smile. Even as he bestowed it, she wondered if he knew what her role was, or suspected her. Perhaps since that moment in the basement when she'd asked whether

212

Huntington was dead? That had been a mistake. She should never have questioned him about that.

Marco had denied it was true, but he must have sensed how badly she would feel if it was. Marco was vain and egotistical, but he wasn't essentially cruel. And he wasn't a true Fascist. He'd become involved in this more from greed for what a Nazi treasure trove might bring him than out of a desire to support the rebirth of Fascism. At least that was what she'd thought until now.

Bach on the other hand was someone to truly fear.

Grazia recalled how Patrick had insisted that she be taken to safety before he would show them where he'd hidden the Madonna. How angry he'd been when the bonehead, as he'd called him, had taken a shot at her.

She'd been taken aback by that herself, expecting only that she might be threatened in order to persuade Patrick to reveal the statue's whereabouts. In that moment she'd known Bach would kill her without hesitation if he had the slightest suspicion she'd betrayed them.

And now he had an even better reason to kill her.

She hadn't been present when they'd pulled the statue roped to Heinrich's body from the water, but Marco had described the scene to her in hideous detail.

She had no doubt that Patrick had disposed of Heinrich. Whether or not it was in self-defence she couldn't say, but the anger she'd seen in his eyes in that basement suggested that Patrick

213

wouldn't miss an opportunity to get rid of his guard if one presented itself.

Her own immediate problem was the need to get a message to Moreaux indicating where they were headed. He would no doubt assume they'd make for Italy, since outside his jurisdiction it would be more difficult for Moreaux to control the search.

For her own part, she'd believed that's what their plan was, so had been surprised when in fact the opposite happened. Arriving in Monaco by helicopter, they'd picked up Bach's car and headed west instead. Moreaux would be chasing them in the wrong direction unless she could tell him otherwise. And to contact him, she needed to be alone and out of earshot.

Quietly she asked Marco if they could stop the car so she could go to the toilet.

'It's better if we keep going,' he whispered back, one eye on Bach in the front passenger seat.

'I'm feeling nauseous. The helicopter ride . . .' Grazia put her hand over her mouth to indicate how bad it was.

Marco looked horrified at the prospect of being vomited on. He leaned forward and quickly explained the situation to Bach. When Bach glanced in the rear view mirror, Grazia upped the ante by making a retching sound, causing Marco to move further away from her.

Bach barked an order to the driver, to find a place to pull up.

Her performance had to last until the next autoroute exit with a Relais.

When the car drew to a halt, Grazia made a dash for the ladies' toilet.

Hearing a toilet flush, she waited for the occupant to emerge. When a young woman and a child of about four came out, Grazia groaned and leaned over the sink as though she felt ill.

'Are you OK?' the young woman enquired.

Grazia clasped her stomach. 'Early pregnancy. Nausea.'

'I know. It's terrible,' the woman sympathized, 'but worth it in the end.' She patted her daughter's head.

'I think I should call my husband and tell him to come for me, but my mobile's battery has run out,' Grazia said worriedly.

'Here, use mine,' the young woman immediately offered.

'I'll just send him a text and let him know where I am.'

'Good idea.'

As the woman washed her daughter's hands, Grazia sent a text giving their location and the registration number of Bach's car.

As she pressed the send button, the door of the rest room was thrown open.

When the woman turned to see who it was, Grazia placed the mobile on the sink and dived for a cubicle.

'Hey, this is the Ladies,' Grazia heard the woman say. 'The Gents is next door.'

Grazia stuck two fingers down her throat, and this time the retching was for real.

The bonehead waited impatiently while she washed her hands and splashed water on her face.

'I'd better check if the shop has something for travel sickness,' Grazia said, playing for time.

'No. We're going.' He pushed her roughly towards the door. The woman and child had left, so there was no one to stand up for her now.

When Grazia emerged, Bach and Marco were waiting by the car.

'I'm sorry,' she said. 'I feel better now. Let's go.'

Bach eyed her as she climbed in the back. As far as she could make out from the low conversation he'd had with the bonehead on their return, her saviour in the toilets hadn't been quizzed, so the bonehead didn't know she had sent a text on the young woman's mobile. He did, however, confirm to Bach that he'd heard Grazia being sick when he entered the toilet.

So she'd got away with the nausea story and sending the text. What Grazia didn't know was whether she'd remembered Patrick's number correctly.

For some reason, Bach didn't direct them back on to the motorway but instructed the bonehead to make for Èze on the Moyenne Corniche. Grazia knew the village well, mainly because it was an artist community and she'd visited most of the small galleries there. Most *perché* of all the perched villages, it was situated on top of a sheer rock face and there was no access for cars.

Why go there?

She shot a look at Marco, but he had lapsed into silent meditation. Grazia touched his arm and mouthed 'Why?' at him.

He shook his head at her as if she was a recalcitrant child. 'Wait and see,' he mouthed back.

If they were intent on Èze, there must be a reason. But what?

Then a thought struck her.

They planned to pass on the statue, and it was the last place Moreaux would think of looking.

Twenty-Two

Moreaux had radioed ahead, intent on making contact with his counterparts in Monaco. Patrick suspected the detective now viewed Le Limier's part in the proceedings as being at an end. When Moreaux abandoned him on the quay, suggesting he return to Cannes by train and await developments, Patrick chose not to argue, intent as he was on seeing whether his own forward planning had come to fruition.

He found the Ferrari exactly where he'd asked François to deposit it, the key stashed in its usual place just above the front wheel. Patrick kissed the key and started her up, noting that not only had François brought her the thirty odd kilometres from the Eden Roc, at what speed he could only imagine, but he'd also topped up the petrol. He vowed to reward the fisherman well when this was over.

A text had arrived from an unknown number as the police launch entered Monaco harbour. Fortunately for Patrick, the sound of its arrival went unnoticed in the noise of docking. The fact that it had been sent to the London mobile convinced him it came from Grazia.

His first plan had been to tell Moreaux. But instinct told him that if he did so the detective wouldn't allow Patrick to accompany him, stating that this was now Police Nationale business and reminding him that he was a private citizen. This way he got a head start, and Moreaux would serve as his backup.

Patrick viewed the cryptic message, then brought up the number and rang it. When a woman's voice answered, he asked for Grazia.

'Your wife?' she said.

'Is she alright?' he said, his note of concern genuine.

'She's OK. She was really nauseated. She wanted to text you to come pick her up. I loaned her my mobile.'

'Where is she now?'

'I assume she is waiting for you at the Relais near the Èze exit. I told her not to worry, the nausea will settle down around three months into the pregnancy. And congratulations, by the way.'

'What time did this happen?' Patrick asked.

'About an hour ago.'

Patrick thanked the woman and rang off.

So Grazia had been at the motorway services west of Nice an hour ago, and according to her text they'd taken the Èze road.

The village they appeared to be heading for was about ten kilometres west of Monaco. Perched precariously on a pinnacle of rock, it had two

218

gates for entry. The jumble of red-roofed houses that clung to the rock were reached only by crooked steps and tiny twisting alleyways, cars had to be parked outside the village walls.

Patrick couldn't imagine why Bach would go there. It would be like entering a castle, but without the possibility of pulling up the drawbridge. They could certainly hide in the maze of little houses, or in the numerous caverns and cellars cut out of the rock which had served as storage places for Èze's medieval smuggling trade. Of course, Bach might be making instead for one of the secluded villas at the foot of the sheer precipice and just above Èze-Bord-de-Mer.

The more he considered the move, the more Patrick was convinced the purpose of going to Èze was not in order to hide. If Bach wanted to do that, losing themselves in Italy would have been a much better plan. Which meant that the choice of Èze was significant.

But in what way?

When Monique Lacroix had accused Patrick of knowing only the tourist stories of Cannes and its environs during the Second World War, she'd only been partly correct. On arriving on the Côte d'Azur, Patrick had spent months exploring the coastline and hinterland of his new home.

Èze had been one of the many places he'd visited, and he'd been fascinated by its past. It was a village that had risen from the dead many times, its inhabitants having been put to the sword on numerous occasions by invading forces, their village razed to the ground. By the 1920s, Èze

219

had been abandoned and was almost completely depopulated. Later, it had been part of the Italian zone and was occupied by Mussolini's troops until the Italians surrendered to the Allied forces in 1943 and the Germans reclaimed it.

Ironically, many thousands of French Jews, fleeing persecution from the Vichy régime in so-called Free France, had sought safety in the Italian-held area. But in truth anywhere along this stretch of coast was significant in the story of European Fascism.

Patrick's conclusion as he left the autoroute was that he had no idea why Bach should come here with the statue, and locating his presence in Èze or its surroundings would be difficult and time-consuming if Grazia didn't make contact again.

Grazia hadn't had an opportunity to question Marco about what was going on until now. Their arrival at the village car park, followed by the walk up the hill to the hotel, had been done in silence.

She was surprised that Bach had chosen a hotel, rather than a private residence. If he didn't want his presence in Èze known, it seemed an odd decision, as was abandoning the plan to drive into Italy. Grazia suspected that Marco knew the answer, but was unwilling to divulge it, until maybe now.

On entry to their suite, he'd gone to take a shower, leaving her alone. She'd contemplated using the phone in the suite, but hadn't had enough time to make the call before he emerged naked from the shower, his intention quite clear.

'I think I should shower first.' Grazia smiled apologetically. 'After that business at the Relais.'

Marco nodded in an understanding fashion. 'I'll open the champagne,' he said, indicating the chilling bottle and two glasses waiting for them.

So this is a celebration, Grazia thought as she entered the bathroom. But a celebration of what exactly? Finding the statue, or something more?

As she showered and washed her hair, taking as much time as possible to delay Marco's plans for sex, she heard him answer his mobile.

When he rang off, he knocked on the door. 'I have to go to Bach's suite. I won't be long.'

'OK,' Grazia shouted back, immediately vacating the shower.

Once she heard the door close behind him, she emerged from the bathroom and headed for the phone.

Her voice was faint, but there was no doubt it was her.

'Where are you?' Patrick asked her, as he steered the car on the mountain road with one hand, the other cradling the mobile.

'Château Èze. Bach has taken suites here. Marco's with him now.'

'And the statue?'

'They brought both the statue and the paintings from the car.'

'They plan a handover?'

'Maybe. But I think there's something else happening. Marco knows, but I haven't got him to tell me yet.'

221

'I'm on my way. And I'll tell Moreaux where you are,' Patrick promised.

There was a short silence as Grazia absorbed the news that Patrick now knew who she was really working for.

'When this is over, maybe we can both be honest with each other,' she finally said.

'Perhaps,' Patrick conceded.

Then he rang off and made his promised call to Moreaux.

Grazia replaced the receiver as the door opened and Marco re-entered. Still dripping from the shower, she secured the towel round her naked body.

'That was quick,' she said.

Marco closed the door, locked it, and stood against it.

'Who were you talking to?'

A hundred thoughts raced through Grazia's mind, none of them good. She had, she believed, managed to fool Marco, at least up until the villa on Torcello. Since then, she'd been extra affectionate, extra convincing.

'Room service,' she ventured. 'I thought we might need a second bottle, if we're celebrating.'

She managed to pour a glass of champagne from the bottle Marco had opened, willing her hand not to tremble.

'Here,' she said, releasing the towel before handing him the glass.

For a moment, she thought it had worked. Marco accepted the champagne and tasted it, his eyes moving over her nakedness. She filled her own glass and stood up, toasting him with it.

'Are you going to tell me why we've come here and not headed to Italy as planned?'

Marco came to stand close to her.

'Because there's going to be a show.'

'A show?'

'We have collectors coming to view the paintings and, of course, the statue.'

'Wouldn't it have been safer to do that outside France?'

Marco raised his free hand and fingered her nipple.

'We can do what we like here. After all, Courvoisier thinks we've headed in the opposite direction, doesn't he?' Marco gripped the nipple and twisted it, hard.

Grazia cried out from the suddenness of the attack, but Marco smothered the sound by pressing his mouth hard on hers. He let go his glass and it hit the deep pile of the carpet, spraying the champagne against her bare leg.

His free hand now found her throat.

'Who were you talking to, Grazia?' he whispered menacingly in her ear. When she didn't answer, he said, 'If I tell Bach, he'll have Jonas tip you over the wall into the valley below. All Courvoisier will find when he arrives is a broken doll at the foot of the precipice.'

'I told you, I was calling room service,' she said, desperately trying to think of a way, any way to get out of his grip.

'I think you're lying.'

Grazia attempted to twist out of his grasp but

223

Marco had no intention of letting her go, so she did the only thing left open to her. She stabbed the champagne glass she still held into his groin. The glass snapped as it met his body and she felt the fractured lip pierce the material of his trousers.

Marco let go of her throat and jumped back.

'So you did call Courvoisier,' he said with a small smile. 'Good. Bach will be delighted to hear it. Now, get dressed. We have a party to go to.'

They left the hotel in single file, Bach leading the way, Marco and Jonas corralling Grazia. She was aware there was a gun pointed at her back, although it would be easy to dispose of her in the way Marco had suggested. At every turn in the twisting narrow street there was a view down the sheer cliff face. Once over the edge, she would descend thousands of metres in seconds, hopefully to die before she reached the foot.

Marco had, she realized, tricked her. They must have suspected her from the Relais stop, if not before. Or maybe they had been playing with her, just the way she had played with them.

Bach obviously wanted Courvoisier here at the finale, maybe more so since he'd killed Heinrich. They now knew she was on Courvoisier's side, but did they know about Moreaux?

If Marco had been listening outside the door, then he knew she'd led Courvoisier here. But she definitely hadn't mentioned Moreaux's name during the telephone conversation, so perhaps her true cover had not yet been blown.

Dusk had fallen on the little hill town, and with night coming the main bulk of the visitors had departed. The number of people actually residing here was small, and once the art and craft shops were closed for the night the winding maze of streets lay empty.

Far below, the lights of Beaulieu and Cap Ferrat twinkled and in the far distance lay Nice and the jutting outcrop of Cap d'Antibes.

A beautiful sight, which is likely to be my last.

They had arrived at their destination. Grazia felt the muzzle of the gun nudge her forward to enter through a low doorway. Dipping her head, she followed Marco into a narrow hall, then down a set of uneven stone steps into what could only be described as a cavern hewn from the rock, ablaze with light.

She came to a halt in astonishment.

Twenty-Three

The car park was practically empty when Patrick drew in, evidence that Èze wasn't a hotspot at night. He made his way up to the lights of Château Èze and came to their unmanned reception, where he found a notice requesting visitors to use the wall phone, then someone would come down and open the door.

Patrick dialled and a man answered.

'I'm here to meet with Herr Bach's party,' he said.

'I'm afraid they've already left, Sir.'

'Damn!' Patrick said. 'Can you direct me to where they're headed? I'm a little lost in the maze of streets.'

'May I ask your name, Sir?'

'Coburn.'

'Let me just check, Sir.'

After a couple of minutes, he came back on the line. 'Follow the wall to your right. The building you're looking for has a plaque above a black door with the symbol of a red phoenix.'

Patrick thanked him. That his name had been accepted suggested Bach was expecting him to turn up, or hoping he would. Either way, it seemed it was now common knowledge that Grazia had contacted him, which meant the danger he'd thought her in before had now multiplied.

Until that moment, Grazia hadn't been permitted to view the golden Madonna. Marco had described the statue to her, but nothing prepared Grazia for its beauty.

A shrine had been set up near the back wall of the cavern. Illuminated by arc lights, the gold shone like a burnished sun. On either side hung the two portraits of Fragonard's mistress. One authentic, the other a good imitation. Directly behind the gold statue was a black-and-white photograph blown up to poster size. Above it were two flags: one the swastika, the other that of the Italian Neo-Nazis.

The large photograph featured a beautiful

dark-haired women and her handsome male companion. The woman's eyes weren't on him, however, but on the smiling man standing before her, holding her gloved hand in his. The photograph, featuring the Duke and Duchess of Windsor being welcomed by Adolf Hitler to his mountain retreat, was a famous one that Grazia had seen before. But at this size, in this place, it struck her even more forcibly.

As Grazia moved forward to view the statue, the group of collectors around the shrine, all male, parted to let her through. With a catch in her throat, Grazia had a close view of what all this had been about.

The figure wasn't, as she'd imagined, a replica of Fragonard's Madonna, although it did resemble it in form, being the upper half of a woman's torso, with her breasts partly exposed. The difference lay in the features of this Madonna. Taken aback by what she thought she saw in those features – the smooth centrally parted hair, the distinctive arched eyebrows, the line of the lips, the shape of the jaw – Grazia looked from the photograph to the statue, then back again in disbelief.

That's why the photograph's up there. Bach wants them to note the resemblance.

It appeared that the gold statue gifted by Hitler hadn't been fashioned to portray Mademoiselle de Sainval of St Honorat but the Duchess of Windsor, Wallis Simpson, wife of the abdicated King Edward VIII.

On the base were engraved the words *Die einst und zukünftige Königin,* below which Grazia read *Von jüdischen Gold.*

227

The once and future queen. Fashioned from Jewish gold.

Now Grazia understood why the British wished so fervently to retrieve and, she suspected, destroy this piece of art. It had never been about the painting that had been gifted to the Windsors by the Führer and hung on the walls of Château de la Croë. It had been about this.

Bach took centre stage and began his speech to camera, in which he explained exactly what they had recovered and its provenance and its significance in the history of the Fascist movement, now being reborn like a red phoenix across Europe.

'Miss Lucca, our art expert, has verified the Fragonard and the rather excellent forgery, done by a German artist at the request of the Duchess of Windsor.' Here Bach paused. 'Of course, the real prize is the golden Madonna. Created to show the Führer's admiration for the woman he wished to place on the throne of England, it is exquisite. The Windsors accepted the gift of this Madonna, just as they accepted the Fragonard. However, on this occasion they did not make the gift known to the British Government, but chose to hide it. Had the outcome of the war proved different, I believe it would have been revealed. The British have been seeking the statue, of course, but have failed in their attempts. It is now ours to do with as we see fit, and we wish that whoever purchases it will use it to further our cause.'

Grazia observed the intent expressions of the men surrounding her, knowing they were only a small selection of the wealthy Fascist sympathizers dotted around the world who would want to bid for such a priceless symbol of their movement.

The black door beneath the red phoenix stood partly open, which suggested that Bach was expecting a further visitor.

Probably me, Patrick thought.

When he'd called Moreaux and explained the state of play, he had felt the heat of the detective's wrath over the phone.

'I told you to return to Cannes, Courvoisier,' he said sharply.

'Grazia managed to get a message to me indicating where they were heading,' Patrick replied, omitting to mention exactly when the text had arrived. 'She wanted me to help.'

Moreaux changed tack. 'Why Èze?'

'Grazia wasn't sure. Maybe for a handover? I'm at the place now. It seems Bach's expecting me.'

'So they know about Grazia?' Moreaux said, concern in his voice.

'They must do if Marco overheard our conversation. But your name was never mentioned.'

'So they may not know her true role in all of this?'

'Let's hope not.'

Patrick opened the door, dipped his head to avoid the low stone lintel, and entered the dark passageway, where he paused to listen. Although the passage wasn't lit, there was a light at the

229

end of it, which illuminated what appeared to be a stone staircase leading downwards. He was aware the rock was riddled with caves, some of the more famous ones between fifty and seventy metres deep, but from the murmur of voices he didn't think he'd be descending that far.

Moving to the top of the staircase, he noted that it wound down in a spiral, thus restricting his view of what lay below, but from here he could make out individual voices, none of them female.

The chatter below ceased and there was a short silence of expectation, followed by an explosion of excited applause. Then Bach began to speak, extolling the virtues of the treasure that lay before them.

Patrick checked his mobile and found there was no signal. If that were the case at the top of the staircase, then it would be the same in the room below. Fortunately he and Moreaux had anticipated they would be out of contact and had already agreed a plan.

Patrick began to make his way down the staircase towards the bright light.

Bach's speech ended to a round of exuberant applause. Immediately it was over, a man approached Grazia and speaking in Italian asked what she, as an expert, believed the Fragonard to be worth. Grazia invented an exorbitant sum and watched his eyes light up.

'And the golden Madonna?' he asked.

'She is worth whatever you are willing to pay for her.'

When he nodded, satisfied, and moved away to view the prize again, Grazia stepped back into the shadows. With Marco engaged in an animated conversation with a collector and Jonas on sentry jury next to the statue, it seemed an appropriate time for her to blend into the background and perhaps even escape up the staircase.

As she made her move, Bach appeared from nowhere to prevent it.

'I suggest you remain here.' He regarded her with displeasure. 'After all, your guest is yet to arrive.'

'I don't know what you're talking about,' Grazia said.

His fingers bit into her arm. 'I have it on good authority that Mr Coburn, or de Courvoisier as he's more commonly known, is in the vicinity and will appear shortly.'

Grazia looked around, but Jonas was still at his post by the statue. So who was watching the door?

'Not everyone here is a dealer or collector,' Bach told her. 'Those who are not, are fully armed.'

Grazia glanced round to discover three men had dislodged themselves from the group and were now focusing on herself and Bach.

'You have the statue,' Grazia said. 'No one else needs to die.'

'You're the one who summoned Courvoisier, remember?'

Bach motioned one of the three men over.

'It's time to remove Miss Lucca.'

At that moment, music blared out like a blast

of thunder. The national anthem of the Third Reich, *Horst Wessel Lied*, resounded round the chamber, drowning any attempt Grazia might have made to scream. In moments, she was hustled behind the display and through an opening in the wall.

Patrick entered the room as the music filled it. He took in the splendour of the brightly lit display as his eyes roamed in search of Grazia. He spotted Marco and then Bach, even Jonas on duty beside the golden Madonna's shrine, but there was no sign of Grazia.

The marching song, complete with the sound of strutting German boots, resounded round the room. It seemed history was repeating itself within these four walls.

'Ah, you've arrived.' Bach approached him. 'We were afraid you might be too late.'

'Too late for what?' Patrick said.

'Not the auction. That has already begun.' Bach paused. 'I refer to Miss Lucca's demise.' He glanced at his watch. 'But there may just be time to view the proceedings.' He gave a signal summoning the remaining bonehead.

'Remove Mr Coburn's weapon and take him to Miss Lucca.'

Patrick didn't argue as they took his gun from his waistband. He had no idea where Grazia was, and the cavern might prove to be part of a labyrinth in the rock. This way they would take him straight to her.

He allowed himself to be bundled roughly beyond the display and through an opening in the back wall that led into a dark passageway. From behind him, the bonehead's torch beam lit their way. It was as though they were back in the underwater cave, but this time it wasn't sand underfoot and they were breathing real air.

Patrick stole a quick glance at the illuminated dial of his watch.

Where the hell are you, Moreaux?

A sudden, desperate thought occurred to Patrick on the steep walk down into what felt like the heart of the mountain. Moreaux wanted his operative alive, but he wouldn't be so concerned about Patrick. If the detective chose to search the hotel for Grazia before coming here, he might lose them both.

Eventually the passageway levelled out. Patrick guessed they'd travelled at least twenty metres down through the rock. During the Middle Ages Èze had become a centre for piracy, and vaulted passageways and storerooms had been created to store booty. Patrick suspected they were headed for an opening in the cliff face from which the booty had been lowered to men on the valley floor. Such an opening, he feared, had also been used for throwing people to their death.

Grazia had hung back as they pushed her towards the opening, fearing there was nothing beyond but a sheer drop. In that, she'd been proved wrong. The opening fed on to a metal platform, two metres in width and waist high. It was a place you might bring someone to gaze at the stars and the sheer magnificence of the deep-blue

233

Mediterranean far below, provided that person didn't suffer from vertigo.

Having deposited Grazia out there, her guard returned to the safety of the passageway, to wait. But for what?

Eventually she marshalled enough courage to check what lay beneath her, and discovered the rock was so sheer that no vegetation was brave enough to cling to its smooth face.

I couldn't climb down there, even in daylight.

Out on the platform, she was as much a prisoner as if she'd been locked in a cell. She sat down in the corner and hugged her knees, as the cool night breeze sent shivers through her thin dress.

Each time Patrick stumbled on the uneven floor, the bonehead jabbed the muzzle of the gun further into his back. Patrick suspected he wanted to do much more with it than that, but was under strict orders from Bach not to. Which begged the question, what exactly did they plan to do with him? And what had they done to Grazia?

They turned a corner in the tunnel and there it was. An opening on to the ravine. The man who stood on guard turned and, seeing the bonehead, exchanged a few grunts with him.

'Where is she?' Patrick demanded. 'Where's Grazia?'

'Through there,' the bonehead said with a smile. 'Want to join her?'

'Patrick?'

The voice was faint, but it definitely belonged to Grazia.

Patrick stepped through the opening and was relieved to find his feet touch metal rather than thin air.

The tunnel had been pitch-black, their way made possible by the bonehead's torchlight. Out here, the light came from a part-moon and a sprinkling of stars. As his eyes adjusted to it, Patrick made out a figure huddled in a corner of the platform.

'Grazia,' he said, overjoyed.

Patrick reached down and drew her to him, enveloping her in his arms.

Twenty-Four

Although the plan discussed with Courvoisier hadn't been what Moreaux desired, he'd had little choice but to agree. Courvoisier's suspicions that Grazia had been outed as a double agent put her in grave danger. Courvoisier's safety wasn't Moreaux's primary concern, but Grazia's was. Unfortunately, their fortunes now appeared to be entwined.

Since the entire operation had been played out under the radar, exposing it now was best avoided if possible. Moreaux had therefore decided to summon backup from Cannes, rather than inform Monaco police what was going on so close to their border.

It was better that way, but reinforcements would take longer to arrive than Moreaux was happy about. He'd brought the marine officers with him, although in his opinion they were better suited to boarding suspicious yachts than storming the Bastille that was underground Èze.

Courvoisier had intimated in his last call that the entire Bach party were assembling in the phoenix house, but he couldn't verify that Grazia was with them. Moreaux instructed an officer to head for Château Èze and make sure that Grazia wasn't being guarded in her room. The remaining officers he took with him.

They met no one on their way, although there were a few lights on in the jumble of houses that clung precariously to the hillside. Èze was like Le Suquet, only more maze-like, with narrower alleyways, the climb to the top steeper.

Moreaux had forbidden any talking, ordering their approach to be as silent as possible. If Courvoisier was right and Bach didn't know about the police's involvement, then surprise would be their biggest weapon.

Reaching the black door with the red phoenix above it, Moreaux stood for a moment listening. There was music being played inside, a military march by the sound of it. Moreaux smiled, realizing that the strains of *Die Fahne hoch* would cover their entry.

Moreaux checked to see if the door was locked. When it proved to be, he ordered it to be forced. With one swing, sixteen kilos of hardened steel hit the door and sprang the lock. The marching music enveloped them as the thick door flew open.

Moreaux dropped his cheroot and ground it

under his foot, then signalled to his men to enter.

Now Bach had both of them out here, what did he have planned for them? Patrick could see no reason why he and Grazia were still alive, except perhaps to be the centrepiece of some future event, maybe the finale of tonight's party.

Both Grazia's betrayal and Heinrich's death at Patrick's hands would require revenge, and Bach would want to be the one to take it.

Huddled together against the night air, Patrick whispered to Grazia that help was on its way. Whether she believed him or not, he couldn't tell in the faint light. His attempt to get a signal on the mobile had failed, so there was no way to find out if Moreaux had reached Èze yet. There was nothing to do but wait.

Or maybe not.

Patrick slipped his hand down to feel for the diving knife he'd removed from Heinrich, which was strapped to his right calf. Now he knew Grazia was alive, it was time to fight back.

A few moments ago, he'd heard what he believed was the departure of Grazia's guard, which left just the bonehead on duty in the passageway. If so, then it was now two to one in their favour.

Patrick pulled up his trouser leg and showed Grazia the glint of metal then, pointing at the opening, signalled that there was only one guard and he was going to try to take him. A few whispered words explained how Grazia might play a part in this.

He was asking a lot of her, and it wouldn't be possible if she didn't have a head for heights. Patrick watched her face in the moonlight for signs of fear and found none.

'Can you manage that?'

Grazia nodded. 'But not in this dress.'

Patrick blocked the opening with his body as she prepared to play her part.

'OK,' she whispered. 'Here goes.'

Grazia swung herself over the barrier and, dropping down, found a foothold in the lower frame of the platform. Now virtually out of sight, she screamed.

The sound was ear-splitting, so much so that for a moment Patrick thought she had really fallen.

The bonehead was out in seconds, gun in hand, to discover a shocked Patrick bent over the barrier, as if watching in horror as Grazia dropped to her death.

Swearing in guttural German, he did the same. Which was exactly what Patrick had hoped for. In seconds he had the knife at the bonehead's throat, its blade breaking the skin.

'The gun,' Patrick demanded, digging the knife deeper. He had drawn blood now. Patrick could smell the metallic scent of it, mixed with the bonehead's sweat of fear and fury.

One deep slice and it's over.

In his former life he would have done the deed by now and offered the body to the ravine. That would have been clean and easy.

This way was less reliable.

The bonehead's grip loosened on the gun and he let Patrick take it from him. He would be

238

planning something, his mind figuring a move that would put him back in charge. If that happened, the bonehead's retaliation would be swift and final. He wouldn't spare Patrick's life, regardless of what Bach's orders had been.

Patrick swung him round and pushed him through the opening. The sudden change in direction, the loosening of the knife from his throat, surprised him.

The butt of the gun met the thick skull in a crunching blow, but it wasn't enough. The bonehead tottered, but he wasn't out. Not yet. Patrick repeated the action, this time twice as hard, and the bonehead sank to the stone floor like a rag doll.

Grazia?

She was already up and over the barrier and pulling her dress back on.

'He's out cold,' Patrick said. 'Are you OK?'

When she nodded, Patrick handed her the diving knife.

'Take this, and use it if need be.'

The music that drifted down had changed from the anthem of the Third Reich to yet another marching tune. Closer to the main cavern, Patrick could make out Bach's deep booming laugh.

Someone's happy. But not for much longer.

Patrick checked his watch.

Where the hell was Moreaux?

The answer came seconds later. Through the opening behind the shrine, Patrick saw the cavern plunge into darkness.

'Cover your mouth,' he told Grazia.

* * *

239

By the voices below, Moreaux judged that there were at least twenty men down there, and with the number of officers at his disposal he couldn't arrest them all. Nor did he have any wish to.

For the moment, he would settle for thwarting their plans and retrieving the goods and his operative safely. Arresting Bach could wait for backup to arrive.

As the power switch was thrown, the tear-gas canisters clanged down the stone steps and rolled into the room, followed by three dive flares taken from the police launch. The mix of gas and orange smoke turned the occupants into mad men flailing around in the darkness of hell.

Patrick flourished the torch he'd taken from the bonehead's body.

'Come on.'

He made straight for the painting, lifted it from the display unit, and wrapped it in the Nazi flag.

'What about the statue?' Grazia said.

'That's Moreaux's,' Patrick said as he made for the stairs.

He found Moreaux waiting at the exit with two armed officers.

'Ah, Courvoisier. How are things down there?' Moreaux said.

'Chaos.'

'Good. My backup team is due to arrive any minute,' he proclaimed, glancing upwards as a helicopter beam lit up the sky above the lower car park.

'I'm glad to see you, Grazia,' he said, his stern face for once softened.

'I'm glad to see you, Sir.'

'Courvoisier has treated you well?'

'He has. Yes.'

'Then I suggest you leave with your souvenir while I clear up the mess.'

Twenty-Five

On the journey to Cannes, the recovered painting sitting on the rear seat wrapped in the Nazi flag, Grazia explained her role in all of this. How she'd been working undercover among collectors and dealers in Nazi stolen art. Moving between Germany, France and Italy.

'That's how you met Marco?' Patrick asked.

She nodded. 'Marco was obsessed with finding stolen art. Not to return it to its rightful owners, but to either keep it for himself or donate it to the cause.'

'Twenty per cent of the Jewish-owned artwork of Europe,' she continued, 'was stolen by the Nazis and secreted away. And most of it has never been found. Beautiful paintings taken from their owners, who were then sent to concentration camps.' She glanced round at Patrick and he saw the tears in her eyes. 'Did you see the inscription? The gold used to fashion the statue of the Madonna was made from the wedding rings and other jewellery taken from those people. *Von jüdischen Gold.*' There was a shudder in her voice.

'What will Moreaux do with it?'

'We would never have known about the statue had the British not contacted us, in search of it. I suspect Lieutenant Moreaux will be obliged to hand it over, in the interest of diplomatic relations with London.' She paused. 'If he does, what do you think they will do with it?'

Patrick found that difficult to answer. The British didn't generally destroy works of art, even if they gave a poor impression of their former Empire and how it got to be so powerful. Visitors to the House of Lords were shown friezes that portrayed the colonization of Africa. Seeing the plasterwork that depicted black men on all fours with a white man's foot on their back had shocked even him, but the guide had simply acknowledged everyone's distaste and pointed out that that kind of thing was all in the past.

'I think they'll simply store it somewhere out of sight.'

'If the recording made tonight appears online, they won't be able to pretend it doesn't exist,' Grazia said.

Patrick had forgotten about the recording. 'Should we let Moreaux know about it?'

'If he's done his job properly, I think it will already be in his possession.' Grazia smiled and it suddenly struck him why she seemed so pleased.

'You think he'll release it?'

'I think he may use it as a bargaining tool.'

She laughed, a sound that was music to his ears.

'You want the abbey to have the Madonna back, don't you?' she said.

'The Fragonard belongs to the monks.'

She countered that assertion. 'My understanding was that it belongs to *your* royal family. Wasn't that why we were sent on this mission, to retrieve it for them?'

'Let them have the forgery,' Patrick replied.

'I don't think Lieutenant Moreaux intends them even to have that.'

Later, on board the gunboat, under the watchful eye of the Madonna, they made love by the light of the moon through the porthole. Grazia's whispered words of love were sometimes spoken in French, sometimes in Italian, never in English.

Looking down at her, Patrick recalled the first moment he'd seen her, when she'd smiled at his kilt in the diplomatic tent. He'd thought her enticing and had hoped to get to know her, then Charles had spoiled it by revealing why she was there.

'I was very rude to you,' Patrick said, 'that day at the garden party. And later in the restaurant.'

'You thought I was there to persuade you to take the job, and you were right. Charles Carruthers is a clever man. And a nice one.'

'I'm not sure it's possible to be nice in his business,' Patrick said.

She laid her head on his shoulder. 'We said that when this was over perhaps we might be honest with each other.' She lifted her eyes and regarded him quizzically.

'OK.' He kissed her lightly on the lips, before

continuing. 'I am Le Limier, a private investigator working from a gunboat in the old port of Cannes. I am also the scourge of Lieutenant Moreaux of the Police Nationale, who would like to see the back of me from his patch.'

'Why?' she asked, raising herself on one elbow.

'You'll have to ask Moreaux that.'

'Perhaps I will,' she said as she drew him to her.

Patrick woke at dawn to find Grazia had gone, although the painting still stood at the foot of the bed. He rose and showered, fetched croissants from the café across from the gunboat, and made himself a pot of fresh coffee, which he took up on deck along with his mobile.

The *Diving Belle* was back in its moorings, but with no sign yet of Stephen. Patrick was anxious to know what had happened after he'd left his friends searching the waters off Château de la Croë, so he gave Jean-Paul a call.

Jean-Paul was, like Patrick, an early riser and was swift to answer.

'We found him,' he said, before Patrick could ask. 'I'm sorry.'

'Where?'

'I told the police divers I'd spotted something under the ledge fifty metres south of the wall. They took a look and confirmed it was a body. When they brought him up, I identified him as Huntington.'

'So he's at the morgue?'

'I assume so. They took him away in the police launch.'

244

'Did they find any other bodies?'

'No, should they have?' Jean-Paul said.

'Hopefully, not,' Patrick said.

'And what of you, *mon ami*?'

'I have the missing Madonna,' Patrick said. 'Miss Lucca and I returned with it last night.'

Jean-Paul swore his delight. 'Miss Lucca is well?'

'She is. I'll come round soon and tell you all about it.'

Patrick rang off and put down the phone.

So Huntington is dead. Wounded and drugged, he should never have made the dive in the first place.

I should have insisted Jean-Paul be the one to come with me, Patrick thought, knowing it would have made no difference, because Huntington would never have agreed.

Patrick's face brightened when the London mobile rang, hoping it might be Grazia. It wasn't.

'Where are you?' Charles's voice was full of concern.

'Home.'

'And the Madonna?'

'Which one?' Patrick replied.

There was a short silence before Charles said, 'Huntington hasn't been in touch.'

'He won't be. Giles is dead.'

Patrick heard Charles's intake of breath.

'How did it happen?'

'He died trying to bring the gold to the surface.'

Patrick sensed how many questions Carruthers wanted to ask, so he waited, knowing which one would come first, before all the others.

245

'Where is the statue now?'

'With the Police Nationale,' Patrick told him. 'I suggest you contact Lieutenant Moreaux. I believe you have his number.'

'Courvoisier,' Carruthers said, as Patrick tried to ring off, 'you'll need to come to London to be debriefed.'

'I don't work for you anymore,' Patrick reminded him.

'Nevertheless, in this case, it's necessary.'

'I'm a private citizen living in France.'

'Who wants to go on living there.'

Charles's tone was mild, but Patrick didn't miss the quiet threat that it contained.

'By the way,' Patrick said before he hung up, 'Miss Lucca is unharmed, in case you're interested.'

Anger drove him below deck, where an empty champagne bottle stood next to the bed he'd shared with Grazia. All London had really been interested in was whether he'd retrieved the gold. Huntington's death was 'unfortunate'. Had it been Patrick who'd fallen in the line of duty, that would have seen a rather awkward situation conveniently resolved.

Patrick contemplated the veiled threat behind his summons to London.

If I don't go, what will happen?

A number of possible outcomes occurred to him simultaneously, ranging from the mild to the extreme. Although Charles might support him, Forsyth could find a way of blaming him for Huntington's death. If Moreaux chose to side with London over that, Patrick would either be on his way out of France or perhaps looking at a criminal charge in a French court.

It was a mess, and not of his making.

Not this time.

Patrick resolved to ignore the London summons for the moment and await the one that would surely come from Moreaux. If Grazia was right, the lieutenant had his own plan as to how to deal with London.

He turned to the Madonna.

'This is all your fault, Mademoiselle de Sainval,' he told her. 'You should have remained hidden in the abbey storeroom for the young monks to gaze on.'

Twenty-Six

Patrick caught the early boat to St Honorat, the Madonna secure in his suitcase. He wanted her back on the island, in Brother Robert's keeping, before Moreaux thought to pay him a visit. Once she was in the care of the abbey, Patrick's job would be done. What was likely to happen after that, Patrick couldn't say, but he would have fulfilled his side of the bargain.

The early boat was captained by Benedict, resplendent with his gold crucifix. Once they were out of the harbour, he summoned Patrick into the cabin.

'We never did meet for that glass of wine,' he said.

'I was called away on urgent business,' Patrick told him.

'And that business is now complete?' Benedict raised an eyebrow.

'It is.'

'I heard you found out about that yacht, the *Hirondelle*?'

'I did,' Patrick said.

'Good. I had planned to tell you about it myself.'

'There are no secrets on this island,' Patrick said with a smile.

'Only the secrets we wish to keep.' Benedict eyed Patrick. 'We all have those, Monsieur.'

'We do indeed,' Patrick agreed.

'Will you be staying at the abbey?' Benedict indicated the suitcase.

'No. I'm just returning something.'

Benedict looked up at the heavens. 'Then thank you, Monsieur de Courvoisier, from the bottom of my heart.'

The small tractor awaited him at the jetty. This time Patrick chose to use it, carefully stowing his precious cargo behind in the trailer. It seemed like a lifetime ago that he had walked this path with Oscar, yet it was no time at all. The day was as fine as it had been then, the scents as pungent, the quiet and industrious tending of the vines by the robed monks an antidote to what had occurred in the last few days.

I should stay here for a while. Eat well, drink good wine. Lay low.

It was an attractive proposition, and Patrick allowed himself a few moments to contemplate it, even though he knew it wouldn't happen.

When the tractor drew up at the entrance to the cloisters, Patrick jumped down and removed his case.

'Brother Robert is expecting you,' he was told by the driver.

Patrick thanked him and entered the building, then made his way up the stairs to Brother Robert's office and knocked on the door.

'Come in,' said the quiet voice.

Sunlight filled the room from the open window. Patrick could smell the lavender and hear the steady hum of the bees feasting on it, below.

Brother Robert rose from his desk, his bright-blue eyes smiling a welcome.

'You have returned safely to us, Courvoisier.'

'With the Madonna,' Patrick said.

He opened the suitcase and extracted the painting, still wrapped in the Nazi flag.

'She comes strangely dressed,' Brother Robert remarked.

'She's been keeping poor company,' Patrick told him.

He removed the flag, exposing the painting to the morning light. As he did so, Brother Robert gave a small gasp.

'I had no idea she was so beautiful,' he said quietly.

'You've never looked at her before?'

'Only once, in the darkness of the storeroom.' Brother Robert gave a wry smile. 'I now see why our young monks sought her company.'

They stood in silence until Patrick said, 'May I ask what you plan to do with her?'

'I wasn't sure, until perhaps now.' Brother Robert came closer, as though drawn to the beauty of the painting and its subject. 'A man who depicts his mistress so exquisitely must have truly loved her, I think.'

'They were together for twenty years,' Patrick said.

'And for twenty years St Honorat was her home.' Brother Robert retreated, seeking his favourite place by the window. Glancing out at the beauty below, he said, 'I have been praying for her return, of course, but also asking God what we might do with her, should He see fit to return her to us.'

'You're considering putting the painting on display here on the island?'

Brother Robert shook his head, though with a wry smile. 'Alas no, I fear there would be no work done by the brothers if we did that.' He paused. 'Although we might display her somewhere close by.'

'Where?' Patrick said.

'I was wondering about the Galerie du Carlton?' Brother Robert looked to Patrick for his reaction to the suggestion.

The famous Carlton hotel had one of the longest-established galleries in the south of France, having exhibited French master painters for over thirty years. But perhaps that wasn't the only reason for choosing it? After all, the Carlton's distinctive domes, on both seaward corners, were reputedly designed to resemble the breasts of the most famous courtesan of the French Riviera during the years surrounding the First World War.

Patrick met Brother Robert's mischievous smile with one of his own.

'An excellent suggestion, and they would be able to protect her there.'

Brother Robert was warming even further to his theme. 'We could have mementos made of her to sell here in the abbey shop. Postcards, posters. Perhaps even a book featuring the story of the painting in the island's history.'

'So you're not averse to making a profit from her?' Patrick asked.

'The Madonna is like one of our fine wines. To be enjoyed, but mostly by others. Besides,' Brother Robert added, 'all profits from our commercial activities support the work of our brothers, both here on St Honorat and throughout France.'

Then they talked of the painting's provenance and what Patrick had learned of it.

'Can this be proved?' Brother Robert said, a little worried. 'Would the English royal family be prepared to take her back?'

Brother Robert had served Patrick a glass of their best vintage, the Syrah, in celebration of the Madonna's return. Patrick sipped it before answering.

'I don't believe Lieutenant Moreaux of the Police Nationale will allow that.'

'Ah . . . And what of Mr Coburn?' Brother Robert said.

'I don't think he'll be back,' Patrick said.

'The Queen no longer desires our Syrah?'

Patrick met Brother Robert's frank gaze. 'They'll send someone else to buy it.'

Moreaux made the expected call as Patrick was on his way back to the mainland with his empty suitcase.

'Where are you, Courvoisier?'

'On the ferry from St Honorat.'

'Then I'll wait for you at the café by the gunboat.'

When Patrick arrived, Moreaux observed his suitcase with a questioning eye.

'You're planning a vacation?'

'I was bringing my things back from St Honorat.'

'So retrieving, not delivering?' Moreaux quizzed him.

'Let's call it an exchange.'

Patrick waited until his espresso arrived, before saying, 'The monks are thinking of displaying the Madonna in Galerie du Carlton.'

To his surprise, Moreaux nodded his approval. 'An excellent idea. She will be very popular, and the hotel will provide excellent security.'

'What of the forgery?' Patrick said.

'Alas, it was damaged in the fracas that followed your departure,' Moreaux said with mock sadness. 'But then it was merely a fake by some unknown German artist.'

'And the statue?' Patrick asked.

'She awaits her fate.'

'Who will decide that?'

'Sadly not I. She is perhaps a little too important for that.'

'So they will have her back?' Patrick said.

'It would seem so. They are very insistent.'

'And what will they offer in return?'

'Probably reminders of how they saved our asses during the war.' Moreaux gave a typical Gallic shrug. 'Then they'll point out the rise of anti-Semitism in Europe and how we must all play our role in its defeat.' He lit a cheroot and inhaled with obvious pleasure. 'But there is one bargaining chip I have yet to play,' he said.

'And what's that?' Patrick asked, thinking he might know already.

Moreaux shot him a keen look. 'They are keen for you to leave France and return to England.'

'I see.'

'I find myself in complete agreement with them. At times.'

Moreaux regarded Patrick with a mixture of irritation and amusement. 'Do you know, when they call they never make the slightest attempt to speak French? Yet we are required to have perfect English.'

'I also find that irritating,' Patrick said. 'If you remember, my father was French.'

'Perhaps that's why I told them I would not aid them in your departure. Not this time, anyway.'

'And they accepted that?' Patrick said, surprised.

'No. Not until I revealed that we had in our possession a video of the golden Madonna that was destined to be put up online. A video that made very plain what her origins were and who the Führer had gifted it to. And told them that, for the purposes of our investigation into the rise of Fascism in France, the video has to remain with the French police.'

'Bravo,' Patrick said.

Moreaux's glance grew stern. 'I'm not your friend Courvoisier, but I am not your enemy either. At least, not for the moment.' Moreaux finished his coffee and rose. 'Grazia tells me you were instrumental in saving her life.'

'She managed that on her own,' Patrick said, honestly.

'Unfortunately the man guarding you wasn't apprehended.'

'How is that possible?'

'We believe he may have copied your trick and hidden below the platform when the passage was searched. When forensic moved into the building, we think he used a suit to escape.'

'Jonas. His name's Jonas,' Patrick said.

'Jonas Engel,' Moreaux said. 'There was a brother, too, Heinrich. Grazia says he was at the villa, but she didn't see him after that.'

Patrick didn't respond to what might have been an enquiry. It seemed Grazia hadn't mentioned how Heinrich featured in the dive for the statue, and he silently thanked her for that.

'I'm sorry about your colleague,' Moreaux said as a parting shot. 'His body was requested by London. In the circumstances, we agreed.'

Twenty-Seven

The market was in full swing, its noise and vitality a welcome reminder of normal life in Le Suquet. Patrick headed up Rue Forville, keen to be reunited with Oscar. He'd missed the little dog more than he thought possible. As he opened the door of number twelve, he heard the welcome sound of Oscar's snuffled bark, but no dog came running to greet him. As he entered the garden courtyard, he spotted Oscar, on a lead attached to the handle of the open front door of the Chanteclair.

Patrick freed him, and a delighted Oscar began racing round the courtyard, tossing a small toy Pascal had given him into the air in celebration, then came to sit on Patrick's feet to prevent another departure.

Patrick laughed and rubbed Oscar's ears, delighting in the dog's happiness at his reappearance.

Pascal emerged from the hotel a few minutes later.

'I had to anchor him, I'm afraid. Since first thing this morning, he's been trying to escape and run off to the gunboat. I know dogs have a strong sense of smell, but how did he know you'd returned from wherever it is you've been?' Pascal said quizzically.

'I have no idea,' Patrick admitted. 'But suffice to say, the job given me by Brother Robert has been done. And now Oscar and I are headed out to lunch.'

Patrick thanked Pascal profusely for looking after his dog.

'Oscar's always welcome here. You know that.'

As Oscar bounced towards the door with him, Patrick didn't look back at what would undoubtedly be Pascal's sad face.

'Pascal makes a better owner than me,' he told Oscar as they headed along Rue de la Misércorde to check if Chevalier was having his prelunch drink at Le P'tit Zinc.

He wasn't, and there was no reserved sign on his usual table either.

'He's gone to see Madame Lacroix,' Veronique told Patrick, with what resembled a suggestive smile. Considering Chevalier was gay and Madame Lacroix didn't supply gay escorts from her Hibiscus agency, Patrick didn't comprehend the reason for the look.

'To view something important,' Veronique added.

'Ah,' Patrick said, although he was none the wiser. 'I'll catch him later.'

Rue Antoine was all set up for lunch, but Patrick didn't view the menus, intent as he was on eating at Los Faroles, provided there was a table free. Oscar bounded ahead up the steep cobbles, turning on occasion to check that Patrick was following.

When Patrick eventually turned into the square, Oscar had already been served a dish of water and something tasty.

'I hope there's some left for me,' Patrick said.

'Chicken or fish?' Fritz asked him.

'Chicken, please.'

'And the wine?'

'Surprise me.' Patrick smiled and took a seat with his back to the outside wall, so he could watch the passers-by. Once Oscar had finished whatever titbit had been given him, he took up residence below the table to await anything that might drop from his master's plate. Patrick

256

thought it unlikely, judging by the extent of his own hunger.

A couple of hours later, he headed for Le Dramont. Seated in the Ferrari, with the warm sun on his head and Oscar in the passenger seat, Patrick was able to pretend the past few days were an aberration. He had delivered the Madonna to St Honorat. The job had been successful. It was over.

Oscar's face was a picture of contentment. His ears pricked up, his pug face turned to the breeze, his ears twitching. The little bulldog could live in the here and now.

Why can't I?

Patrick drove down the dirt track and parked the car next to the restaurant. Lunch was obviously over for the day. Those customers still on the deck were having coffee, beer or a glass of wine. Entering the kitchen, he found Jean-Paul preparing tonight's speciality, which was *bouillabaisse*. The scent of herbs and garlic made Patrick's mouth water in anticipation.

'You're here, *mon ami*. Have you eaten?'

'I have.'

Jean-Paul bent to greet Oscar, ruffling his ears and immediately finding something tasty for him as a treat.

'I don't know why he isn't fat,' Patrick said.

'Because that breed of dog is all muscle. Like me.' Jean-Paul grinned. 'Life is returning to normal?'

'I hope so,' Patrick said honestly.

'And the lady?' Jean-Paul asked, with a twinkle in his eye.

Patrick didn't answer. The truth was he feared that the previous evening had been a one-off. A way to celebrate survival. Courting death required a celebration of life in its aftermath. Patrick had been surprised at the strength of his feelings about what had happened between them. Grazia was a beautiful woman. Sexy, intelligent, brave. What man wouldn't relish making love to her? And they'd faced death together and survived. He'd met that type of love many times before, but once complete it was over, like the danger that had been faced.

Patrick found himself acknowledging that he didn't want it to be over with Grazia. But, maybe she did.

'She works for Moreaux.'

Jean-Paul's eyes flew open in astonishment. 'For the Police Nationale?'

'Undercover.'

'I thought she was with the English,' Jean-Paul said, puzzled.

'So did I.'

Jean-Paul stirred his pot. He tasted the contents, added something, then put the lid on and left the soup to simmer. After which he brought a carafe of wine to the table, and two glasses.

'My advice is to find another woman immediately and make love to her.'

Patrick laughed. 'Does Joanne know you give such advice?'

'Joanne is more than enough woman for me,' Jean-Paul admitted. 'So what will happen to the gold Madonna?'

'The Brits will reclaim it.'

258

'It was their fault it existed,' Jean-Paul said. 'But Vichy France has a responsibility, too.'

'It was a mess,' Patrick said. 'All wars are.'

'Do you believe the Windsors, as you call them, thought they would be placed on the throne of a conquered England?'

'Who knows what they thought?' Patrick said. 'And who cares?'

He stayed on into the evening, when they all sat outside eating *bouillabaisse*. Daniel and Fidella joined them, and Patrick learned that the garage, despite its state, would be back in operation in a matter of days.

'I'll work outside in the street if I have to,' Daniel told Patrick. 'The flat will take longer to fix, but Jean-Paul has offered us a place to stay until it's ready.'

Patrick glanced over at his friend and said a silent thank you.

They talked of holding a party in the garden courtyard of the Chanteclair to celebrate the reopening of the garage and the return of the Madonna.

'Pascal would be up for that,' Patrick said.

When the meal was over, Patrick went down to the beach. Instructing Oscar to wait for him, he stripped off and took to the water, swimming straight out past Île d'Or before treading water to look back at the shore, where the little dog sat patiently awaiting his return.

Twenty-Eight

She called at midnight. Patrick was sitting under the awning with a whisky, Oscar spread out at his feet.

'Where are you?' she said.

'Sitting on deck, enjoying a dram. Are you coming to join me?'

'Alas, no. Not tonight, anyway.' She hesitated. 'I wonder if you would like to invite me to dinner tomorrow evening? I've heard you're a good cook.'

'Did Moreaux tell you that?'

She laughed. 'No. He's not complimentary about you at all. It was Madame Lacroix who told me.'

'I'd be delighted to cook dinner for you,' Patrick said. 'What time suits?'

'Seven,' she said.

'Seven it is, then.'

Patrick lifted his whisky and toasted whatever deity had permitted such a thing to happen, then calling Oscar, went below to bed.

Next morning, his dinner menu in mind, Patrick headed for Marché Forville, Oscar trotting alongside. Patrick's dreams had been punctuated by images of Grazia, dressed in red, then in green, then stripping off on the platform to climb over the barrier and drop into space.

260

He'd known only one other woman with Grazia's beauty and courage.

And look how that turned out.

Patrick had woken with that warning in his head. A warning he chose to ignore. Wandering the market, he set his mind on the meal for tonight instead, aware that he was hoping to impress.

Having purchased clams for *spaghetti alle vongole*, he headed for the fresh pasta stall. A visit to the cheese counter and then the fruit stall, to purchase fresh figs and strawberries, saw his meal complete. An Italian speciality dish plus a malt whisky to follow would pay homage to Grazia's Barga connections, Patrick thought.

Happy with his purchases, he whistled to Oscar and made for the Cave Forville for a light lunch of oysters and tapas. He was lucky to get a table, the Cave being thronged with a mix of early tourists and locals who, like him, had already shopped in the market and now sought a glass of wine, a coffee or lunch, before heading home.

Patrick ordered the current wine of choice to go with his oysters, then settled down at a pavement table. Oscar, realizing Patrick was planning to stay, surveyed the surrounding clientele for someone to perform for.

An elderly lady at a neighbouring table proved to be Oscar's choice of the day. The small dog took up residence between her and Patrick, so that he might keep an eye on his master while ploughing his own furrow. Patrick, admiring his determination, let him get on with it.

Patrick had finished the tapas, and was enjoying an espresso while contemplating an afternoon swim, when a figure arrived to stand between him and the sun. Thrown suddenly into shadow, a surprised Patrick looked up to discover Charles Carruthers.

'May I join you?'

'Can I say no?'

'You can, but I hope you won't.'

Of all the things Patrick thought might happen in the aftermath of the Madonna, this hadn't been one of them. Carruthers would normally never consider visiting an operative in the field. They were always required to report to him.

After the case of the black pearl Patrick had answered a summons to London, delivered by Forsyth in person. Perhaps this was Carruthers' way of making things even.

Oscar, observing the new arrival, came to check him out. Carruthers did the honours by rubbing Oscar's ears, thus immediately endearing himself to the dog.

When the waiter approached, Carruthers ordered a coffee in fluent French and made a joke in passing. The waiter's response suggested he believed Charles was French.

Patrick waited for the waiter to depart before saying, 'Lieutenant Moreaux says that when London calls they always expect the conversation to be in English. Why, when you speak French like a native?'

'Protocol. I don't agree with it, but you know what they're like,' he said with a shrug.

'Conversing in the language of the natives gives the impression they might be your equal?' Patrick said.

'Good diplomacy requires that you should always appear to hold the upper hand,' Carruthers said without a hint of irony.

Patrick cursed, in French, under his breath.

'I should warn you I swear well in French, too,' Carruthers said with a wry smile.

Patrick laughed. He'd always found it difficult to be angry with Carruthers for long. He had to admit he liked the man and, for the most part, trusted him.

'Friends?' Charles tried.

'Not enemies,' Patrick responded.

Charles's expression darkened. 'Not that, Courvoisier. Never that.'

They sat in silence for a moment, before Charles finally said, 'I came because I need to hear from you personally how Huntington died.'

'I told you on the phone. He died trying to bring the gold to the surface.'

'But I understood *you* were the one to carry the Madonna from the cave?'

'Huntington was injured. Quite badly. He wanted to do it. I wouldn't let him. He shouldn't even have been diving.' Patrick shook his head at the memory of the scene in the cave. 'We rescued the statue, but he was running out of air. I sent him up while I hid it in the sea wall. I don't know what happened to him after that. I came to in a cellar to find I'd been picked up by Bach.'

He glanced at Carruthers, who was listening intently.

'When Bach didn't mention Huntington, I hoped they thought I'd been on my own. After all, they'd left Huntington for dead back on Torcello.' Patrick paused. 'The plan was, if I didn't make it to the surface and Huntington did, he knew where I'd hidden the statue. It turned out I was the one to survive after all.'

Oscar, sensing the tension between the two men, had come to sit on Patrick's feet. He felt the soft snuffle of the dog's nose against his hand when he reached down.

'I should have ordered him home from Venice,' Charles said.

'You did try, but he'd already left the hotel,' Patrick reminded him. 'And he kept the bullet wound secret, even initially from me.'

In the quiet moments that followed, Patrick had a powerful sensation that he was under close observation. And not by either Oscar or Charles. The feeling was so strong that he felt the hairs on the back of his neck react. A flash of light, as if the sun had been reflected off a mirror, was followed by a swishing sound, as a bullet skimmed Carruthers' ear, pinged off the metal table, and embedded itself in the shopping bag of their elderly neighbour.

Patrick knew that sound too well. As, it was clear, did Carruthers.

Both men shouted simultaneously, in French, at those around them to take cover.

A second bullet pinging off the sign offering today's specials forced the issue, and the screams

264

of the women and the frightened shouts of the men saw them scrambling for cover.

Patrick was in no doubt who was shooting at them.

'I'm the one he's after,' Patrick told Charles. 'I have to get away from here or someone's going to get killed.'

Opposite Café Forville was a staircase that led to the flat roof of the market building. Patrick vaulted the locked gate and climbed to the top. Up here was nothing but empty space. A car park at one time, it had lain unused since the building was refurbished. He was a sitting duck up here, but at least no one else would get hurt.

Staying low against the outer wall, Patrick ran his eyes around the neighbouring buildings. From the angle of the bullets, the shooter had been above them, which meant he was possibly at one of the windows overlooking the north side of the market.

Below him, panic had followed his escape. The street below was rapidly emptying, the alarm now spreading into the covered market below. A siren screamed its approach, someone had had the presence of mind to call the police. Patrick scanned the neighbouring windows for the glint of a weapon, but found only the frightened faces of occupants checking out what was happening below.

Then he saw him, and realized that the perfect place from which to take out someone sitting in the café below was here, on the roof of the market. The remaining bonehead was walking towards him across the tarred surface, a smile on his face.

By now he knew that Patrick was unarmed and that, even should he have a knife, he would never get close enough to use it. He could have taken Patrick out from where he stood, but preferred to come close enough to look into his victim's eyes before taking his shot.

This is it, Patrick thought.

He might vault the waist high wall and fall six metres to the street below and survive the impact. Then again, the bonehead had only to lean over and shoot him where he lay.

It seemed he'd run out of options.

They say the moments before death are extended, as the fevered brain becomes reconciled to its own departure. So it was with Patrick. Regret swept over him. Not regret at what he'd done, but regret at what he had not.

Jonas, two metres away now, had come to a halt, his eyes burning with the righteous wrath of the avenger. It seemed there were to be no words exchanged between them. In that moment Patrick didn't blame Jonas Engel for what he was about to do, because he knew he would have done the same if he'd come face to face with his brother's killer.

As Jonas levelled the gun, Patrick squared his shoulders but didn't close his eyes. If he was to meet death, then he would stare it straight in the face.

'Get down,' Moreaux shouted from behind.

As Patrick dived for the ground, a volley of shots exploded simultaneously. Skimming through the air above him, the police bullets hit home, exploding in the bonehead's chest, piercing his

266

brain, tearing through the swastika tattoos on his arms. They forced him first on to his knees, then face down, never to rise again.

Twenty-Nine

Skin on skin. Just as it had been in the cellar, although this time they shared each other's warmth. Her long dark hair fell on either side of his face like a silk curtain. Her breath brushed his lips, before she kissed him lightly then rolled to lie beside him.

'I take it my attempt at seducing you with good food was a success, then?' Patrick said.

Grazia pulled a face. 'The spaghetti wasn't homemade.'

'What?' Patrick said, as though affronted. 'The stall I bought it from in the market assured me it was.'

'Apart from that,' she conceded. 'It was very good. As was dessert,' she added, with a smile. 'And now breakfast.'

'Coffee and croissants to follow?' Patrick said.

'Perfect.'

After the incident in the Marché, he, Moreaux and Carruthers had adjourned to *Les Trois Soeurs*, where Carruthers had thanked Moreaux, in perfect French, for the input of the Police Nationale in retrieving the golden Madonna, and indicated that Her Majesty's government

267

didn't intend to pursue the repatriation of the Fragonard.

At this declaration Moreaux's lip curled, but he said nothing.

'We would expect, however, that you would hand over the video made at the auction,' Charles said.

At that point, there had been an impasse. Patrick, his only interest in the matter being that the Fragonard should remain with the monks, left the two men to fight it out and, whistling to Oscar, departed from the gunboat.

En route to Le P'tit Zinc in search of Chevalier, he received a phone call from Madame Lacroix, inviting him round for a glass of wine.

'To celebrate the fact that you're still alive,' she added.

Patrick was pleased to accept the offer, although the tone of her voice suggested that wasn't the only reason for the invitation.

The market having finished for the day, the cavernous space had been cleared and hosed down. The restaurant was back at work, the customers' conversations animated, with much gesturing at the roof of the nearby market. Patrick suspected they would be dining out on the story of the gunman for some time.

Patrick chose to avoid any questions or interested enquiries by going through the empty building. Emerging on the other side, he headed for Rue d'Antibes, where Madame Lacroix had obviously been anticipating his imminent arrival as she immediately answered the buzzer and invited him up.

268

Brigitte Lacroix's dark eyes were sparkling when she opened the door to him, her kiss on both cheeks positively affectionate. As she drew him inside, Patrick registered that he wasn't her only visitor. Chevalier rose to greet him with an equally wide smile on his face. It seemed his brush with death had reached everyone's ears.

Madame Lacroix indicated the open bottle of St Honorat Syrah and offered him a glass. It was obviously a celebration that demanded a fine wine.

'A gift from Brother Robert,' she explained.

Patrick almost said 'For what?', then remembered it was Madame Lacroix's knowledge of the history of the Fragonard and Château de la Croë that had led them there. When Patrick tried to make a toast to her contribution, she raised her hand to stop him. 'Come, Courvoisier, I have something to show you.'

Patrick glanced quizzically at Chevalier, who merely smoothed his moustache and smiled. At that point, Madame Lacroix indicated that Patrick should follow her into her bedroom.

The room was everything Patrick had always imagined it might be, from the Louis XIV bed to the crystal chandelier. But it wasn't the furniture, beautiful as it was, that dominated the room. It was the painting that hung there next to the miniature Madame Lacroix had shown him on his previous visit.

Grazia had declared it a forgery, yet Patrick could hardly believe that to be true. It was in essence a twin of the Fragonard, apart from the shape of the land mass at its foot.

'Isn't she beautiful?' Madame Lacroix said.

'She is.'

'I wanted to say thank you for rescuing her. For rescuing them both.' She turned to Patrick. 'As for that other thing,' she growled. '*Von jüdischen Gold!*' She uttered an expletive even Patrick hadn't heard before. 'My grandmother who worked at the château was Jewish.' She laughed up at Patrick. 'She would have been very pleased that this Madonna has found a home here with her granddaughter.'

'I thought the second painting had been damaged in the fight in the cave?' Grazia said, as he topped up her coffee and finished his story.

Patrick explained Madame Lacroix's role in the search for the Fragonard. 'Added to that, Brigitte Lacroix is Lieutenant Moreaux's mistress,' he said.

'Really?' Grazie smiled. 'Then I'm certain Mademoiselle de Sainval would have approved.'

At that point, Oscar indicated that they had a visitor.

Charles Carruthers stepped out of the black chauffeur-driven limousine on to the *quai*. Dressed in a smart grey suit, he looked every inch a member of Her Majesty's diplomatic service. Patrick wondered if the golden Madonna resided in the boot, or if it was already on its way to London by special courier.

'Will you come on board?' Patrick asked.

'My apologies, but I have a plane to catch.' Charles smiled over at Grazia. 'I wonder if I might have a few moments alone with

Courvoisier?' When she nodded, Charles indicated that they should talk in the car.

As Patrick climbed in, he had a fleeting image of being whisked away from the gunboat, then put on a private jet and taken back to London. Something of this must have shown in his expression, for Charles said, 'I assure you I have no intention of kidnapping you, although I believe Forsyth would have jumped at the chance.'

In the privacy of the car, out of earshot of the driver, Charles said his piece.

'We couldn't have done this without you.'

'And my reward is?' Patrick said.

'We leave you alone.'

'For how long?'

'That I can't say. Although I would hope for some time.'

'Not indefinitely?'

'It can never be that.' Charles shook his head. 'You know why.'

'There were three of us that day on the mountain,' Patrick said. 'I'm the only one left alive.'

'Which is the reason.'

Charles opened the door, indicating that Patrick should get out. They shook hands, as they had done on the day of the garden party.

'I wish you well, Courvoisier. And good luck with Madamoiselle Lucca.'

As the car drew away, Patrick could see nothing through the smoked-glass windows, but he sensed that Carruthers did not look back.

Thirty

That evening he and Grazia attended a different kind of garden party. One that didn't demand the wearing of a top hat and tails, nor the equivalent expensive female outfit. That's not to say the guests weren't well dressed, in particular Chevalier.

'They should invite you to a Buckingham Palace tea party,' Patrick told Chevalier when he arrived.

'Who is to say they haven't done so already?' Chevalier said mysteriously, before heading off to greet their host, Pascal.

Grazia was wearing the green dress Patrick had first seen her in, but she had unsuccessfully tried to persuade Patrick to don his kilt.

'I'll wear it for you later,' he promised, with a glint in his eye.

'Like a true Scotsman?' she enquired.

'*Naturellement*.'

Oscar was off on his rounds, gathering approbation and titbits with equal enthusiasm. Patrick helped himself to a *verre de rosé* and chose a seat, just outside the circle of light, from which to observe the party. The scent of roses hung heavy in the still night air. Above him swifts skydived through the tumble of buildings that formed Le Suquet, crying their joy.

Patrick couldn't think of anywhere he'd rather

be at that moment than in this courtyard with all his friends about him.

When Fidella spotted him in the shadows, she loosened her arm from Daniel's and approached. Patrick gestured she should take a seat beside him.

'Jean-Paul tells me you were born in Casablanca,' she said.

'My father was a doctor there. My mother worked as a teacher.'

'Casablanca was my home before I came to France.' She faltered a little on that.

'You miss it?' Patrick said.

'I miss my family, but now there is Daniel.' She glanced over at him and, as if he sensed this, Daniel turned round and smiled.

'There have been no more problems with those men?'

She shook her head. 'Although I fear they may make trouble for my family in Morocco if word gets back about what happened here.'

It seemed the cycle of revenge kept on turning, whatever was done.

Patrick spotted that Moreaux had arrived with Madame Lacroix. The detective acknowledged Patrick's presence, but made no effort to come and speak to him, choosing to greet Oscar instead.

According to Moreaux, the police had been close on Jonas's trail.

'In truth, he hadn't been in hiding,' Moreaux had told Patrick. 'He was more interested in getting to you than saving himself.'

'He expected to die?'

273

'I don't think he cared, as long as you died first.'

Patrick had thanked Moreaux for saving his life.

'I think this time we're even,' Moreaux had said. 'I should warn you that Miss Lucca will be leaving Cannes soon.'

Patrick didn't ask why, or where Grazia might be going. Those questions he would have to direct to her.

And I haven't. Yet.

Patrick glanced over at the tall figure next to Madame Lacroix's much slighter one. The two women were deep in conversation. About the forged Fragonard, Patrick suspected.

At that moment, he saw Oscar detach himself from the group and sprint through the passageway to the outside door. Assuming more guests had arrived, Patrick went to let them in.

But the door stood open and there was no one there.

Then Patrick noticed that Oscar had something in his mouth.

'Here, boy,' Patrick said. 'What's that you've got?'

Oscar wasn't keen on giving up his prize, which was an envelope.

Patrick shooed him back into the courtyard, fetched a titbit from the table of food, and offered it to him in return for the envelope. Oscar thought about it briefly, then relinquished his prize, accepted the treat in return, and took it elsewhere to eat.

Patrick glanced down at the envelope to find

it was addressed to Le Limier. Intrigued, he looked at the back and found the envelope was sealed.

Anyone in Le Suquet would be aware of the party and that he would be at it, so it was no surprise a message should be delivered there. But why run away afterwards?

Patrick contemplated opening the envelope, then decided it would keep until later. Slipping it into his pocket, he went in search of Grazia.

They walked back to the gunboat in silence, Oscar at their heels. Patrick already knew this was to be Grazia's parting gift to him. She would return to Italy in the morning.

'For how long?' Patrick asked.

'I don't know.'

Patrick didn't question her any further. Given the little he knew about Grazia and the little she knew of him, they had done well to get even this far. The look she bestowed on him suggested she felt the same.

'Then let's make it a night to remember,' he said.

Patrick woke before dawn to find Grazia gone, the place beside him already cold. Oscar had made no sound when she left, he imagined Grazia signalling the little bulldog to be silent.

He rose and checked the cabin briefly, hoping to find a note from her. There wasn't one. Because, he realized, they had said all there was to say.

Patrick dressed, made a pot of coffee, and took

it up on deck. The rising sun had painted the sky above the castle a bloody red, reminding him of the intensity of the sunrises and sunsets of his Moroccan childhood.

Until his conversation with Fidella, he hadn't recalled that time for many years now. He wondered about his family's house, still there, waiting for a return visit that would never happen. Both parents now dead, there was no reason to go back.

Thinking about Morocco and Fidella reminded Patrick of the previous evening's delivery. He went downstairs, retrieved the envelope from his trouser pocket, and brought it up on deck.

Whoever had sealed it had done a good job, aided by the application of adhesive tape.

When he finally managed to tear it open, Patrick found a single sheet of paper, with a name on it. A name he recognized.

'Took your time opening that.' Jack Brooke's loud American twang resounded across the *quai*. 'Gone native, I see.' He indicated the gunboat's name.

'When in France . . .' Patrick said with a smile. 'Are you coming on board?'

'I sure as hell am.'

Patrick lowered the gangplank and the big American stepped aboard.

He glanced at the coffee pot. 'Got anything stronger?'

'It's eight o'clock in the morning,' Patrick remonstrated.

'For me it's the night before.'

Patrick ushered Jack to a seat and went down

for the whisky and two glasses. He suspected they might both need a stiff drink. A visit from the jovial American, though welcome, was unlikely to herald good news.